The Morning Bell Brings the Broken Hearted

The
MORNING BELL
brings the
BROKEN HEARTED

JENNIFER MANUEL

Douglas & McIntyre

Douglas and McIntyre (2013) Ltd.
P.O. Box 219, Madeira Park, BC, V0N 2H0
www.douglas-mcintyre.com

Edited by Barbara Berson
Cover design by Dwayne Dobson
Text design by Carleton Wilson
Printed and bound in Canada
Printed on paper made from 100% recycled fibres

Supported by the Province of British Columbia

Douglas & McIntyre acknowledges the support of the Canada Council for the
Arts, the Government of Canada, and the Province of British Columbia through
the BC Arts Council.

LIBRARY AND ARCHIVES CANADA CATALOGUING IN PUBLICATION

Title: The morning bell brings the broken hearted / Jennifer Manuel.
Names: Manuel, Jennifer, author.
Identifiers: Canadiana (print) 2023013369X | Canadiana (ebook) 20230133711 |
   ISBN 9781771623193 (softcover) | ISBN 9781771623209 (EPUB)
Classification: LCC PS8626.A67683 M67 2023 | DDC C813/.6—dc23

To my grandchildren, Arthur and Ripley,

May you be treated by the world with grace and respect.

May you always be told stories that make you believe in yourself and in all the possibilities and choices you have in this world.

And may you be given the very best teachers with the very best hearts in the very best schools with the very best resources.

Because making things good for Indigenous children is good for all of Canada.

Teacher, teacher, let me in,
My feet are cold, my shoes are thin,
If you do not let me in,
I'll knock your window outside in.

—English playground song

1

From the front door of my grey trailer home, my commute across the old logging road to the school took precisely forty-six steps. Forty-six steps I no longer wanted to take. Forty-six steps I counted every dreaded morning to keep from thinking about those children and my failures and my desire to be back home and my mistaken belief that I had what it took to be a teacher in a place like this. Forty-six steps that I counted to keep from thinking about the rainforest that loomed all around me. It was on blustery mornings like this one, when the forest seemed charged with an awakening, as though it stirred with the stories I had obsessed over as a child—stories of forests riddled with darkness and deceit, where beautiful flowers were promised to red-cloaked girls if only they went farther into its depths, where witches cast spells to make it always winter but never Christmas, where wolves waited in disguise and crones lured children with the things their hearts longed for, things no one in this world could ever give them.

At the end of the dirt path from my porch, my boots crunched onto the gravel of the old logging road, the sound muffled by the roar of the wind through the cedars, and as the pages of my students' notebooks riffled under my coat sleeve, I felt a sudden chill. My eyes darted to the trees in spite of my counting. Since arriving in Tawakin last month at the beginning of September, that forest had haunted me. Why this was, I could not say. There was, of course, my natural concern for the creatures that roamed there, the black bears and the cougars. I halted in the middle of the logging road at the thought of this, my boots skidding slightly. A small spray of pebbles bounced and rattled, and in the quiet that followed, I checked for any signs of movement around me.

The empty logging road snaked between the small cluster of the teachers' homes and down the hill to the shoreline of the tiny Nuu-chah-nulth village: twenty-five houses the colours of blue jays and daffodils and ferns, woven into the rainforest on a remote northwest corner of Vancouver Island, stitched to the rest of the world by only air and water and the satellite signals captured by the grey discs mounted on every roof. Beyond, the Pacific Ocean stretched out to the horizon, marked with thin lines of white-crested waves, dotted with small islands of cedar and sharp stone, a few of them visible from here above the village on clear days if you looked past the descending tree tops of the forest.

Gazing over the ragged fringe of hillside cedars was the closest I ever wished to come to exploring the forest. While I had used every shred of rational thought to fight off my fear of what might lurk inside there, I had no intention of ever stepping into that darkness, its undergrowth thorny and tangled, its canopy so thick not even the sun could guide your way, each fibrous giant connected, as if by magic, through a fungal, subterranean circuit like the neural pathways of our own minds, able to warn one another of threats and dangers or perhaps whisper an enchanted "wisha, wisha, wisha" into its shadowy maze. If I were to believe the folktales that consumed me as a child, then I knew a person could lose themselves in the dark woods if they weren't careful. In there, evil forever chased. The good forever fled. Children forever dared one another to enter. Deep enough inside for us to realize that the woods played with children as much as children played with the woods.

*   *   *

"Redneck bitch."

That morning, eleven-year-old Hannah Charlie showed up to my classroom wearing long sleeves stretched over her hands. She was a tall girl, always angry, and as she often had before, she called me a redneck bitch because I was a *mamulthni* and because I extended my hand out to her. Hannah was first in line in the hallway outside my classroom when the morning bell rang, and it wasn't like I was signalling her to stop or to be quiet. I only wanted to shake her hand, which I'd tried to do at the start of every school day for the past month, a tiny exercise in manners, a small connection, but Hannah didn't want anything to do with me, not before and especially not today.

With my hand stuck out in midair, I glanced at the rest of the class, which included children in grades three, four, five and six, all fifteen of them stretched out next to the wall in a ragged line. A large space between them and Hannah already kept them out of her reach, yet they now shifted their gaze to the floor, pretending not to have heard Hannah, and nudged themselves even farther away, if only by inches. I didn't condone swearing in school, of course not, but if Hannah was made to leave the moment she swore, she would never complete a full hour of school never mind a full day, and there certainly weren't any alternate institutions or programs available in Tawakin. Besides, if I didn't conserve my energy when it came to Hannah, it would be depleted by recess, meaning I'd have nothing left for the other children, and they already got so much less from me on account of her. What was I supposed to do? Prepare better? That's what teacher training had said, after all. Prepare your lessons, prepare your materials, prepare your transitions. This was the key to a well-behaved class! Yet how does one prepare for Hannah Charlie?

All I had ever thought to do was to wait for a quiet moment in the afternoon when I knew I'd made it through another day with Hannah and when Hannah was exhausted from another day of trying to fit into this world. Then I would give a gentle yet firm reminder about her language, and Hannah would respond in her usual manner:

"Fuck you, Teacher."

And I would remind her: "My name is Ms. Royston."

As the children waited to be let into the classroom, I took sidelong glimpses at Hannah's shirt. It was unlike anything she had ever worn.

Long sleeves dangling past her hands, loose hem draping her thighs. Translucent patches of grease or oil on the stomach. A faded yet large beige stain on the chest. Yellow patches under the armpits. Tattered cuffs. The neck hole stretched out of shape. Normally Hannah wore crisp, clean shirts tucked neatly into her pants. She coordinated colours, she matched her socks, she kept her running shoes as bright and white as her scrubbed teeth. Her black hair always washed and combed. For Hannah, her appearance was perhaps one of the only things she could control with certainty. Through a tidy wardrobe and careful grooming, she disguised herself at school as orderly, unsullied, balanced. It was her way of showing that she belonged.

"I'm happy to see you at school today, Hannah." I could hear the strain in my voice, my own uncertainty ringing in my ears. I kept my hand extended.

"Real dumb," Hannah said. She knocked the back of her covered hand against the wall, repeatedly and with increased volume. "Get your ugly hand out of my face or else."

My hand briefly clenched. "Or else?"

"What's your dog's name, Ms. Royston?"

"You know I don't have a dog."

"Good," Hannah shrugged, "or something bad might've happened to it."

A wave of discouragement washed over me. This was not what I had imagined when I decided to become a teacher. "Threats don't work on me," I said. I took a breath.

"It's not a threat," Hannah said. "It's a fact. Bad stuff happens to things."

"True." I didn't lower my hand and although I could feel myself wavering, I moved next to her. Not facing her, but side by side. Never had I thought it possible that a child could make me so timid, so jittery, and at the same time so resentful that this was her effect on me. In a quiet voice, almost under my breath, I asked her in the most casual tone I could manage: "Is there something wrong with your hands?"

"Is there something wrong with your face?" Hannah asked.

"Not last I checked," I said.

"Nothing wrong with my hands neither."

"It seems like you're hiding them. Are you hiding them?"

"I'm not." Hannah kept her gaze fixed on the opposite wall where artwork was displayed in neat rows. The tiny handprints of the primary students, whose classroom was across from ours, had been pressed onto paper with brown paint, each finger a feather on a turkey, each thumb decorated with an eye, a beak and a fleshy red wattle.

Even though I knew I was pushing the limits of her patience, I asked her, "Then why won't you take them out of your sleeves?"

"This shirt is too big."

"Why are you wearing it, then?"

Hannah turned and glared at me. "I'm cold is all."

Once more Hannah called me a redneck bitch and also a fat cow and then she punched the wall with the cuffs of her shirt wrapped around her fists like mittens. She dragged the back of her knuckles across the roughly textured wallpaper until her face contorted into a grimace that seemed like relief. I tried to get a look at her hands but not once did Hannah uncurl the cuffs from her fingers. I wasn't going to push. If you pushed, Hannah erupted, and if she erupted, she always got sent home in the past, and if there was one thing I'd figured out during my short time in Tawakin it was this: Hannah Charlie wanted desperately to be at school, wanted to be seen as a normal eleven-year-old girl, as a real person, something more than a walking, breathing vessel of rage.

Although I had only known Hannah for a month now, I had read her thick file within a week of my arrival. I knew about the first incident of the crayon self-portraits, how she had lit a cigarette she'd stolen from home, and how she'd pressed the burning end into the waxy cheeks of her classmates until their faces smouldered to black. How everyone said it was just an accident, but that maybe Hannah wasn't ready to start grade one yet. Everyone hoped it was only a phase, but Hannah spent the rest of the year learning at home. In grade three, she threatened to kill the teacher's Jack Russell terrier and throw it into Dog Ditch. When nobody could find the dog, Hannah was interrogated. She admitted nothing, though the transcripts in the report made it clear that she looked at her teacher and laughed. The school suggested that Hannah receive an examination by doctors, but her mother, Patty, refused and accused the school of overreacting. In grade four, Hannah cooked the class hamster in the school kitchen microwave. This time her mother told the school, "Kids will be kids." A week later, Hannah defecated on the free throw line in the gym. She said she was only kidding around. Child Protection Services flew in from Port Hardy and conducted a brief investigation, but then they left the community and did nothing. At that point, Hannah's mother told the school that Hannah only acted out because the teachers didn't know how to do their jobs properly and that if Hannah didn't get an education, she'd sue the school board. The following year, after getting sent home almost every day of grade four, Hannah entered grade five in my class.

Across the hall, the first and second grade students shuffled into their classroom. Ms. Smith, the primary teacher, looked at Hannah and smiled.

"Hater," Hannah said to Ms. Smith, punching the wall hard.

"Please don't talk to Ms. Smith like that," I said, trying not to sigh in exasperation.

Hannah shrugged. "Wasn't talking to her."

"Oh? Who were you talking to, then?"

"Myself."

Joan Smith was a young teacher of twenty-four, about fifteen years younger than me, and over her black tights she wore long, bright green socks that matched both her sweater and the thick elastic that pulled her brown hair into a high ponytail. Some days she wore deep burgundy socks that reminded me of the red wine that stained her lips after we'd hung out together some evenings, for escape and lonely commiseration.

Hannah glared at Ms. Smith and repeated, "Hater."

As Joan led her students into their classroom, Hannah punched the wall a third time. Then a fourth.

I felt my face grow warm, flustered at looking inept in front of the primary class despite the fact that everyone in Tawakin acknowledged the unfixable problem of Hannah Charlie.

Quit. This was the thought that kept poking at me lately. Quit this job. Just quit and pack your belongings and go back to the city. But I pushed the idea out of my mind. I sighed. "I swear, Hannah—"

"No," Hannah said. "I swear: shit, damn, fuck."

"I swear, Hannah," I repeated, gritting my teeth, "if I said black, you'd say white."

"Nope," Hannah said. "I hate whites."

My face turned hotter now, and I tried not to flinch at this, how it embarrassed me in front of the class. A few of the girls played with the ends of their long black hair while several of the boys pulled the hoods of their sweatshirts over their heads to hide their eyes. Kenny Frank kicked his sneakers so that the wet rubber soles squelched repeatedly on the linoleum. Odelia Joe tugged at the straps of her old backpack, the one with the pink and red flowers, the pink and red faded from walking day after day in the pouring rain. Between her fingers, Candice Henry rubbed the small photograph she carried everywhere. Not one of the children looked at me. What did they think of me? With the exception of a few, they were as shy and quiet as that first day of school when they had hidden under their hoodies and avoided making eye contact. It was moments like these, these moments of withdrawing, that made it hard to imagine that I could ever become more than the familiar stranger, the white teacher, the outsider. And if I could never become more than that, what difference could I ever hope to make?

Finally moving past Hannah, I went down the line, repeating with a listless cadence, "Good morning, good morning, good morning," shaking each child's limp hand.

Inside the classroom, as the children hung their backpacks on hooks, Hannah crept close behind Kenny, slightly off to the side, and stared down at the back of his head. Without turning around, Kenny strained to see Hannah out of the corner of his eye. Like a puppet string, the pull of Hannah's close attention held Kenny in place. She was taller than him by a head, and Kenny didn't move a muscle, his arm frozen in mid-air with his jacket in hand. Finally, Hannah stepped away, but the moment Kenny moved to hang his jacket, she sidled up to him again.

"Hannah," I said from the doorway. "Don't."

"What am I doing?" Hannah asked.

I said, "You know exactly what you're doing, Hannah."

"I'm only kidding around," Hannah said. "Right, buddy?"

Kenny stared at the floor. "My dad says he'll come up here if you pick on me."

"Fuckers." Hannah went to her desk, picked up her chair with her covered hands and slammed it down. "Fuckers. Haters."

In my classroom, there were short desks for the children in grades three and four, taller desks for the children in grades five and six. These desks were arranged in a semi-circle, except for Hannah's, which she kept turning outward from the others no matter how many times I moved her back into the group. It was one of the many things I could not at first puzzle out about her—why someone who wanted so badly to belong would turn themselves away like that. Yet she had also made it so that anyone who wanted to sharpen a pencil, or get something from the coat area, or leave to use the washroom had to pass by her. Her desk was like a tollbooth: the payment was your full, frightened attention.

Once more I studied Hannah's shirt from my spot in the corner by the door. Her hands were still buried inside the sleeves so that the cuffs dangled. It was more a matter of curiosity to me than concern. Chances were, Hannah had tagged some of the larger logs of driftwood with graffiti again, like the giant *FUCK U* she'd sprayed in orange neon on the shore next to the dock. Or maybe she had suffered mostly harmless yet incriminating burn marks from playing with fire as she had apparently been seen doing on several occasions in the past. For all I could guess, Hannah had used her mother's nail polish and was ready to punch out anyone who complimented her about it.

After the children had settled at their desks and I had taken attendance, I asked them to take out their novels and reading journals. Hannah tilted her desk onto two legs until her journal—a thin notebook—fell out, then she let the desk crash back down onto all four legs. Then,

The Morning Bell Brings the Broken Hearted

as the other children tried to read, Hannah teased them with random intervals of silence. That was how she controlled the room: by creating silence and then filling it with her own unique brand of sounds. It was as if she waited for slack in the room's tension before pulling it tight again with her wild noises. Sometimes she barked. Sometimes she growled. Occasionally she snorted like a pig with such volume and intensity that I wondered if it were possible for a person to snap their septum.

Suddenly, in a high pitch and with great volume, she yipped like a poodle, the sound like a sharp crack in the air.

My shoulders tensed. I resisted the urge to spin around and glare at her. But I held firm and still in my spot, determined not to give her the reaction she hoped for: a sign that she was getting under my skin, which she was, there was no denying it. But I would not let her know it. Who did she think she was, anyway? Who was she to make the rest of us suffer?

Several children twisted in their chairs and read with their backs to her. Most only pretended to follow the lines of text, not just because of the distraction, but because nearly all of them struggled to read. Kenny picked his nose, which he did whenever he was nervous, holding his book upside-down in front of his face. Candice wedged her small photograph into the binding of her paperback. Odelia stood her book up on end to hide the fact that she was drawing. So far my classroom was a place where my students pretended to learn and I pretended to teach, and in those moments when I decided to stop pretending, I made myself promises that tomorrow I would do better. But tomorrow had not come yet.

I opened my desk drawer where I kept Hannah's Safety Plan, an official list of appropriate responses to her behaviours. Her school file revealed no formal diagnosis, though there were unfulfilled requests from past teachers for Hannah's parents to take her to town for testing. Scattered on top of this document were Hannah's straightened paper clips, her confiscated elastic bands, her whittled pencil stubs she called her prison shivs. There were scraps of paper with Hannah's drawings, each one the same: a lacerated head, blood spilling around a woman's body, contorted limbs. Depictions of a movie, Hannah claimed, though she couldn't ever recall the title. Hannah's reading book was also in the drawer. It was an early-level text intended for readers in grade one. Poor attendance was a perennial issue at Tawakin School, children often travelling out to Port Hardy with their families for days of appointments and shopping. But Hannah's case was far worse on account of her lengthy suspensions, and she'd never attended school long enough to learn how to read more than the handful of words she must have puzzled out on her own. On the cover of her book there was a picture of waddling ducks, but I had ripped this off and replaced it with *The Call of the Wild*.

Whenever Hannah thought I wasn't looking, she made slow throat-cutting motions at the others with her covered finger. Admittedly, I should have stopped such violent gestures. Truth be known, though, after a month of these mimed assaults, I was too relieved by the accompanying silence to do anything but pretend not to notice. And I wasn't the only one. The entire class acted as if they could not see Hannah. Hannah narrowed her eyes when her classmates refused to look at what she was doing, and she held that squinted gaze as if shooting invisible lasers into their ears. Finally, she gave up and slapped her notebook onto her desk. It was crisp and clean and hardly used except for the rows of *hannah* she kept printing on the cover, without any capital *H*'s, even though I had taught her about proper nouns. You're more important than that, I had told her many times in the hopes of softening her edges. Don't you think you deserve a capital?

I took the reading book from my drawer, placed it on her desk, and as I retreated without a word, I tensed slightly in preparation for a smack of the book onto the floor, or a shout, a swear, a slander against me. There was nothing. From the corner of my eye, I watched Hannah. You had to do it like that, watch her without her knowing you were, which was no easy task because Hannah Charlie had a strange way of knowing exactly what you were doing and why. The way butterflies can detect the smallest changes in air pressure with the tiny hairs on their wings, or the way dogs can smell that you're scared of them. She stared at the book for a long time, then fumbled to get it open with her covered hands. It flipped to the page where the ducks go swimming.

The last time Hannah swam was four years ago. I knew this from Sophie Florence Joe, who was the school secretary and also Hannah's auntie. One day, two of Hannah's older cousins dared her to jump off the dock. So, she did. And they cheered. But when she tried to climb out of the ocean and back onto the dock, they stomped her hands with their boots.

"Let me up," Hannah said.

"Stupid mutt," they said. "Maybe if you drown, we'll drag you up the hill, dump you into Dog Ditch with all the other dead dogs. You know what that'd be? Justice. We heard lots about what you like to do to puppies with pins and rope."

"Let me up," Hannah said. "It's cold."

"Don't worry," they said, "your mother Patty is a big, fat whale. She'll come swim with you and keep you warm."

"Please let me up," she said.

Her cousins sat on the dock for hours, fishing for rock cod and keeping Hannah in the water. Tired and cold, Hannah wrapped herself around one of the pilings under the dock where she shivered and cried and bled against the barnacles until the sun set and her cousins went home.

Hannah now read about the ducks, sounding out the first words slowly. Something was wrong because Hannah never read out loud. True, she was unpredictable and surprising, rarely falling into discernible patterns from one day to the next, but she knew that her ability to read was far lower than her classmates', even those two years younger than her, and she avoided the humiliation of the printed word at all costs. But she didn't stop. She kept reading out loud. A few of the students watched her with furtive, sidelong glances. By the end of the second sentence, Hannah was shouting.

"Look in the water. One fuck, two fucks, THREE FUCKS IN THE WATER!"

From my desk I waited, carefully assessing whether there was any need to navigate Hannah's behaviour. During the first week of school I had tried to put a stop to her outbursts by exhausting a number of approaches. I warned of consequences. I gave choices. Twice I lost my cool and outright yelled at her to stop, which only made her smile and become quieter and more eerily calm yet even more vulgar.

For several minutes after Hannah's reading performance, all the children remained silent, even Hannah, who squeezed both hands between her legs and stared intently at her desk. Out of the stillness, Odelia rose from her seat. Chewing at her bottom lip, Odelia took a few small steps toward my desk. Then she stopped, glanced at Hannah and turned back toward her desk. She stood there for a moment, seemingly unsure of her next move. Finally, she turned back again and shuffled to my side and whispered, "Can you catch a curse from another person?"

"What?" I put down my book.

Under her breath Odelia asked, "Is a curse the same as a cold?"

I looked over at the Beverly Cleary book on Odelia's desk, *Ramona the Pest*, and smiled. "She's just a girl who makes a great big noisy fuss all the time. She's not cursed."

"She is," Odelia insisted.

"Keep reading," I said, "you'll see."

Odelia leaned over so that her mouth was next to my ear. I could smell peanut butter and toothpaste. "She's got a curse. That's how come she's hiding her hands."

I kept my eyes from moving in Hannah's direction. On a piece of scrap paper I printed Hannah's name, followed by three question marks, then tapped the name with my pen.

Odelia looked down at it and nodded.

Motioning for Odelia to follow me, I went and stood outside in the hallway where I could keep an eye on the class through the window. I left the door partway open for extra measure.

"Why is she hiding her hands?" I asked.

Odelia cast her eyes to the floor. "I told you. She's got a curse."

I winced in disbelief. "How'd she get a curse?"

Chewing on her bottom lip some more, Odelia peered through the narrow space of the open door. "I can't talk about it."

"If it's a matter of keeping somebody safe, it's not tattling."

"I can't talk about it because it's a very old secret."

Rubbing a tense band of muscle at the back of my neck, I tried to think of a question that might pry open this secret but came up with nothing. In the awkwardness of the silence that followed, I glanced around at the walls. A long row of framed photographs placed just under the ceiling adorned the top strip. The photographs depicted the entire school for each year—every child, teen and staff member—everybody always situated next to or on the playground equipment, several piled on the yellow slide, others draped over the monkey bars. In the middle of the hallway, across from the school office, were the photographs of past graduates. Each year there were only a few graduates, some years only one, and from what Joan Smith had told me, only a tiny percentage graduated with a full diploma, even though the formal graduation robes and caps suggested otherwise.

Turning back to the classroom, I watched Hannah from the corner of my eye and I wondered, What are you up to now? She was hunched over, and even though her back was to me, I could tell by how her arms twitched and jerked that she was frantically doing something in her lap.

Turning her face to me, Odelia gave me a worried look, and for a moment it appeared as though she might cry.

"We're not supposed to talk about her," Odelia said, though her voice hinted that she very much wished to talk about it.

"About Hannah?"

Odelia wrinkled her nose.

"About who, then?" I asked.

"I told you. I'm not supposed to say."

"Alright then," I said, gently turning Odelia by the shoulder, aware that the Shape of the Day on the chalkboard said that it was almost time for cursive writing. "Back to class. There's only one curse to worry about right now. The curse of writing."

I glanced at Odelia to see if she caught my pun.

If she did, she wasn't impressed. She just looked at me with worried eyes.

As we entered the doorway, Hannah stood up, kicked out her chair and marched to the front of the class. She pressed her back against the chalkboard.

"Look!" Hannah yelled at me. She held her hands up as if she were under arrest. Her bare palms were coated in thick, dark scribbles of ink. "See? Nothing wrong with my hands. Are you happy now?"

Hannah stomped back to her desk, a great big fussy noise, pulling the cuffs of her sleeves over her hands once again. Then she picked up her chair and flung it sideways into the air, spinning it end around end. It crashed on top of the counter, one of the metal legs obliterating three glass jars filled with paintbrushes. The plastic back of the chair let out a crack as it collided with the sink faucet.

Every part of me tensed. For a brief moment no one moved. Then, out of the stunned silence, I heard a tearful sniffling. It was Kenny. He hung his head so that no one could see that he was crying, but there was no mistaking the tremor in his shoulders. As I looked around at the faces of my students, it was immediately apparent to me that their usual fear of Hannah had now turned to sheer panic. Hesitantly, I returned my gaze to Hannah, unsure what she might do next, and when I saw how she narrowed her eyes at me, something inside of me snapped.

"Get out," I said.

Hannah jerked her head back slightly. "What?"

"I said: GET. OUT."

"But—" Her voice seethed with indignation. "But you promised my dad you'd never kick me out."

"Get out," I repeated, pointing firmly toward the door.

Hannah drew a sharp breath into her nose. "Where?"

"I don't care where. Right now, you do not belong here—" I stopped abruptly. I knew I was saying something intended to cut her to the quick. "The principal's office. Go see Mr. Chapman. Now."

Hannah looked sidelong at the floor, her eyes still narrowed. She seemed to be trying to check the faces of her classmates out of her peripheral vision. Maybe she was trying to buy some time, too. Time to figure out how to leave with the upper hand, or time to see if I might change my mind. A moment later, she made her way toward the door, staring intently at me the entire way. No longer did she narrow her eyes. Now her droopy-lidded gaze gave the impression of dull coldness, an indifference that bordered unnervingly on lifelessness. As she neared me, she stuck her tongue into the side of her cheek and gave me a look as if to say that I was the brazen one here, and that I would come to regret this decision. As she passed me, she came so close that she nearly brushed against me, a last grasp at power, and once she'd passed by me without further incident, I felt all the tension loosen in my shoulders. Then I tiptoed to the doorway where I peeked down the hallway until I was sure that she had turned into the office.

*   *   *

Each night I drew small portraits of my students, four or five sketches overlapping one another on a single page as I tried to capture them from different angles, in different lights, different moods. I kept my sketchbook under a Japanese fishing float on the windowsill among the abalone and moon snail shells, the clam shells filled with beach glass and willow charcoal sticks. My artist mother told me as a child that charcoal was for big sketches, sketches intended to create the illusion of motion and vector, but I loved how the rough lines and the smudges of black dust opened my yolk-sized portraits to interpretation, like tiny Rorschach blots. Whether it was the lack of realism and definition I embraced or the ability to inject my interpretations with hope, I did not know. But as I sketched my students' portraits that evening, I found myself searching their faces for cracks of innocence, traces of what was once whole among all those broken lines, as if their true child selves were buried somewhere beneath the frowns and the scowls and the furrowed brows, the cruel smirks, the seemingly unkind intentions, the scathing mockery of everything, the immeasurable hurt, the angry blood rushing out of their broken hearts.

Once again that nagging thought sprang to my mind. Quit. Quit this job. Just quit and pack your belongings and go back to the city. But what would my friends think of me? Would they even believe it if I told them how the first month—just the first month—of teaching in Tawakin had taken the ground out from under my feet? And it wasn't just Hannah Charlie. There was Candice Henry, and her photograph of her father, drowned in the Pacific, her mother living on a beach somewhere in Port Hardy. There was Odelia, and her father who had been kicked out of the village for something only said in whispers. There was Kenny, and his mother who had obliterated their television with a shotgun one night two weeks ago. Even those children who sometimes laughed quietly at my jokes or flashed a small smile when they understood a math problem or showed a hint of excitement for an art project, even those children erected walls around themselves that left me believing I could never teach them in a way that might make a difference.

As I roughed out the structure of Hannah's face, I rubbed the charcoal until the lines of her face became soft and peaceful, a vision of what I dreamed she might become. Normally, the more serenity I depicted in her face each night, the more my feeling of defeat and futility faded. Tonight, though, no amount of alterations seemed to lift up my spirits. After school, the principal, Mr. Chapman, had asked me to fill out an incident report, which I did while John, the school custodian and maintenance worker, picked bits of glass off the counter. Turns out, Hannah had spent the rest of the day in Mr. Chapman's office, where they played checkers and he promised to move her on to learning chess in the school's chess club if she in turn promised to never hurl furniture in the school again. This surprised me, that Hannah had been keen to learn how to play chess. What surprised me more was that Mr. Chapman had managed to extract this information out of her back in early September when she was spending every day fighting and taunting me.

I could leave here tomorrow, or next week, or at the start of Christmas holidays, wishing everyone felicitations only to never return.

And what would it matter? Even if I felt shame for leaving, I would never have to see any of these people ever again.

There were practical matters, of course, some more insurmountable than others. For starters, I came here because there were no jobs in the city. And I had student loans to pay. And now I had no apartment to go back to. For another thing, how would I get all my belongings out of the community if I wished to leave without anyone knowing I was leaving? Maybe the answer was to admit it. Admit that I was not cut out for this. Admit that this was not a life I could understand. Admit that I was sorry, but this wasn't for me. Me, who grew up on a quiet surburban street where people manicured their lawns and where children sat so still in their school desks you would think their chairs were made of flowers.

It was almost midnight by the time I had drawn over half the class. Where mouths turned downward in actuality, I had curved lines upward. Where shadows darkened their eyes, I had depicted light. Where eyelids drooped in apathy, I had lifted their gaze wide. Where expressions showed fear, I had injected hope.

As I leaned back and stared at my work, it occurred to me that some might think it dangerous to contort my students' reality in this way, but over the past month my sketchbook had become a rock of faith, a source of strength, and it was at nightfall when I needed this the most. It was at nightfall when I felt most uncertain about living on an edge of the world where dark rainforest met ocean, the precise place where two unknowable things came together. It was at nightfall when the darkening forest left me alone with my uneasiness, my mind going over the day, trying to figure out how I could out-teach the broken lines, the frowns, the fears. That was when the strange light changed the cedars and the firs into creatures that seemed almost heartbreaking to me, in their hugeness and their sense of purpose.

2

Tuesday was Hot Breakfast Day for staff, students and the village elders. As usual, the same three women were in charge of the cooking: Sophie Florence Joe, the school secretary, and Gina Joe and Margaret Sam, two of the teaching assistants. They wore grease-stained aprons with sayings like "Fry Bread Queen" and "I'm such a good cook even the smoke alarm cheers me on," and as they whipped up scrambled eggs and turned bacon with tongs and flipped the fry bread in splattering oil, the three women chatted and giggled and tousled the hair of the small children coming through the door.

The large table in the school kitchen left little space for the women to squeeze past one another along the counter and the two stoves. Today, extra chairs were crammed tightly around the table, each seat filled with young and old. Those who did not have a seat hovered in what little space was left, dodging out of the women's way. On top of the chest freezer against the wall, Hannah Charlie squatted on her haunches like a frog of a girl, ready to stick her tongue out at whatever moved past, wearing that same shirt as yesterday with the cuffs curled around her hands. She gave me a quick look that might have been a glare, but otherwise she acted as though nothing had happened the day before.

Since the tiny school did not have a staff room or a large office, the small set of teacher resources was stored on two bracket shelves in the back corner of the kitchen. I squeezed past everyone to retrieve a book on science experiments. With the book in hand, I started to make my way back to the classroom to finish preparing my lessons but was intercepted by Mr. Chapman.

"You can't run off now," he said with a smile. "Stay. Have some breakfast."

I smiled and shook my head, averting my eyes to the cover of the book in my hands. Whenever I looked at Mr. Chapman's pale, translucent skin, I found myself tracing the path of his circulation along the bright blue veins in his face and neck and arms. I guessed him to be over seventy years old. He'd come out of retirement from back east somewhere in Ontario, stopping for a year or two to teach in northern British Columbia along the way. How desperate must the school district have been to fill the principal position with a man who regularly forgot the names of the teachers and the students, where he'd placed certain files, why he'd called certain meetings, and that the school boat needed to be tied to the dock or it'd wind up in the middle of the cove.

"Sit. Eat," he insisted.

I looked at the clock. Forty minutes until the morning bell. "I really can't. I need to get ready to teach."

Chuckling, Mr. Chapman shook his head. "Nonsense. This is what you need to do right now. Sit with everyone. Eat. Am I right, Gina?" He called out across the kitchen. "She needs to sit and eat, am I right?"

"Ay-ha," Gina called out over her shoulder as she flipped rashers of dripping bacon, "you are so right, sir. So right. She needs to sit and eat."

Mr. Chapman pushed a chair toward me. Taking one more glance at the clock, I sat down reluctantly. With a satisfied nod, Mr. Chapman sidestepped his way twice around the big table as though he were doing laps, stopping to talk about basketball with the teens or to tell the younger children a knock-knock joke. Like me, Mr. Chapman had arrived in Tawakin last month, yet already he appeared to have made a connection with the children, despite their eyerolls at his corny jokes and the way he mispronounced the names of their favourite NBA players.

Someone behind me tapped me on the shoulder. I turned to see an elderly man grinning. His tongue poked out of a toothless gap.

"Ernie Frank," he said to me, patting me on the back.

"Molleigh Royston," I said. "Pleasure to meet you."

As I turned back around, I felt another tap on my shoulder.

"Just wanted to thank you," Ernie Frank said with a nod. "For coming here and teaching our children."

"Oh—" I uttered, unsure what to say. I knew enough about the effects of colonization and the history of residential schools, most likely attended by Ernie Frank, that I had assumed the elders of Tawakin would not want an outsider like me here. I took a quick glimpse at Hannah, who was sneering at one of the high school students. I thought of how I was considering quitting tomorrow, next week or by Christmas at the latest, and I felt a splinter of guilt. I smiled at Ernie and said, "It's my honour."

Across the room, one of my students, Candice Henry, guided her grandmother to a place next to her grandmother's sister, Nan Lily, who was the oldest elder in Tawakin. Carefully, little Candice draped a thin blanket over her grandmother's brittle legs, even though the kitchen was hot and humid with cooking. Candice Henry, who was ten years old and carried a photograph of her dead father everywhere, lived with her grandmother, who was also named Candice and who was blind.

Behind me Ernie muttered, "I can't tell who it's coming from."

I turned to him, in case he was speaking to me again, but he didn't look at me. He sipped his coffee and rotated his gaze around the crowded kitchen, locking his eyes for a moment on each person.

"But it's dark," he said. "And sharp as broken glass."

I turned my head slightly to hear him better, but he said nothing more. Mr. Chapman had made his way back and sat in the chair next to me.

Nan Lily passed a basket of fry bread to the children gathered around her and elder Candice. "Good lessons," Nan Lily said, "always happen over food. As you take in the food, you take in the lesson. You digest what you've learned. It becomes a part of you."

"The Basket Lady," elder Candice started. "She is big and fat, tall as anything, and ugly, too."

"And covered with hair, right?" Julian Henry asked.

Elder Candice nodded at the second grader. "Covered with hair from her head to her yellow-nailed toes. She steals children who are bad, so always listen to your parents. She steals children who are bad and rubs chewing gum over their eyes and tosses them into the big basket she carries on her back."

Candice paused so long between her sentences that I wondered if she was in fact taking a brief nap. Then she suddenly started up again.

"She thumps around the forest behind the village in her bare feet, all those naughty children on her back, blind and forgotten, wriggling inside her cedar basket, their limbs tied up in knots. Tangled up like a nest of snakes."

As they listened, the children clutched their fry bread like squirrels, nibbling tiny bites. I, too, was on the edge of my chair now, intrigued by the story, by the image of the Basket Lady, by the thought of her thumping around inside the surrounding forest, that forest that troubled me. I was so enthralled that I didn't notice Hannah standing in front of me.

"Did you hear what I said?" Hannah asked me.

Looking up at her, I shook my head.

"Nan Lily keeps glaring at me," Hannah said.

"I don't think that's true," I whispered. "Why would she do that?"

"Because she thinks the Basket Lady should get me," Hannah said.

Mr. Chapman leaned over to catch Hannah's eye and said, "The Basket Lady is just a story."

Hannah stuck out her chin. "It's *not* just a story."

As Hannah returned to her spot on the freezer, Ernie leaned forward and whispered to me, "I tell you, there's a bad energy coming off somebody."

My eyes moved to Hannah.

Ernie shook his head. "Not her. She's got a darkness for sure, but hers is more like an emptiness. That girl's got no hope."

Whether Ernie meant that he had no hope for Hannah, or that Hannah had no hope for herself, I couldn't guess. But it brought to mind a painting that I first saw on a Jordanian 30 fils stamp I found inside a used copy of *Foucault's Pendulum*. The book was monstrous in size and convoluted in style; I never did come close to finishing, but my discovery of the stamp between pages 454 and 455 made my attempt worth it. The figure of Hope sat on top of an orange globe, her eyes bandaged as she played a lyre of broken strings. With the single fragile string that remained, Hope strained toward the lyre to hear the sound of music. At the top of the painting a distant star shone, as if to say there was always the existence of more hope, even beyond Hope herself, although the poor woman couldn't possibly see it past her blindfold. If only somebody could tell her it was there: this was what had struck me most profoundly.

"One time," elder Candice said to the children, "the Basket Lady stole a boy. His mother loved him very much and she could not ever forget him even though he had been very, very bad. Every day the mother sat on the shore and prayed to the Creator and cried."

Hannah returned to me a second time. "I hate the part about Mucous Boy. I don't want to hear it."

"Why not?" Mr. Chapman asked. "It's just a story."

Hannah scowled at him.

"Tell you what, Hannah," Mr. Chapman said, "sit back down and we'll have our chess club twice this week."

"You promise?" Hannah asked.

"Cross my heart," Mr. Chapman said.

"Alright, but it's *not* just a story." Hannah stomped back to the freezer with her sleeve-covered fingers in her ears.

"That poor mother," Elder Candice said, "she cried so hard that snot came out of her nose: first as a trickle, then as a bubble and finally as a thick strand. The snot fell to the ground. The mother thought nothing of it. But soon she saw a face in the snot. The snot grew into a boy, a boy made of mucous. And the mother was not sad anymore. *Chuu*," she said, which simply meant: done.

"*Klecko, klecko*," said the children. Thank you, thank you.

Sophie Florence went to the garbage bin next to Ernie and tossed in a tower of eggshells. She nodded at Ernie, her nose dusted with flour. Even though she was the school secretary, Sophie Florence spent most of her time in the kitchen making food for the children or pounding her fists into a pillow of bread dough, a portable phone stuck in her apron or wedged between her shoulder and her jaw as she talked to parents or the school district office. As far as I could tell, Sophie Florence was the heart and soul of Tawakin, as well as auntie to many of the students, grandmother to others. She lived with her four brothers and her granddaughter Odelia Joe in a tiny house that overlooked the mouth of the cove.

The women announced that breakfast was ready and Sophie Florence asked Nan Lily to say a prayer. Although I found it strange to hear prayer at a public school, I lowered my head anyway. While Nan Lily murmured something in Nuu-chah-nulth, I found myself believing that I could feel the energy Ernie had mentioned. Ever since I was a child, I had always sensed those dark currents that moved invisibly underneath everything, rolling the round pebble of my life downstream.

Nan Lily ended the prayer with "*chuu.*" Several children rose to fetch plates of food from the women, which they delivered to the elders before getting their own breakfast.

As the children stuffed bacon and eggs into their mouths, I caught snippets of their conversations about video games and horror movies, the boys imitating guns and explosions while the girls shrieked and cried out in mock disgust. All fifty students from grades one to twelve at Tawakin School lived in the village, some even sharing the same crowded house, all related to one another—some closely, others distantly—by blood or by marriage.

Ernie shook his head and murmured to me. "Somebody in here needs to get cleansed. I just can't tell who it's coming from. Too many people in here. But I can feel it, the bad energy. It's a gift I got. My sister got it, too, after our father pushed us off his boat when we were young to swim with the killer whales. Except hers is in her vision, not in her feeling like mine. She can see when somebody needs to get cleansed. She sees it around the edges of people. A kind of aura. Not me. Me? I feel it in my skin when somebody needs to get cleansed."

"Cleansed?" I asked.

"Some brush with cedar. Others brush with the wing of an eagle."

"And that cleanses them?"

Ernie nodded once. "Can clean the dust right off their spirit."

❊   ❊   ❊

I had left my home in Surrey on the first of September and eventually drove my rusted minivan across the north of Vancouver Island along a logging road heading west. It was a rough gravel route surrounded by endless wilderness, with tall cedars bristling the mountains and steep ravines descending to the river far below. For two hours, I travelled the remote road, thumping into potholes and over large stones, the summer dust wafting through the vents and the windows and the rusted hole in the floor. The dust coated my hair, my face, the lining of my throat. It crept under my cuticles and it dried my eyes. It powdered the woods on either side of the road so thickly that it was difficult to make out the green of the foliage.

Why did the forest always make me think of childhood? Why did it always make me feel like I was ten again, wanting but not allowed to go outside, wishing to be sunburnt, in striped tube socks, with an ice cream pail of grasshoppers throwing themselves against the punctured lid? Forests should be dappled with sunlight and streaming with radiance but whenever I tried to recall the hours I used to spend perched high in a tall tree, the woods below me always appeared murky and dark, and in that darkness I could hear the trees rustle with a noise like newspapers and the pages of fairy tales.

At thirty-nine years of age, becoming a teacher was admittedly a late career choice. But there was my seven-year marriage to Mark, and then there was the divorce, and in between that was my career as an artist, though Mark would scoff at anyone who called it a career. "You don't get how the real world works, Molleigh. How are you going to make a living painting?" Then he always added with a derisive head shake, "You see the world through rose-coloured glasses."

Art critics agreed with Mark. My work was called vacuous. Devoid of substance. All surface with no depth. All light with no darkness. A saccharine optimism at best. One particularly scathing review called me an artist whose eyes were closed to the world. Someone who has yet to learn how to see. Still I carried on for a few more years, despite never selling enough pieces to make a living from it. Though I tried new approaches and focused on new subjects, I came to believe that the critics were right: I couldn't ever seem to capture any truth about life. Finally one day, not long after the divorce was finalized, I remembered the time, as a child, when my mother packed away my paintings, her voice shaky as she said, "Promise me you'll never make paintings like these ever again. There's too much darkness in them." It made no sense. I could recall painting pictures of animals and cars, but I had no idea what my mother saw in those paintings that upset her. The memory was enough, coupled with my string of failures and unsold work, to put my paints away for good.

For as long as I could remember, there were only two desires that had ever filled me with a sense of purpose: to become an artist and to teach children, in that order. Since being an artist had proven to not be my purpose in life, I now imagined a classroom filled with wonder, an emporium of exploration, and I'd packed my minivan with fossils and ostrich eggs, magnifying glasses, old cameras, geodes and other minerals, animal bones, glass beakers and test tubes, tanks for live frogs and other creatures, rock picks, trowels, sifting screens, archaeological maps. I imagined a classroom in which the drawers and cabinets were crammed with curiosities and creativity. Paintbrushes and easels and lumps of fresh clay ready for artistic hands. Artwork in neat rows along the walls, the children's names printed in the lower corners, the letters shaped with innocence and pride. The buzz of stories being read and told every single day. Questions and laughter wrapping around my students every moment. A classroom part Picasso's studio, part Edison's workshop and part Marie Curie's laboratory, minus the radioactivity— and, in my vision, it was a place the children would never forget. Sure, my rose-coloured vision might seem far-fetched to the Marks of the world, something out of an old movie, but it was what I imagined. I dreamed of building science projects and chatting about *Harriet the Spy* and *Harry Potter* and why the sky is blue. Children would say to me, Ms. Royston, quick I need magnet wire and a diode, and I would nod and say, third drawer under the trilobite case.

Of course, within a week of starting in Tawakin, I quickly became too overwhelmed to do much with my classroom. When I brought my gyroscope to school, the janitor found it later that day at the bottom of a toilet in the girls' washroom. Still, I promised myself that I would fill them with hope and curiosity and excitement; I said this, I said I would, and I drove that day brimming with optimism and the promise of possibility and no idea of what it would really be like.

Eventually the logging road ended at a dirt parking lot beside an uninhabited harbour. Empty boat trailers and cars, some with smashed windows or flat tires in tufts of long grass, lined the lot. On the ridge above the parking lot was a trailer partly concealed by trees. Large painted signs about moorage fees and boat fuel adorned the panel siding. No one was there, and nothing moved except the poplars bending in the wind and the swans drifting among the reeds in the estuary, turning in the breeze like paper boats.

On the concrete wharf I stacked all my cardboard boxes plus the large wood box that had belonged to my mother. About five feet long and four feet wide and just over half a foot deep, the box had not been easy to cart along. Yet that was exactly what I had done for the past twenty years. I knew what was in it, of course I did, but the key had gone missing years ago, which allowed me to avoid looking at the paintings which my mother, long dead now, had locked inside so many years ago.

I paced the wharf, back and forth among seagull droppings and squashed cigarette packs and plastic coffee lids, searching the channel of water. By the time I had graduated, there were no teaching jobs to be found anywhere, so instead of staying put and hoping for calls to substitute occasionally, I applied wherever there was work. I thought about this as the wind swept under the wharf and into the metallic shells of boats docked below, as it trumpeted through a pile of scrap metal. It made the whole place feel hollow. Everything rusted and broken, forgotten. There was always work in the most remote corners.

For a long time, there was no sign of anybody, not even a faraway speck on the water. From there the journey was supposed to continue by boat for another half hour. Somebody, according to the school, would pick me up at noon. Finally, a young man arrived in a twenty-foot fishing trawler at two o'clock. He wore a green ball cap pulled low over his eyes and he gave me an almost imperceptible nod as he asked, "You my daughter's new teacher?"

"Are you Chase Charlie?" I asked.

Chase Charlie's seat was the only seat in the boat, so I sat on an upside-down bucket facing the stern, surrounded by my boxes of belongings. As we drove along the stretches of open water, the silence between us continued, the roar of the motor and the wind over the open deck making it impractical to talk. To my right, the Pacific Ocean stretched to the distant horizon, and I imagined it stretching like that, unbroken by land, all the way to Japan. To my left, the rugged stone of the shoreline was etched with scars, beaten by violent storms, everything upon the stone and the earth deep and dark, a fibrous mass without a hint of humankind to be seen. No glints of glass panes in the tangled trees, no docks along the shores, no swatches of colour other than green upon darker green, browns and greys—overcast grey, granite grey and somewhere in there, grey wolves.

When we arrived at last, passing slowly into the mouth of the cove, the sudden sight of Tawakin startled me. As Chase slowed the motor to a creeping putter across the cove, I tried to take in everything: the village, the house on the rocky ridge with a large red cross painted on the cedar siding, the long wharf with creosote-stained pilings, the yellow and purple cabins hiding in the trees of a narrow island across the cove from the village, the red canoe resting on the shore. After nothing but stone and cedars and firs for miles and miles, the suddenness of bright colours had appeared to me like a secret hidden at the edge of the world.

"What kind of teacher are you?" Chase turned to me.

I looked at him blankly, wondering what he meant by the question. Elementary or high school? Strict or permissive? Mean or kind? I squinted and looked intently at the water, as if to convey my deep consideration of a question I didn't understand.

"They kicked my daughter out of school lots of times before," he said, sounding defensive. "You gonna be the kind of teacher who kicks her out?"

Now it was my turn to feel defensive. His question felt like an accusation, as though I was being blamed for something I had not yet done. I readjusted one of the teetering boxes in front of me, taking a moment to figure out my answer. I shook my head. "I am not the kind of teacher who kicks a child out."

"Not ever?"

"Not ever," I said.

"Even if she swears?"

"Even if she swears."

Immediately I regretted saying this. At that point, I knew nothing about this child, yet I had made a promise I possibly couldn't keep.

Chase cranked the boat toward the concrete dock at the bottom of the village. At the sight of the boat, children dumped their bicycles and scattered along the low ridge of the crescent shoreline. From the corner of my eye I could see them peeking from behind propane tanks and between thistles growing from the cracked hulls of overturned boats.

Once my boxes were loaded onto the pickup truck, which was the only other vehicle in the whole place besides the school truck, I climbed into the passenger seat next to Chase. The truck was rusted, and its lights were smashed out, the passenger door attached with rope. We drove along the dirt road that circled the inner row of houses, my boxes rocking in the back of the truck with every dip and bump.

Two women in bloodied aprons peered through the smoke seeping from a fish shack as the truck went by. The bright colours of the houses were duller than I had first thought, revealing themselves to be a patchwork of repairs and peeling paint. In one yard, a large depression in the ground was filled with dozens upon dozens of empty milk containers, a pond of plastic. Elsewhere, the grass grew thick and lush around forgotten bicycle wheels, discarded motors, broken laundry baskets, coils of rope, prawn traps.

Shadows moved across the house windows that day. Two faded Canada flags parted like curtains in one window, then quickly closed again. As the truck left the village and headed up a steep road rising into the forest, I spotted an animal skull above a shed door. Its flesh was rotting off in long shreds, its mouth gaping, its eyes gone. As we passed, those empty sockets seemed to gaze at me, following my every movement, and I got the eerie yet exhilarating impression that this place, like me, was full of searching.

*　　*　　*

At lunch that Tuesday, Chase Charlie came to see me in my classroom. I was seated at my desk, exhausted after a long morning of the class shutting down and refusing to do any work. The moment I saw his face, I grew nervous. He narrowed his eyes in that same way Hannah did.

"You said you wouldn't never kick Daughter out of your classroom," he said, his arms folded across his chest.

I stared down at the row of blue check marks in my open attendance folder. "I did, yes. I did say that." Looking up, I pointed at the counter across the room. "But she threw a chair and smashed our paintbrush jars."

"Sometimes she can't help it," Chase said. He pushed the green ball cap higher up off his forehead and tried to fit into one of the grade-three desks without thinking. He got stuck but persevered, wriggling into the tight space. Something about the look on his face—a sincerity—was endearing. "You made a promise," he said firmly.

My body slumped in my chair. He had said the word *promise* with such weight. Yesterday I had thought sending Hannah out of the classroom was the right thing to do. Now I wasn't so sure. "I'm sorry," I said.

"What can we do about it?" he asked.

"What do you mean? She's back at school."

"About your promise? You going to keep it from now on?"

I stared at him as he tried to turn sideways in the too-small desk. The whole front, hooked on his thighs, lifted off the floor. I tried not to smile, but then he laughed, and so I laughed, too, except his laugh sounded wholesome while mine sounded nervous.

Once he was free, he said, "She talks about you at home. All the time."

"What?"

"All the time," he repeated.

My stomach fluttered. The thought of what Hannah might have said about me at home horrified me. "You know how kids can exaggerate things sometimes," I suggested. "Maybe we could agree that I'll take what I hear about home with a grain of salt, if you take what you hear about me with a grain of salt."

He shook his head thoughtfully. "She's never talked about any other teacher as much as she talks about you. She says, Teacher said this and she said that, and it was so funny, Dad, she's so funny, and then we did a science experiment with pop and candy and it was the best! It was such a great day, Teacher is the best."

I raised my eyebrows in disbelief. What Chase was saying couldn't be true. It had to be a ploy on Hannah's part, I was certain of it. She was fooling her parents for some reason.

"She likes you so much, Teacher," he said, and in his voice I heard the same sincerity I saw in his face. His eyes looked like they might be moist with tears, but it was hard to see in the shadow of his ball cap. "She likes you so much. And she don't like any teacher. I don't know what you do in here, but all she does is come home and talk about you and I never seen her so happy."

I pressed my palm against my forehead, trying to make sense of it. All I could recall in that moment were the times Hannah had told me to fuck off or called me a redneck bitch or a fat cow, and I couldn't help but continue to feel that what Chase was telling me was impossible.

"And then you kicked her out," he said. "And she came home and she cried the whole night." Chase pulled off his ball cap, scratched his head, then wiggled the cap back on. "My wife Patty wanted to come up and bang on your door, but I said, hold on, we don't know the whole story yet. So, that's why I'm here. To get the whole story."

"It started with her hands," I said.

"Her hands?"

"She's been hiding them all day long at school," I said. "She refuses to show me or tell me what's wrong."

Chase laughed. "Who knows with that girl. If something was wrong, she'd tell me for sure. She trusts me. And I trust her."

I nodded.

Then he asked, "Do you?"

"Do I—?" I trailed off, uncertain what he was asking.

"Do you trust her?"

My mouth opened a little, but no words came out. How could I trust Hannah? I could list for him all the names she called me, or all the ways she intimidated her classmates, but Sophie Florence had made it clear to me that Hannah's behaviours were common knowledge. If Chase had done nothing about Hannah yet, it felt pointless to give him an inventory now. Instead I scrambled to think of a diplomatic answer but I must have been taking too long because he repeated his question and in that certain kind of challenging tone that could only come from a parent. Then he asked a third time, rewording the question.

"*Are* you going to trust my daughter?" Before I could answer, he added, "Are you going to be different than all the other teachers who come here?"

"What do you mean?" I asked.

"Are you going to leave her wondering why you left? Are you going to leave her thinking you left on account of her?"

"I—" My breath caught in my throat. "I hope not."

"Me too."

There was a long pause.

"Because," he went on as he made his way to the door, "we've never seen her this happy about school." He stopped in the doorway, turned to me and took off his cap. He clutched it with both hands, wringing it slightly. "Please don't leave."

I didn't know what to say to this. I squeezed my hands together underneath my desk, looking at the chalkboard across the room. I felt his large essence, and I pictured briefly that a cedar tree stood next to me, one that was not large in stature but in its determination to push its branches through anything, fixed in its spot, almost heartbreaking in its sense of purpose.

"Teachers always leave," he said. "Please don't leave. Promise you'll stay."

I looked at him and nodded.

He flashed a wide grin at me, gave me a firm nod in return and said *klecko, klecko*, then dashed out the door, his cap still twisting in his fists. As his footsteps shuffled quickly down the hall, I felt stunned, wondering what had just happened. Had I just agreed to something? I had only meant to nod in acknowledgement of what he'd said, nothing more. There was no promise in my nod. I never meant to promise. I stood to hurry after him, to tell him that he mistook what I meant, but I hesitated and turned back toward my desk, petrified at the thought of explaining to him that he'd misunderstood, that I couldn't possibly make such a promise—not when I wanted more than anything to go back home, not when I believed I might not last another week in this place, not in the same classroom as the ticking time bomb that was his daughter. Yet how could I face that sincere father, that cedar tree of a man determined to keep his daughter in school? I didn't have the heart to correct him. I should have been more careful because, while it felt good to be wanted—didn't it?—I had accidentally given him my word and your word to another human being was, to me, different than accepting a job from an institution—my job was nothing more than an impersonal, economic agreement. I sat back at my desk and stared out the window at the trees across the logging road, my mind flitting to the darkness and deceit of forests, and as I waited for the school bell to bring back the children from the village down the hill, I lamented how much I wanted my word to be worth something.

3

On Friday little Candice Henry asked if she could tell me a secret. It was early in the morning and I was in my classroom finishing last night's portraits in my sketchbook. As I shaped the crown of Kenny's head out of the white space of the page, I contemplated the nature of edges. How all edges, no matter how thick or razor thin, light or heavy, rough or smooth, never belonged to a single object but were always shared between things. The precise place and moment when two things came together.

"You can tell me anything," I said.

Candice stood in the doorway of the classroom, the hood of her black sweatshirt covering her head, the darkness of the empty hallway framing her shoulders. Early morning rain glistened on her cheeks. In one hand she held a wet, limp envelope and in the other, the photograph of her dead father.

"Promise not to tell anybody?" Candice glanced down the hallway, but we were the first to arrive that morning.

The last thing I wanted to think about was another promise. I told her, "I can't promise that. As a teacher, there are rules about the kinds of secrets I'm allowed to keep." I rested the piece of charcoal in the binding of my sketchbook and leaned back in my chair. Out the window, I could see my grey trailer home across the gravel road, the hard rain pricking the puddles on the asphalt basketball court, the wind pushing against the swings on the playground. On the chain-link fence, a child's forgotten jacket.

Candice narrowed her eyes at me. "Then I won't tell you."

"Alright," I said.

Candice pouted, which was nothing new. She was sad most of the time. She sat near the front of the classroom, easy to forget with her quietness. Sometimes I tried to coax her across the room to play games with the others on the carpet, but her desk and what she kept inside it seemed enough company for her. In the pencil trough, she always tilted upright the small photograph of her dead father. At recess, whenever she was made to go outside, Candice put the photograph in her back pocket and took her father on the swings and down the yellow slide. There was also the stack of letters from her mother, who left Tawakin to go to a party in Port Hardy two years ago. Now Candice lived with her grandmother in the blue house at the back corner of the village.

"I got another letter." Candice held up the envelope. "Do you want to read it?"

"I sure do," I said.

"Read it out loud." Candice handed the envelope to me, then went to the corner of the classroom and sat cross-legged on the large rug. "Don't forget your special glasses, Teacher."

I went to the chalkboard and took the pair of cat-eye glasses from the ledge. The thick black frames, sweeping up into giant curves in the corners, were decorated with tiny fake diamonds. Despite being two-dollar costume glasses without real lenses, my doctor had prescribed them to me for reading aloud. Almost magically, according to this doctor, they electrified the words on the page, bringing them to life and causing me to read with great fluidity and feeling. This was what I'd told the class, drawing the details out into a long, elaborate story, and so far, none of the children had doubted me, not even Hannah, who believed everybody in the world lied most of the time.

Wearing glasses three times too big for my face, I stood next to the window where the floor vents blew warm air up my pant legs and across the sandals I always wore in the classroom. I started to read the letter.

Deer Candice—

"You're not supposed to read over there," Candice interrupted. "You're supposed to read over here. On the Read-Aloud Rug."

"It's fine where I am," I assured her.

"But I'm already sitting on the rug. How come you can't meet me over here?"

"I'm more comfortable here. It's warm." But that was only half the reason. Truth was, I couldn't bear to sit that close to Candice while I read her letters. The words were hard enough to read without feeling Candice's quivering sadness next to me. "You can hear me perfectly fine from there."

Candice frowned, but I stayed next to the window and read her letter, and although I paused to puzzle out misspellings and occasionally stumble over missing punctuation, I tried to read with an air of great importance.

Deer Candice I cry every nite becuz I miss you reel lots. But don't worry I allmost haf enuff mony to cum bak to Tawakin when I cum bak I will teach you how to mak bred becuz I promised you we wood mak bred it will be reel gud. Love Mom

"Can I answer her during writing time today?" Candice asked.

"You can answer her," I said. "But after school. I have lessons planned for writing time today."

More than once I had wrestled with how to handle these letters. This was the fifth one Candice had brought me. Every single one of her mother's letters, including this latest one, was written in Candice's own handwriting with those looping *t*'s and *i*'s dotted with tiny, plump hearts. The shaky *w*'s as wide as whales.

"It's a real good letter, huh?"

I looked at her. "Yes, it really is."

While Candice crafted her mother's letters in this simple, awkward fashion, Candice's replies were vastly different. Unlike anything she wrote as an assignment, Candice's return letters, despite the grammatical errors and misspellings, were bone-shiny vessels of yearning, pieces of prose that plumbed the deepest caverns of human feeling, intimate tangles of fact and fiction, the details raw and visceral. Where she mailed these letters, I never knew, but each one burned brightly with the promise of a writer who might someday turn an entire nation inside-out with her voice.

There were moments, however, when Candice did not mask her mother. Sometimes, she stayed after school and helped me clean the paintbrushes or tidy the books. For a short while she'd open her clenched fist and show me the heat of adult truths she kept hidden there. She told me that her mom lived in Port Hardy so she could get money from her boys. She told me how the boys party and get *naqcuu*—drunk—with her mom on the beach where her mom lived in a tent she had stolen from Canadian Tire. She whispered to me that her mom does stuff for the boys. Gross stuff. For money. Then Candice would tell me that someday she'd find money of her own.

"Because then," she'd said, "my mom will like me better than her boys."

I slid the letter back inside the envelope and put the envelope on Candice's desk. Candice remained on the carpet with her arms wrapped around her bent legs, her forehead resting on her knees. She stayed like that for several minutes, silent, the clock on the wall the only sound in the room.

Then she said, "There's a woman."

"A woman?" I asked, sitting back at my desk.

"A woman in a box." Candice's voice sounded careful and low, as if the information was both a secret and a warning.

"A woman in a box?"

"With a baby," Candice said.

"A woman in a box with a baby?"

Candice lifted her head. "Don't tell nobody about it. Please."

I was intrigued to hear more, though I wondered if this wasn't, like her letters, another one of Candice's fabrications. I looked out at the woolly, grey sky. "Where?"

"In the middle of Fossil Island. Over by Nurse Bernadette's place."

Fossil Island stood outside the village cove. The Pacific Ocean threw itself against the low-lying bluff of sharp rocks there. Black stones imprinted with scallop fossils older than the moon fringed the shores, that's what Chase Charlie had said.

"You been on it?" Candice asked.

"I've only boated past," I said.

"Well, the island isn't too big but it's real thick with trees and there's moss and lichen hanging everywhere like an upside-down garden. Makes it hard to get to the middle of the island, with the trees all tangled up." Candice lowered her voice. "That's where she is, in the middle there."

"The woman in the box with the baby?"

Candice nodded.

"You can get lost in the woods, you know," I said. I could hear the uneasiness in my voice. "It's not safe."

Candice nodded again. One of the outside doors opened with a clatter, then footsteps. Across the hallway I could see Joan Smith wriggling her key into the primary classroom doorknob.

"There's an open spot," Candice said. "In the middle of the island full of ferns and skunk cabbage. And there's this giant cedar tree that fell into that open spot a long time ago." Her voice became airy with a sense of awe. "A beam of silver light pours like water through the hole in the treetops where the giant cedar used to stand. A bunch of spruces are growing out of the cedar. All them spruce roots hold on to the cedar trunk. Just like fingers around a paddle. One of the fingers pushed right through the bottom of the cedar box. It pokes out between her leg bones. It pokes out so much that it broke the lid of the box into two pieces. Both pieces fell to the ground. Now the woman in the box with the baby aren't even covered no more. Now they just stare straight up at the heavens."

I dwelled for a moment on Candice's description, how much the imagery reminded me of the stories Candice wrote in class. I asked, "The woman is real?"

Candice nodded. "And her baby."

As I thought about whether to believe any of this, I went to the bookcase and straightened the tattered novels on one of the shelves—several copies of *The Bridge to Terabithia* and *Holes*. I asked, "Who are they?"

Candice shrugged. "Don't know."

There was a sudden change in Candice's tone, and it surprised me. She now sounded matter of fact, as if the subject was mundane and not a bit mysterious.

"When it rains," Candice said, "the rain knocks on her hollow skull and rattles against her bones and fills her mouth right to the ends of her broken teeth, to the two big ones in the front, the silver one and the one made of wood. You probably don't know the story about the wood tooth. Only a few special people know it. And there's another story about the silver one, too. A different story that's sort of the same."

I glanced at the clock. Soon the others would arrive.

"Is it a long story?" I asked.

"Kind of," Candice said.

"Tell me."

"No," Candice said. "I can't tell it right."

"I'm sure you can," I said. "You are an amazing writer."

I picked up a book off the shelf. Somebody had scribbled boogers into Brian's nostrils on the cover of *Hatchet*. With a pen, I quickly turned the graffiti into a moustache, then slipped the book into place on the shelf.

"A treasure is there," Candice said. "In the box. With the woman and the baby."

"What kind of treasure?" I asked.

Candice went silent for several moments.

I asked again, "What kind of treasure?"

Candice said softly, "My mom's going to like me better than her boys."

The quiet desperation in her voice struck me hard. I turned away from her, not sure how to react. I wanted to help her somehow, to make things better, to make her mom return, to make it so that Candice didn't think she needed to seek a treasure. Nothing good ever came of a child seeking what their heart longed for inside a dark forest.

"Are they supposed to be there," I asked, "the woman and the baby?"

"Don't know," Candice said. "I guess."

"If they're supposed to be, then how come it's a secret?"

"Because—" Candice looked away. "We're not allowed to go there."

Somewhere down the hallway, I could hear the cheerful whistling of Sophie Florence Joe. It grew louder as she neared the office next to my classroom.

"Have you ever gone there?" I asked.

"I told you. We're not allowed."

Candice and I stared at each other, and as I floated in the silence of a secret I didn't understand, I considered asking Candice how she'd come to know so many details if she'd never been there before. But I could feel the bristling of Candice's nervousness from across the room and it made me anxious, too. I was starting to realize that this part of teaching had been kept from me: all the training, all the books, all the mentoring in the world could not have prepared me to teach children who cursed at me with spit in their words one day, then spilled out their private selves the next. Who hurled chairs across the classroom one day, then went home and cried all night because you rejected them when all they wanted was acceptance. Who hid their faces behind hoodies one day, refusing to answer your simplest questions or requests, then trusted you to join their pretend game of fake letters from an absent mother the next.

After school that day I went to the office and asked Sophie Florence, "Who is the woman in the box with the baby?"

Sophie Florence leaned back in her swivel chair and folded her hands on her belly. "Where'd you hear about that?"

"One of the students told me."

Sophie Florence nodded. "The kids got a story that there's treasure there."

"Yes."

"There's no treasure," Sophie Florence said with a grin.

"Why do they think there is?" I asked.

"You know how kids make stuff up. To test each other. Like a dare. But they know they're not allowed to set foot on that island."

"How come?"

"When a loved one passes, we have traditions to make sure their journey will be complete," she said. "When a family can't finish what needs to be done, it can be dangerous—" The phone on Sophie Florence's desk rang. She paused to pick it up, explained that Mr. Chapman was not available at the moment, then scribbled down a name. Hanging up the phone, Sophie Florence shook her head. "Hannah's mom, Patty, calling to complain again."

My stomach tightened. I thought of Hannah crying. "About me?"

"Not you." Sophie Florence motioned her head slightly in the direction of Mr. Chapman's office. "But I'm sure you'll get your turn soon. She complains about anything and everything. Anyways, where was I? Right, we were talking about *isaak*. The elders have always told the kids: Have *isaak*—respect—for the dead. Never disturb the dead. It can lead to *numak*."

"What's *numak*?"

"Bad things," Sophie Florence said.

"What kind of bad things?"

"Things get broken, accidents happen, dogs get spooked, strange sounds haunt people." Sophie Florence sighed and added, "Another loved one can be taken."

She said this last part so solemnly that I fell silent.

"The kids might like to tell stories about a treasure," Sophie Florence said, "but they know it's not to be taken lightly. It's not to be made fun of. Our stories are the way they are for a reason. They shouldn't be changed like that. If they hear that treasure story too much, they'll start to believe it. We need them to believe the stories of our elders. They are the stories of who we are and how we are to be."

"So what is the story of the woman in the box with the baby?" I asked.

"I don't know," Sophie Florence said.

"You don't know?" I asked in surprise. "Well, has she been there a long time?"

"As long as I can remember," Sophie Florence said. "Only a couple of the elders know the story, I think. I don't ask. They'll tell it if we need to know it. But bad things can happen if you disturb the woman and her baby. That's the story the elders do tell."

✻   ✻   ✻

At home that evening, I stood at the living room window. The rented teacherages were provided by the school board, as were the sparse furnishings, though a few of the makeshift pieces had been left by previous teachers. In my living room there was a greasy green armchair, which I never dared to sit on, not after finding a dead mouse in a crack of the cushion, and a coffee table made from a warped sheet of plywood set on top of four yellow milk crates. Black mould dotted the walls and occasionally mouse droppings dotted the floor corners.

The windows in the living room looked up the gravel road. Nearby were the trailers of the other teachers, plus Mr. Chapman's place, our quiet cluster of homes high above the village on the shore below. Next door was Joan Smith's trailer; across the road farther up were the trailers of Diane Rickman and Timothy Ness, the two high school teachers. A half mile separated the teachers from the community. Of course you never got to choose your colleagues, I knew, but there was really no escaping them here, not even when your time was supposed to be your own. I was used to the anonymity of surburban apartments, with neighbours who scarcely gave you a nod in the hallway. Now? Go for a walk, there they were. Go to the market, there they were. Go to a community dinner, there they were. Look out the living room window, there they were.

All the damn time.

And then there were the students and their parents. Already I felt the squeeze of what Joan had pointed out to me the first week: that being a teacher in Tawakin was like being on call twenty-four hours a day. No matter where I went, be it on a Monday or a Saturday, I was never not the teacher. I couldn't step outside without having to look at the school, a constant reminder of all the daily stresses and workload.

At nightfall, I sat at the kitchen table with my sketchbook, feeling a profound sadness that Candice longed for a treasure that didn't exist. I imagined the woman and her baby out there across the water on that thickly forested island. The thought of a child like Candice trying to make her way through those woods troubled me. Did she understand how dangerous a forest could be? Did she know how easy it was to mistake one sound for another in the woods? To mistake figures for mere shadows? Maybe Candice needed to hear the story of Erlking, king of the fairies. It was a story I knew by heart, having asked my mother to tell it to me many times as a child. In my sketchbook I started to draw the boy and the father riding by horseback through the forest at night, the boy's face frightened when he heard Erlking coming for him. It was only the wind, his father told him. And when the boy saw Erlking, his father told him it was only the shadows. Then Erlking said, "Come away little boy, come and play with me and my daughters on the shore." The boy cried out again, yet his father rode on, leaving the boy behind, not understanding how sinister the forest could be.

I turned to a fresh page, leaving the father and the boy with their tragedy. I thought of drawing another portrait of Candice, but my mind kept turning to an idea that had been slowly blossoming inside me all week. With my charcoal, I sketched a picture of Hannah as the figure of Hope. I planned my version to be more hopeful, without bandages to blind Hannah from the many stars of hope surrounding her head in the distant sky. Instead of setting her atop an orange globe, I perched Hannah atop a tree, and as I shaped her face to gaze skyward, I wondered how one could teach hope. How could a message of hope be delivered to students like Hannah and Candice so that it implanted in their thoughts, their feelings, their flesh, their bones?

Hunching over my sketchbook, I fell into a state of concentration of such intensity that the rest of the world slipped away and these questions of hope flowed in and out of the back recesses of my mind. After some time, I leaned back to survey the drawing and it struck me h Hannah's legs settled deep into the branches, strangely so. It looked as though Hannah was, in actuality, becoming the tree. I stretched my fingers, tight from clutching the charcoal, then I went about adding squiggled patches of foliage on the branches of the tree. I imagined this tree standing in the middle of an expansive field. There was nothing I loved more than the sight of a single tree in the middle of an expansive field, ideally a willow or an oak, something that could cast a large circle of shade with its wide branches. For many years, I had thought it was the simplicity and the symmetry of this image that I cherished, but recently I'd come to believe that it was the grace and mercy of it all, that such a singular object was left to stand for no other reason than the fact that it existed.

quite
ow

4

"The dark woods remind us of the darkest places of our minds."

I dropped a stack of math sheets that were still warm from the photocopier, startled by how the words seemed to have been plucked out of some place deep inside me. It was after school, and I was alone in the main office, checking my pigeonhole for any memos, when Mr. Chapman made this declaration out loud. He stood at the window of his office, a large closet of a room located at the back of the main office.

Crouching, I gathered the math sheets from the floor and wondered why his declaration sounded so familiar. "Jung?" I asked Mr. Chapman.

"Young. Old. The woods touch something deep in us all."

I went and stood in his doorway. "Since I have you here, I'm wondering if you've had a chance to consider the book order I proposed. I could really use some resources that don't refer to our students as Indians. Maybe some stories with Indigenous characters?"

Continuing to gaze out at the thick forest across the road, Mr. Chapman nodded. "Stories transform the dark woods."

"So that's a yes, then?" I asked, trying to ignore how strange it felt that he was discussing the woods in this way. As if he somehow knew how much they haunted me every evening.

Mr. Chapman nodded enthusiastically. "Yes, they need stories of hope. Stories that they see themselves in. Because you know what kids like them are used to? A whole lot of judging, condemning, blaming. What they need is reassurance. They need to believe that every day is a new chance. Every breath is a fresh start."

I felt a small surge of excitement for his optimism, and was suddenly invigorated, lifted momentarily out of my desire to leave this place, and I could hear the renewed energy in my voice. "And you're still okay with me renovating the old smokehouse next to my trailer for our chicken coop?" I asked. "The baby chicks are coming this week, and they'll have to be moved to the coop about two weeks after that."

"They're hatching in your classroom?" Mr. Chapman asked.

"No. If you recall, we tried to hatch chicks in the incubator but none of the fetuses grew to term. Saul Finkler is bringing day-olds in from town."

"Day-olds? Like doughnuts?" Mr. Chapman said, and I couldn't tell if he meant it as a joke. Then he said, "That will be good for the children, I think. It will make them happy, little chicks."

Hesitantly, unsure how to broach the subject, I asked, "Can I get your advice on something?" When Mr. Chapman nodded, I continued. "Have you heard about the woman in the box with the baby?"

Mr. Chapman narrowed his eyes. "Can't say I have."

After giving him a quick summary of the story that Candice had told me, I got straight to the point: "If I think that any of my students are planning to look for the woman, should I do something?"

"No," Mr. Chapman said flatly. "The kids here explore little islands on their own all the time, so it's not a safety issue as far as I'm concerned. And if it's not a safety issue, it's none of the school's business."

"But the elders said—"

"That's between the people down the hill," Mr. Chapman interrupted. "Besides, it's just a story. Let them pretend. Sometimes that's what they need."

Outside the window three dogs from the village ambled past. One with only three legs had mud or something worse matted in its black fur. It veered suddenly from the small pack and grabbed a soggy, half-eaten sandwich with its jaws. Wet pieces of brown bread fell to the ground.

The dog with thick yellow fur jostled for the scraps while the one with a face like a wolf mounted the three-legged dog from behind while it ate.

"Horrible creatures," Mr. Chapman said under his breath.

"They're mostly harmless," I said.

"Truth is, they scare me to the bone," Mr. Chapman said. "In Bodder they were particularly vicious, roaming in packs around town and snarling in their bloodied fights, afraid of nothing except the wolves that also wandered the town, coaxing the dogs away from their homes. Cousins for devouring. Wolves," he muttered. "Savage. Traitorous."

Mr. Chapman took a seat at his desk and motioned to the empty chair on the other side. Reluctantly, I sat and hoped our conversation would be a short one. As friendly as Mr. Chapman was, he was prone to long, rambling discussions, and I thought of all the things I could be doing instead. Preparing tomorrow's lessons. Boating over to the Tawakin Market to check my mail. Drawing in my sketchbook.

"It's a desolate place, Bodder. Ever been?" he asked.

I shook my head.

"Terribly desolate. Up in the far northwest of British Columbia, just south of the Yukon border. Hardly anything up there. A couple of small stores, a greasy roadside diner—" Mr. Chapman paused and looked up at the ceiling as if trying to access his mental inventory of the town. "Gas station, tiny post office, RCMP detachment. And the school. Kindergarten to grade twelve. One hundred and thirty-two students. Some of them bussed from the Tasset Reserve forty miles away. In the winter. In a bus with a broken heater."

"That's impressive," I said.

He gave me a perplexed look. "How so?"

"Their commitment to attend school. In conditions like that."

"Right. Well, all the kids nicknamed the town 'Badder' because they thought there was nowhere shittier, and every week somebody in my grade six and seven class bragged that they were finally moving out of that place—'thank fucking God,' they'd say—but nobody ever did, so they kept spending their days playing pool at Louise's Store or jumping their snowmobiles over ditches filled with empty bottles of Fireball."

"No wonder you're a natural with the kids," I remarked. "You've taught in some challenging places. Tough when the winters are so long."

"And the remoteness," Mr. Chapman added. "Worse than here, far worse. More people than here—four hundred—but there were four hundred miles of icy highway until the next town. Except for the health clinic and the garbage dump up the highway, we were surrounded by nothing but snow and icy lakes and stumpy trees. It was like being surrounded by death."

I had seen places like that on television, panoramic shots taken by low-flying planes. Endless tracts of spruce zipped inside white cadaver pouches, every body of water covered in a mortuary sheet.

Mr. Chapman spun in his chair to look out the window. "The town didn't become any more interesting when the snow finally melted in May. The kids then spent their days jumping their bikes over ditches filled with empty cans of Budweiser, or they'd hide in the woods, swarmed by bugs as they waited to throw rocks at Americans in Winnebagos. Those Winnebagos—" Mr. Chapman puffed out his cheeks with a gust of breath. "They'd show up at the end of May and they'd stream past the town from morning to night, one after another after another."

I pictured kids near the edge of the dark woods, their faces covered with balaclavas of black flies as they hurled stones at the white metallic whales migrating along an asphalt channel to Alaskan vacations.

"You'd think the spring sun would've brightened that town," Mr. Chapman said, "but it was a menace like everything else. It didn't even grow anything. The whole place was a scouring pad of rock and scraggly shrubs. Scarcely a blade of grass anywhere. And try teaching when the sun stayed in the sky until two in the morning, shining into bedrooms around the edges of aluminum foil taped over the windows. My students were bored and bitter to begin with. Add sleepless nights..." He trailed off.

I was entranced by this faraway land that seemed so brutal and unforgiving, and I found my respect for Mr. Chapman's experience deepening. There was a lot I could learn from someone who had managed to stay so full of hope after all his years. How did he do it when my hope was fading after one month?

Mr. Chapman smiled or winced, I couldn't tell which. "At least in the winter there was a good chance of a truck sliding off the road and toppling over."

I frowned. "A truck sliding off the road doesn't sound like a good thing."

Mr. Chapman shook his head vigorously, perhaps impatiently, as if to suggest it should be obvious to me. "No company ever bothered to recover cargo from the middle of nowhere. So, as soon as the truck driver flew home from the tiny landing strip, the whole town picked clean the truck's load of hothouse tomatoes or breakfast cereal or cartons of milk. Otherwise local authorities would burn it. Besides that, hothouse tomatoes and breakfast cereal and cartons of milk cost a bloody fortune at the Super A. You know what I'm saying, Sarah?"

"Molleigh," I reminded him.

Just then the VHF radio mounted to the underside of Sophie Florence's desk in the main office blared with a woman's voice: "Cinnamon buns for sale at Ella's today. Four dollars for one bun. Come and get a cinnamon bun."

Another woman demanded to know, "They got raisins, or nah?"

"Big raisins, yeah," said Ella.

"Ay-haw, don't like raisins," said the other woman.

"You can have them for only three dollars, then."

"Alright, I'll take three," agreed the other woman.

Most houses in Tawakin didn't have a phone. Instead, everybody communicated over Channel 14 on the VHF radio. On the VHF radio, parents called children back home at night. Women asked to borrow cups of sugar. Men warned about incoming weather or looked for somebody with gas to sell them for their boat. All kinds of familiar voices announced bread sales, pizza sales, Indian taco sales. From across the cove, the Tawakin Market let people know the store hours that day. When the power was out, which was often, the whole community played bingo over the VHF. It was like a string that tied the people together. Yet twice I had been awakened at night by darker sounds that came over the little handheld VHF radio I kept on my kitchen counter. Angry voices. Scared voices. A cry for help with a medical emergency the first time. A distressed report of a fight or domestic assault the second time. Shouts of panic in a place with no doctor, no police, no fire department.

When the cinnamon bun transaction was complete, Mr. Chapman continued. "In the coldest days of winter, there were men who wandered up and down the highway in blue jeans and thin jean jackets. Their eyes always half closed. Tiny bottles squeezed into their breast pockets."

The VHF radio went *click click click click click click click*. Somebody was rapidly pressing the button on their VHF radio. Somebody who the village called Buttons, an anonymous nuisance who seemed to find great amusement in pressing the TALK button repeatedly in quick succession. Days and weeks would pass without any sign of Buttons. And then, just as the community got used to the peacefulness, the noise would begin again. *Click click click click click click click.* For hours at a time, for several days in a row, the irritating noise filling every household and preventing others from talking on the community channel. Nobody had ever figured out who the culprit was, and I was told it was a mystery more than a decade old.

Mr. Chapman gazed out the window. "You ever have a moment when everything becomes clear and magnified and it shifts your thinking forever?"

I nodded, even though I wasn't sure it had ever happened to me.

Mr. Chapman patted a red notebook on his desk. "Happened to me a few times in Bodder. In fact, Bodder turned me into a poet. Started writing down these moments in my notebook. It's how I learned to cope."

"I do that, too," I said. "But not poetry. Drawings. Portraits, mostly."

"Perhaps you will show me sometime," Mr. Chapman said with a smile. Then he opened the notebook and set his palm flat on the open pages but didn't look at it. "One afternoon at the Super A, I asked one of these men how he could stand the cold dressed like that. It was minus thirty-two and the man was leaning against the empty ice machine outside. He looked at me with vacant eyes and, despite the fact that the sun was right there above our heads, he said, 'I wonder if you could tell me, brother, is it day or is it night?'"

I stifled a small laugh. While I did not know whether it was supposed to be funny or not, there seemed to be something comical about it, if darkly so.

"I remember that day clearly," Mr. Chapman said. "I remember how I turned away from the man and looked across the highway at the large mound known as Suicide Hill. Named that mostly because of the high-speed tobogganing done there in the winter. It was the most interesting thing to look at in that place. Everything rock and ice and leafless willow trees. Nothing in the distance to help you daydream, you know what I mean?"

I knew exactly what he meant. To me, nothing was more conducive to imagining than the sight of the vast ocean, and I couldn't fathom a place without such a focal point. A place with no landmarks to occupy your soul, no faraway shapes or colours to free your mind and let you dream something more than the gritty details of reality, only endless bars of ice and rock and leafless willow trees whose gunmetal branches I envisioned as bent and broken bayonets. Swatches of the same two spaces: the immediate grey and white here, the distant grey and white over there. Bleak tessellations.

"A thought grabbed me just then: When had I last seen a daisy, a rose, a blade of grass?"

"Unless you don't like rain, we are lucky here," I said, thinking of the rich variations of green upon green everywhere you looked.

"Well, imagine this. On the ground a few feet away from me was a thick femur of a moose, partly stuck in the snow. Bones like that fell off pickup trucks all the time. Anyway, I stared at its big knot of knee cartilage and I tried to imagine a daisy, then a rose, then a blade of grass, but I couldn't picture a thing except grey, which made my thoughts even darker, I'm not ashamed to tell you."

I inched forward in my chair. "Did you ever want to just quit and take off?"

"Oh, every day. In fact, that day outside the Super A somehow reminded me what a wraith I'd become teaching up there. I was a shadow of my old self. I turned back around and told the man, it is day, and I watched his face, but I couldn't figure out what this meant to him, if it pleased him or not."

At the image of such bleakness, I thought about how I had accidentally given my word to Chase Charlie and I wondered if I might also become a wraith, a shadow of my former self. I said, "It sounds like such a hopeless place."

"Yes. And it didn't take me long that day to recognize that this was the season—" Mr. Chapman stopped abruptly, looked down at his notebook, then smiled at me as if enticed by a thought. "Would you like to hear what I wrote that evening? It's just a ragged bit I might build into something bigger someday."

"Yes, please," I said.

Mr. Chapman slid the notebook in front of him and cleared his throat. "This was the season that mixed apathy with alcohol, stirred isolation with anger, bred unwanted children across the bare-boned, half-dead land."

I listened to Mr. Chapman's voice, how it lifted and fell in an almost Biblical cadence, and I thought, Who are you? I knew the man had a wife and grown children somewhere, but what was his story? Not the story everyone could see. Not the timeline of his life. Rather, the secret story hidden within the story. The secret story that lurked within everyone's private self.

* * *

Once at home, I went to the sink to fill the kettle for tea. As the kettle started to stir, I picked up the Japanese fishing float from the windowsill. The float was a hollow glass ball the size of a large orange, and I rubbed my hands around the smooth blue-green surface. Small bubbles of air were trapped inside the glass and on one end was a bump of extra glass, like a nipple or a wart or a knot. Peering into the empty sphere, I saw a ghostly globe, a crystal ball, a glass balloon, a hollowed womb.

Some years ago I heard a story about an amputee who believed that his phantom hand was perpetually clenched into a fist. It tormented the man every second of every day. No matter how hard he tried, he could not make himself imagine his phantom hand opening. He used mental tricks to no avail. After nobody was able to help him, he consulted the world expert on phantom limb pain. A mirror box was constructed. The man was told to clench his existing hand into a fist and insert it into the box, which gave him the illusion that both his hands were there before him. Then he was told to open his hand. Instant relief. For him to believe he could unclench his phantom hand, the man had to first suspend his disbelief. He had to see the thing not for what it was but rather for the things it wasn't. Pretending was what he needed, and that box created the lie that he possessed both hands. Sometimes it took a lie to reflect the truth.

When the tea was steeped, I took my sketchbook to my usual spot at the kitchen table next to the window and thought about Candice, the adult truths she kept hidden. I scanned the room as I rolled the stick of charcoal between my thumb and finger. The kitchen had come furnished with a table and four pine chairs, though one of the chairs had been pushed to the corner because it only had three legs. An orange plastic chair with *Tawakin School* written on the back with black marker had been put in the broken chair's place. A child's desk held a small microwave next to the table. The walls were the colour of concrete, the whole trailer a dim, gloomy box except on clear days when I could see an expanse of the Pacific Ocean out the window—an expanse so big it made everything about my life feel small and easier to grasp onto.

5

After dinner that night, fifteen yellow chicks arrived at my door in a Rubbermaid tote with a bag of feed, a bag of wood chips, two bales of hay, a roll of chicken wire and a plastic swimming pool—the type small children splash around in. The bottom of the pool was decorated with a giant purple octopus whose cartoon face looked uncannily like Mr. Chapman's.

"Think you could open the gym for basketball tonight?" Kevin Sam asked me. The grade eleven boy leaned on my deck railing.

"There's no one to supervise," I said, handing him a twenty-dollar bill for his efforts in boating the chicks and supplies across the cove from Saul Finkler's place. Saul Finkler was an American who ran a seasonal restaurant on Mitchell Island. Whenever he returned from Seattle, he brought back anything locals needed. Like plastic pools and chickens. In the darkness of the covered tote, the fuzzy creatures were quiet and still.

"You could supervise," he suggested, a small smile across his lips.

That night Joan was coming over for a visit.

"Or I could spend my Friday night relaxing," I said.

He clasped his hands together and made a begging gesture. "Please."

"Why don't you play on the outdoor court?" I asked.

Kevin grimaced. "Too many puddles. And you could sprain an ankle on those roots coming up through the asphalt. Please, Ms. Royston?"

"You know our deal." I raised my arms and pretended to shoot a basketball, flicking my wrist at the end. "Beat me at a game of Twenty One and I'll sacrifice my free time to open the gym on a Friday night."

Kevin groaned. "I'm never going to beat you."

"Probably true," I teased.

Kevin was tallish, at least in comparison to his classmates, and he had a decent free-throw shot, but I had played two years of varsity basketball and could still drain it from anywhere on the court.

"Now if you don't mind," I said, "I have a brooder to build."

As Kevin headed up the dirt path, the nature of his request suddenly struck me, and I felt a twinge of guilt when I thought of how seldom Kevin, who loved basketball more than anything, got to play in the gym. How could I say no to a teenager who wanted to spend his Friday night doing something other than drugs or drinking or video games? I thought about calling him back but didn't. I needed to keep some time for myself.

When the door knocked again later that evening, I fumbled my way through the dark trailer, the lines of furniture faint in the hint of sunset that remained. Opening the door, I squinted into the glare of the outside light. Joan Smith stood there with a mischievous smile on her face, holding a canvas bag. She wore a loose towel draped over her head. Underneath it, something large protruded.

"What's with the towel?" I asked.

"In case I ran into a student." Joan stepped inside then yanked the towel off with a flourish as she said, "Can't have them seeing this!"

I smacked my forehead. "You actually ordered it."

"Cost twenty-six dollars. Plus another thirty-two dollars of STT charges."

"STT?"

"Shipping to Tawakin," Joan said.

"You paid fifty-eight dollars for a plastic construction hat?"

Joan took the rubber tube that hung from the hat, put it in her mouth and sucked. From the two beer cans nestled in plastic rings on top of the shiny red hat, yellow liquid moved through the transparent tube.

"Tell me that's not worth it. Oh, and check this out." Joan unzipped her jacket to reveal a fanny pack with six pockets, each one containing an upright beer can.

"You look like you're going to a country music festival," I said.

Joan shrugged. "Got to do something to survive the dull days here."

"I can't believe you teach primary."

"Better fucking believe it." Joan walked past me into the kitchen. "Why is it so dark in here? You've got every single light off."

"The chickens," I said. "They're driving me nuts already. Peep, peep, peep. All fifteen of them, constantly. But the second it's dark? They sleep."

Joan flipped on the light and held out the canvas bag. "This should help."

Inside the bag was a box of Pinot Grigio. Although Tawakin was a dry community and alcohol was not permitted, this didn't include the teachers' homes up the hill. Still, we were discreet out of respect, especially after eating pieces of sobriety birthday cakes during lunchtime with Sophie Florence and Gina Joe to honour their many years alcohol free. Joan and I had agreed to always bring back a box of wine or a case of beer whenever we returned from town for medical appointments, holidays or professional development workshops. The wine in boxes, the beer always in cans. Never bottles. Bottles clinked in the boat and on the village dock.

I poured wine into a Mason jar that still smelled faintly of salmon, then we went into the living room and stood in the middle of the brooder supplies.

Joan sucked on her beer tube. "A kiddie pool?"

"It's the bottom of the brooder we're going to make," I said.

"We?"

I put my jar of wine on the coffee table and tore the bag of wood chips open. "You're going to help me."

"Alright. But we're still going to drink, right?"

I picked up my jar. "You can't brood without drinking."

By nine o'clock, Joan had ditched her beer helmet and both of us were onto our fourth jar of wine. Together, we'd measured and cut a length of chicken wire, using the wire cutters I had borrowed from John, the school custodian. Curling it into a large circle, we set the tube of wire just inside the wall of the pool. We wove pencils through the wire holes so that the ends of the cage held together. At the top of the wire we clipped a small reading lamp and shone it on the chicks for warmth. Then we sat on the floor drinking our wine, our legs splayed. We watched the chicks meander around the wood-chip terrain, bumping into each other at times, the sound of peeping as relentless as ever, yet now more bearable due to the warmth of wine in my head.

"You find out yet what's up with Hannah's hands?" Joan asked.

I let out a groan of frustration. "No. She refuses to talk about it and I can't get a look under those sleeves of hers."

Joan shrugged. "It's probably like you guessed. Paint or something."

"I wonder if I should ask her mom about it," I thought aloud, though the idea of approaching Patty didn't thrill me.

"Patty? Don't bother. Mention anything about her daughter and she'll rip your head off. Trust me. I've seen many teachers try to get Patty to take Hannah to town for a diagnosis so we can get her the right resources, but all she's ever done is scream at them that she didn't drink a drop while she was pregnant and how dare they suggest she did. There's no way her daughter has fetal alcohol syndrome—you just need to learn to do your job, that's what Patty will tell you."

"But she does, though. Right?" I asked.

Joan closed her eyes and raised her brows. "Apparently Hannah showed some physical features of FASD in her face when she was little. But it affects kids in so many different ways, physically and mentally. So who knows for sure. Not me. I'm not a doctor. Have you thought about how she'll be with the chicks in the classroom?"

"What? Because of the hamster incident last year?" I asked. "I've thought about it. But I decided that I want to show her that I trust her. And I want to show her dad that I trust her."

"Do you?" Joan asked.

Over the past month, Joan and I had rapidly formed a close friendship, the type that felt as though it had always been a part of our lives.

She possessed a keen ability to detect what I needed—when I needed her to challenge me and when I needed her to back off—and perhaps that was why she changed the subject after a long moment of awkward silence. Because she not only knew that I did not trust Hannah, but that any efforts to falsely declare that I would trust her were nothing more than a desperate attempt to keep my head above water when I was in fact drowning.

"Hannah's dad," Joan said, nodding thoughtfully. "He's a good one to have in your corner. He's a lot more reasonable than Patty. But he's also *very protective* of his daughter."

Very protective. Joan had said this with the weight of a warning. I thought of the promise Chase seemed to believe that I had made, yet instead of feeling anxious about it, I felt surprisingly irritated. What did I owe Chase Charlie, after all? Certainly not a promise to stay in a place that might very well turn me into a wraith. Into a shadow of my former self. For crying out loud, it wasn't like he had simply asked me a small favour. He had made a request of me, and requests carried ideas of obligation. But what obligation did I have? Did I owe it to him or anyone else to stay? This was my life. These were my choices to make. I took a large gulp of wine, then another and another until my jar was empty.

"But be aware," Joan continued, "that he can be a hard one to get hold of, always out in his boat fishing. To get away from his wife's yelling, would be my guess. Patty yells round the clock. Thinks she's entitled to everybody's undivided attention."

I poured more wine. "She called the school the other day to complain. Sophie Florence indicated it was something to do with Mr. Chapman. Can't imagine what for. I was just relieved it wasn't about me."

"Actually, I've heard murmurs from down the hill," Joan said.

"About me?"

"About Chapman," Joan said.

From what I could tell, Joan was greatly respected by the community. She must have been, as she had her finger on the pulse of village rumours and relationships.

"Some people don't like him," Joan said.

"Really? Why not?"

"Not sure. Not even sure if they know why not. A few people just have a bad feeling about him."

From the way Mr. Chapman treated the children, it was hard to believe anyone could think poorly of the man. Then again, Patty was apparently ready to bang on my door with her complaints.

"How long do you think you'll stay here?" I blurted out.

Joan grinned. "You're kicking me out already? The party just started."

"In Tawakin," I said.

Joan lifted her shoulders slowly into a long shrug. "Can't say for sure. This is my fourth year and each year I wonder how I'll ever make it to Christmas holidays. Doesn't get any easier. If anything, it gets harder the longer I stay."

Nodding, I stared down at my jar of wine, running my fingertip thoughtfully around the wet rim. When I finally looked up, Joan was eyeing me with a look of suspicion.

"You're not thinking of quitting, are you?" Joan asked.

"No, of course not," I lied, too ashamed to admit it. "It's just so draining already and it's only been a month. Sometimes I wish I was in your classroom, where the kids are still so innocent."

"Ha!" Joan laughed so hard she sputtered out a small spray of wine. "Innocent? You know what I read the kids today? A picture book filled with photographs about people who work at night. You know, nurses, fire-fighters, that sort of thing. I was getting the kids to guess what each worker was. When we got to a picture of a man with a big black moustache, you know what Julian guessed? And with great confidence, I might add."

"Please don't tell me porn star."

Joan shook her head. "He shouted, 'I know! I know! DEALER!'"

"Shit. That's worse than porn star."

Joan agreed. "At least if he'd guessed porn star, I might have been able to think he got that from some stupid show and that he probably didn't know what it actually was. But dealer? That requires a different level of familiarity."

We both sat silently, thinking.

"It was a bus driver," Joan said finally. Then she pointed her jar of wine at the brooder. "Maybe we should add stuff to do in there."

"What? What do you mean?"

"Stuff for the chickens to do in there," Joan said.

"What, like a deck of cards? A jigsaw puzzle?"

Leaning back, Joan topped up her wine from the box we'd moved to the coffee table. "Haven't you ever heard about Gus?"

I shook my head.

"Gus was a polar bear that lived at Central Park Zoo," Joan said. "One day he started swimming laps back and forth in his small pool. Back and forth, back and forth. He then started doing this every single day. In the same figure eight pattern every time. Some days he spent twelve hours swimming like that." Joan took a long sip. "Visitors from the zoo complained that Gus appeared unhappy. Reporters called him neurotic, flaky, depressed—"

"Bipolar?"

"Funny," Joan said, rolling her eyes. "Actually some people said Gus's behaviour proved that no creature could escape the stress of living in New York City. The zookeepers admitted that something was definitely wrong with Gus. He became the first zoo animal in history to be treated with Prozac. Eventually, the zoo brought in an animal behaviourist. The guy who trained the killer whale in *Free Willy.*"

"I've never seen that movie," I said.

"Me neither," Joan said.

"We should show it to the kids."

"We should," Joan agreed. "So anyway, after watching Gus's daily routine of swimming, the behaviourist concluded that Gus needed greater challenges. He needed wider opportunities. He needed a choice in his swimming path."

I pondered this with the kind of philosophical consciousness that comes after several glasses of wine. I wondered what it was like for a polar bear to be a polar bear, but the presence of my own mind and all that it contained got in the way. I raised my jar, clinked it against

Joan's and said with a hint of slurring, "Gus needed to feel control over his own destiny."

"Every day," Joan said with nod.

After Joan left that night and I fell into bed, the trailer dark and the chicks quietly sleeping, I stared at the barely visible ceiling and pictured the wood box I kept under my bed. Ever since my mother had died when I was eighteen years old, I had slept with the box beneath me. Many nights I imagined that I could hear the pulse of the box, made from the heartwood of a magohany tree, beating life into our possessions. I knew this was far-fetched. I knew that the sound of a tree's heartbeat was only a myth. I knew that whatever pulsing sound might be heard from pressing an ear against the trunk of a tree was only water passing through the cells of the xylem tubes. And I of course knew that it had been many years since anything, water or otherwise, had moved through the wood below my bed. Nonetheless, the idea that the mahogany box was still vibrating with life, and that through years of touch my mother's genetic code might have entwined with the heartwood's, gave me comfort in the enduring resonance of things.

Tonight I found myself thinking about the period from my child-hood I only vaguely remembered, of staying locked inside my house for several weeks. Whenever I tried to remember this period of time, I always entered my memories from high above, a bird's-eye view of my quiet street and the surrounding neighbourhoods. I saw roof shingles and treetops and rectangles of mowed grass and the circle of asphalt where I played road hockey with the other kids. I saw a cowhide patchwork of bright areas and dark areas. Some of the dark areas were unfamiliar to me, adjacent streets I never had reason to visit. But the narrow strip of woods behind the houses where I climbed trees and built forts, and the large grass field lined with hydroelectric poles on the other side of the woods where I imprisoned snakes inside ice cream pails, were also blacked out, as was the shortcut to school through the empty parking lot behind Safeway. These spaces appeared in my aerial view like splotches of black ink spilled on a map. They'd been blotted out in my mind since I was ten—the year the Beast of BC moved in an unknown vector toward my neighbourhood.

What shone brightly on my bird's-eye map was my house. Inside was my mother, a strangely solitary woman. She wore glasses the size of saucers, and she'd slide them down to the tip of her nose as she read Alice Munro stories or painted a portrait from memory or practised her calligraphy. I could remember her with perfect clarity, particularly how I loved to sit in the evenings at the kitchen table listening to the scratch-scratch of her steel nibs on sheets of vellum. Back then my mother made some extra money by penning high school diplomas, and each year she'd have to start early in October if she had any hope of finishing by June convocation.

Occasionally, I would press my ear against the table and guess each letter based on the stroke length and the susurration of the broadly sweeping loops. If it wasn't too late and I wasn't too tired, my mother would give me a pen and a piece of vellum to practise one of the easier styles, Chancery or maybe Gothic. But mostly I was content to watch my mother, admiring the care she put into the names as well as her courage in starting each stroke, the ink clutching to the nib, dangerously close to dripping, and I marvelled at how much my mother trusted her own hand. It took commitment, I knew even back then, to set ink down on a page like that, unable to erase it or adjust it after the fact. Whatever way it turned out, you had to accept it. If my mother had lived to see computers take over her job, this would have been the thing she would have missed the most. It was the tiny human irregularities, she told me, that made the letters so beautiful.

Sometimes while my mother worked, we played a game we called Dream Up My Destiny. For each name my mother scribed, I would decide what sort of life the person would have after graduation. Girls with the name Sarah or Tammy were always nurses who had at least five children and a house near the beach. Hanks or Henrys were mechanics or grocery store managers. Evelyns, Carolyns and Sherilyns were bound for Broadway. Together, we would take turns telling elaborate stories about each destiny. Sometimes the stories were so richly detailed that they seemed wholly true to me, stuff not just from our daydreaming but from reality. Yes, my mother once agreed when I told her this, that's because a life fully and truly imagined *is* a life lived. At the time, this declaration from my mother appealed to my love of illusion and invention.

Often I projected my own aspirations onto these stories, and future graduates became detectives, international spies, mad scientists, archaeologists, marine biologists, artists, Wimbledon champions, inventors. My dreams were ambitious and wildly varied for one simple reason: my mother had convinced me it could be this way. That I could become whatever I dreamed my own destiny to be. But I couldn't remember playing that game after the Beast of BC arrived in our neighbourhood, and I came to believe that his presence undid my mother to the point that she no longer wanted to talk about the destiny of children.

*　　*　　*

That night I dreamed that a swarm of bees as big and dark as a storm cloud chased me. I tried to hurry away but my legs were too slow, as they always were in dreams about fear of failure, and eventually I fell to the ground, startled to see that the bees were not bees but children. Suddenly I awoke to the sound of a loud roar outside my window. Lights streamed across the bedroom curtains. I tried to make sense of the noise. It was a rumble that didn't stop.

Climbing to the edge of the bed, I kneeled at the window. When I pulled back the curtains, the sight on the school soccer field across the logging road was like a movie scene about extraterrestrials. Surrounding the perimeter of the field were quads and dirtbikes, all with their headlights shining toward the centre, where Chase's truck stood, its headlights also on. As I stared at the strange scene, I realized that the bees I thought were children were not children but the drone of motors.

There were smaller beams of light, too. People, invisible in the darkness, with flashlights. At that moment the school truck drove past my window, Mr. Chapman at the wheel in his pajamas. He turned down the grassy embankment and onto the soccer field to join the others. I spotted a figure that looked like Joan walking across the logging road from her trailer. Her flashlight beam disappeared as she too went down the embankment to the soccer field.

After throwing on some clothes, I grabbed my flashlight and headed outside. I watched my steps in the beam of light, careful not to trip in the potholes, my head still spinning from the wine earlier that night. The crowd was much larger than what I had witnessed from my window. It seemed that nearly every person from the village was there, including many children. There were murmurs here and there, but mostly everyone stood in silence. Several teens straddled their dirt bikes, keeping their headlights steadily pointed. Looking at the field, I tried to see what all the headlights were pointed at, but all I could see was the scruffy grass.

I asked a woman next to me, "What is it?"

Scrunching her eyebrows, she shrugged one shoulder and shook her head, as if she didn't understand the question.

I motioned toward the lit patch of grass. "Are we waiting for something?"

The woman stared at me for a moment, then she pointed at Chase Charlie's pickup truck. Six men and women were seated on the sides of the pickup so that their legs were inside the cargo bed. All of them stared down at whatever was at their feet. The tailgate was down, and from where I stood I could make out the shadowy image of something wrapped in a light-coloured covering.

A man's voice called out, "I hear something."

Everyone looked skyward.

After several moments, the same man called out, "Nope."

"It'll never get through," another person said. "It's too windy."

I looked up again at the sky. Earlier in September, when the sky was clear and the moon's full familiar face gazed upon me, the brightness of a Tawakin night and the crispness of the moon shadows had been astonishing. But when the sky was thick with clouds, as it had been lately, the darkness of a Tawakin night was blacker than any darkness I had seen before. Blacker than my mother's calligraphy ink.

I started to shiver in the cold, so I decided I needed to move and warm up. Making my way around the large circle of vehicles and people, I found Joan.

I asked her, "What's going on?"

"It's Candice," she said, pointing at Chase's truck. "The elder."

My stomach sank. From where we stood, I could no longer see into the cargo bed. There had been something wrapped in the back. "She's—?" I also pointed at the truck for confirmation. "She's in the truck? That's Candice in the back?"

Joan nodded.

"What's the matter? Is she—?" I didn't want to ask.

"She collapsed in her kitchen. Nurse Bernadette rushed over from the outpost and gave her CPR. To be honest, I don't know much else. I don't know how she is." Joan's voice cracked with worry. "The helicopter from Port Hardy is on its way but I don't know if it can land in this weather."

"Coffee?" Mr. Chapman asked.

I turned to see him with a headlamp shining from his forehead. He carried a large tray of paper cups steaming with coffee.

"No, thank you," I said.

"You sure? We could be here a while," he said.

I took a cup to warm my hands and waited, my eyes fixed on Chase's truck. After twenty minutes or so, someone spotted a light in the sky. It was small and diffused behind the clouds, then it was gone. It returned a few minutes later in a different spot in the sky, then disappeared again. By this point my coffee was cold and my fingers were icy and numb. As I poured my coffee onto the grass, it occurred to me that my little flashlight was not much of a contribution to the beacon offered by the circle of quads and dirtbikes.

"I'm heading back," I whispered to Joan. "How about you?"

Joan shook her head. "I'm going to stay."

When I got back home and started the wood stove, I immediately felt guilty for leaving. How could I go back to my warm bed while others were out there guiding the way for poor Candice? Yet what use was I out there?

The cold had made me hungry, so I checked the fridge for a snack but it was almost bare. I grabbed the last bit of cheddar and wished for an apple to go with it. For the past two weeks, the only produce available at the Tawakin Market had been a wilted head of celery with pale green ribs that drooped over the bars of the refrigerator rack. It was the only store there unless you counted those in the basements of houses in the village, but they didn't sell vegetables, only candy bars and homemade pies and sometimes jugs of milk for eight or twelve dollars, depending. Yesterday afternoon, after two weeks of violent gales and high crests on the Pacific, the *Sojourner II* finally delivered a shipment of food. Tomorrow I planned to take the school boat across the cove to the Tawakin Market. I imagined carrots and cabbage and lettuce and oranges and pears. Maybe even cantaloupes.

I spent the first half-hour in bed watching out the window. I thought about poor Candice in the back of that pickup truck, not knowing if she was okay or not, and I thought about little Candice, too, how worried she must be. Soon my eyelids grew heavy. I finally gave in to my urge to sleep, crawling under my blankets while the village waited together in the cold. Just as I was drifting off, it struck me how pitiful I seemed in that moment. Here were these people sticking by one another while I fell asleep.

6

The next morning, as I untied the school boat from the government dock, I looked around the village for someone with news about Candice, that the elder was recovering in a hospital bed somewhere, but there was nobody to be seen except a small figure in the distance. It was seven-year-old Julian, making his way along the trail to the dock. Though the air was cool, he wore thin Batman pajamas and rubber boots so large they must have been his father's. He saw me and started to run down the ramp, shouting something frantically that I couldn't make out until he reached the dock.

"She lost her name for a whole year!" He pointed to a figure, a girl maybe, sitting on a log or something that looked like a log in the middle of the cove between the Tawakin village and the small arc of islands that sheltered the village from the Pacific Ocean. I hadn't noticed her off in the distance. From here it looked like a hood was draped over her head. "She's going to the island with the fossils to find the woman in the box with the baby but she's not supposed to, she's not supposed to!"

He sucked in a tremor of air.

"Have you heard about your grandmother yet? How is she?"

"She's not supposed to look and now I don't know how to call her back."

"Who is it?" I asked.

Julian stared at me but didn't answer.

I squinted at the figure in the distance. It looked like Candice Henry, but I couldn't tell for certain. It wasn't unusual to see a child alone in the cove, going to the market in some tiny bucket of a boat to pick up the mail or a jar of yeast for baking bread, but this appeared to be something else entirely. It looked strange, almost surreal, as if she were a monkey in an ancient animal fable, crossing a river perched on top of a crocodile.

I asked, "Where is her boat? Why is she on a log?"

"It's a canoe," Julian said. "Except it's not done being carved."

Nothing yet moved in the village along the shoreline except a knot of dogs and the tendrils of smoke that rose from shacks where fish hung over sticks of cedar. The other dock at the end of the village was crowded with windblown boats that creaked and knocked against the pilings even though it was a day when everybody should be boating across to the Tawakin Market on Mitchell Island. Abandoned bicycles and toys were scattered in the grassy yards. Saturday afternoon, and there were no children except this boy and that girl.

"You should stop her, Teacher," he said.

My rubber boots squawked against the aluminum hull as I climbed inside the boat and tried to keep my balance. It was a wobbly ten-footer, as light as an old metal washtub, puddled deep with rainwater. I sat on the bench at the stern beside the motor and started to bail out the boat with the top half of a bleach bottle.

"You have to make her come back," Julian said through clenched teeth. He stomped his foot. Something fell from his fists and hit the dock like rain. Little drops of silver and blue. "She'll upset the spirits, my grandma says so."

He and Candice were cousins. "How *is* your grandma?" I asked again.

More tiny drops of blue and silver spilled from his fists and scattered into whole constellations. "My grandma died last night in a pile of beads," Julian said.

The bleach bottle went still in my hand, stopped in its perpetual scoop-and-swing. "Oh, Julian—" I felt a wave of sympathy for him and for the community. Then I thought of little Candice, all alone, her father dead and her mother on a beach in Port Hardy. "We should go and get your dad."

Julian's lip quivered. "He's still sleeping."

"Then your mom," I said.

"She's sleeping, too."

I looked at the poor girl paddling in the distance, then I surveyed the houses on the ridge of the shore. In most every window, the curtains were closed. "We should get somebody. Maybe Sophie Florence."

Julian breathed fiercely through his nose. "They're all sleeping!"

I took hold of the starter cord. "I'll try to get her to come back," I said. In an effort to clinch his faith in me, I gave him a firm nod.

But Julian wanted more. "You can't just try, Teacher. You have to get her to come back. You have to." A seagull circled overhead and dropped a clam shell to the dock where it shattered beside Julian. He flinched. Tears filled his eyes. Some of the icy water splashed out of the bleach bottle and streamed down the inside of my coat sleeve. Julian punted his boot at the broken bits of shell, grunting with each kick: "Get—her—to—come—back—Tea—cher!"

*   *   *

Whoever had been carving that log into a boat, just as Julian had reported, hadn't finished yet. As I boated closer, I could see that the inside of the canoe was rough and shallow and barely cradled little Candice on her journey. It was more like a narrow raft on which she sat huddled with her knobby knees bent skyward, the splashes of water from the carved paddle soaking into her pants. The blade of the paddle was not much wider than its handle. When Candice pulled it through the water it looked about as practical as stirring a pot of fish-head soup with a needle.

"Candice!" I called out.

Candice did not stop paddling, did not turn to look around. Her face was hidden by the hood of her sweatshirt.

The Morning Bell Brings the Broken Hearted

"Candice!"

"Shut up!" Candice shouted.

I blinked in shock that she would say such a thing to me. But I wanted to be gentle with her and her grief. In a friendly tone, I called out again. "Candice!"

"Ay-haw!" Candice slapped the paddle flat against the water. "Stop it, you're being dumb!"

My mouth dropped open. I didn't know what to say to that. Across the water, at the end of the wharf on Mitchell Island, grey smoke rose from the chimney of the Tawakin Market and disappeared into the grey clouds hanging low over the cedars. The clouds appeared to form a wall around the islands, a barrier between the cove and the rest of the world. On the other side of the grey wall, the Pacific Ocean heaved all the way to Japan, from where glass balls and chunks of tsunami-torn homes and Kawasaki motorcycle wheels washed onto Tawakin shores.

"Where are you going, Candice?" I shouted.

Candice turned to look at me with eyes as red and swollen as plum tomatoes. "Don't call me that! You're being—" She stopped and growled with frustration. There was spit in her words: "If she hears her name, she'll think we're calling her back and then she'll turn around and she'll get lost and then she'll never get over to the other side. We can't say her name until she's finished her journey. Don't you know anything?"

"You need to come back with me to the village," I said.

Candice shook her head vigorously.

"I'm your teacher, and I'm telling you: you need to come back with me."

"It's Saturday," Candice said. "You're not my teacher on Saturday."

"Still—" I didn't know how to counter this. "Still, you should listen to what I'm saying. For your own good."

The wind picked up, lifting and chopping the dark ocean into triangles. Wet palms of water slapped the aluminum hull. I rocked back and forth while the boat drifted away from Candice's half-dugout canoe. A few moments passed before I shifted the motor out of neutral and circled closer again. It started to rain, soaking Candice's sweatshirt and her pants and pelting against my aluminum hull, my yellow rain jacket and my matching yellow rain pants.

"The sky's getting darker," I yelled into the wind.

"I don't care."

"If you don't come back with me, I'll tie a rope onto your canoe and pull you back myself," I warned, knowing very well that I hadn't thought this over. "You think I won't, but I will."

"You can't do that," Candice shouted. "You can't touch this canoe. Don't you dare touch this canoe. It isn't yours to touch." She reached into the giant pocket at the front of her sweatshirt and pulled out the photograph of her dead father. She waved it at me. "This is my father, and he was making this canoe for *me*, not *you*."

I looked at the half-dugout canoe, never to be finished by the man in the photograph, and the bittersweetness of it pierced me. I felt my whole body slump in my wood-planked seat as Candice slipped the photograph back into her front pocket. Impulsively, my hand went to my own pocket. I felt the perimeter of my small sketchbook. There was only one blank page remaining, and I'd planned, if the weather turned nice after shopping, to sit on the outside shore of Mitchell Island and finish my first Tawakin sketchbook with whatever came to mind.

Candice stuck her paddle back into the water.

The truth was that I had no intention of wrangling that canoe and pulling it back to the village. At the very thought of it, all I could picture was bumping my boat accidentally against the canoe as I drew close with rope in hand, sending Candice into the cold water. And even if I did manage to tie up the canoe without tipping it, what disaster might occur as I towed the wobbly vessel back with Candice perched on the top?

"Don't try to stop me, Teacher."

At first she paddled like a small ferryman, slow and steady, trance-like. I imagined the grief the girl must be feeling, the numbness of it all, the uncertainty of what was to now come.

"Please stop, Can—" I caught myself. "Please."

From here I could see Candice's blue house at the back corner of the village. Julian, now only the size of my thumb in the distance, stood around the outside corner in the pouring rain, waiting, his fist probably still squeezed around those blue and silver beads.

"You shouldn't be doing this," I yelled to Candice. "You'll upset the spirits, your grandma said so."

Candice froze for a brief moment, then paddled harder. The canoe wobbled from side to side.

The least I could do was to follow her. But I hesitated. Chances were there was no need to follow her. Chances were she'd be perfectly safe on her own, or better yet, someone else would come along at any minute to take her back home. But when I surveyed both docks across the water, there was nobody coming to help, and I realized that I was it, I was the only one, and in fact it was even possible that this was my purpose in life, that my sole purpose was to make sure that this girl stayed safe today, the day after her grandmother died in a pile of beads.

"Ha!" I laughed out loud at myself. It was only a single snort of noise at first, but it quickly turned into a quiver of giggling, a full-bodied release of everything that had been tightening inside me. Had I really become so desperate to feel a purpose in my life that I could be this dramatic? That I could think, like a fool, that this moment had anything to do with my life? It was definitely not something I wished to believe anyway, that one's purpose could be pinned down to a single day. If that were the case, what would be the point to all my days thereafter?

I looked once more at the smoldering chimney above the market. The first time I'd met elder Candice we were standing outside the market in the September sun among the shards of clam shells on the wharf.

"It was a hairy *puukmis*," elder Candice had told me that day. "When I was a child, I lived on Toomista Island. Before we all had to leave that place. Something was stealing our vegetables from the patch my mother had dug into the earth. Back then we had no other way to get fresh vegetables and even that was hard with the *muwach*. But it wasn't no *muwach*—deer—nibbling our lettuce but something with hands that could tug the vegetables out of the ground. One night my sister said I was a baby and that I was too scared to go out in the dark and get a good look at the thing stealing our potatoes and lettuce. Ooh, she could get me real mad! So, I went." Elder Candice paused for a long time then said, "Don't ever point at an eagle, it's bad luck."

For the next while, elder Candice told me about eagles and the eagle feathers she owned, and about how the hippies used to drive to the reserve back when there was a logging road connecting Tawakin to the rest of the world, but now the road was grown over and she was glad for it.

"So, what happened? Did you go out into the dark?" I asked.

"A hairy *puukmis* has eyes like diamonds that glow real bright, like this…" Elder Candice gestured imaginary beams from her own eyes. Then she described her favourite recipe for fish-head soup in great detail and told me how she was going to teach her granddaughter how to bead abalone shells and that she was knitting a new style of hat for the Christmas Craft Fair this year. Shaped like a limpet shell, she said, and then explained how she liked shapes because she could trace her fingers along edges she could not see. Then she said, "It was as tall as a piling."

"I'm sorry, you lost me," I said. "What happened exactly?"

"When you get lost you go around and around in circles, don't you? And sometimes you pass over a part of another circle you already been on, but you still keep going around anyhow. You got to get lost first because when you get lost you can only find your way back by looking real close and listening for everything. Everybody's got to get lost before they truly look and listen. That's the way it is."

I thought about how the kind old woman's spirit was already gone, set off on a lonely and nameless journey, and here was her granddaughter moving across the cove at a slug's pace to find a woman in a box with a baby that I wasn't sure even existed.

I could hope Candice would change her mind, that was a possibility too, although what if she didn't and I found myself on a shore filled with fossils? And what if I then found myself pushing through a forest thick with cedars and firs, the trees all tangled up, moss and lichen hanging everywhere like an upside-down garden? I shuddered at the thought.

Then I remembered my VHF radio. I had left it on the kitchen counter. Who would rescue us if we both got lost? Then again, what kind of attitude was that, and what did my mother used to say? I tried to recall her exact words as I shifted the motor into drive and steered the boat around a bed of kelp fronds, avoiding the long fingers of green ghosts that clawed at the surface. You could always measure the humanity of a person by how they treated a child, that was how my mother had phrased it. I certainly didn't wish to fail measuring up, I only wished to avoid the measuring altogether, although that in itself was measurement enough.

I turned toward the Tawakin Market, which closed in an hour until Wednesday, and I thought of romaine lettuce with crisp, verdant leaves and ribs that spritzed out moisture when snapped in half, soft yellow bananas with no bruises and Spartan apples with shiny red covers that punctured loudly under the weight of my teeth. I could practically feel the vitamin A, the potassium, the vitamin C coursing through my blood, rejuvenating my cream-of-something-soup-and-saltine lethargy.

Was my hesitation to follow Candice merely a matter of convenience? I had to consider the possibility. But if I was indeed reluctant to miss the store hours for the sake of a grieving girl, what kind of person did that make me? That was simple enough to answer: It made me a small person living a small life when I wished to have a large life and be a large person who was even larger than her large life.

I lifted my face and let the rain spill over my closed eyelids.

Still, I thought, what would the community say if they learned I had found the woman in the box with the baby? I didn't believe in *numak*, those bad things that supposedly would happen if we visited the woman, but I didn't want the community to think I didn't respect their ways. Wouldn't they understand, though, that I only did it to keep Candice safe? Of course they would.

Along the Vancouver Island coastline, the edges of the forested mountains were shaped like profiles of faces reclined to the heavens.

For a brief spell, as I turned the boat slowly in Candice's direction, I studied the mountain edges from skyward down, to discover what new shapes might be revealed. Like Rubin's vase, that optical illusion that forms a vase one way and two faces another, depending on whether you perceived the edges from inside out or outside in. As I puttered slowly in pursuit of Candice, I pointed my index finger in the air and traced the shapes of the mountains, the ridge of a forehead, the peak of a pointed nose, the divot of a philtrum. Next to that a wide valley, like a mouth gasping in suffocation, opened and gulped up the sky.

7

We dragged our boats onto the narrow beach of Fossil Island. The wind snapped at my jacket and battered my ears. It pushed the rain horizontal. A rush of tidal water washed over the indentations of Precambrian life, over my rubber boots, over Candice's running shoes. Candice stepped onto a flat spot of a wet, black rock. Next to her, the edge of the forest was thick and tangled with no obvious point of entry. The thought of stepping inside prickled the hair at the nape of my neck. I shouldn't go in there, I thought. Not because of the woman but because of something else. Something I couldn't give shape to. A feeling burrowed deep within me. From left to right I looked along the edge of the forest. I suspected it was the type of forest that would swallow us whole and give us no clues for exiting back out at the right spot, and the right spot was crucial: I could see that the shoreline was dangerously narrow and rocky in places, making circumnavigation of the island along its outer edges impossible.

I unzipped my rain jacket. "Take it, you're soaked."

Candice wrinkled her nose. "I don't want it."

With a sigh, I zipped my jacket back up. I pulled the long chain from the boat and hooked the small anchor under a driftwood log. Squinting into the rain, which pecked at my eyelids like tiny ravenous birds, I peered at the grey and landless horizon across the ocean. Would elder Candice's journey be as cold and grey? Or as far? Little Candice had lost her name for a whole year, that's what Julian had said, and a tenacious spirit such as elder Candice's—a spirit that had finally shed its sagging vessel, its bad back, its crippling bunions, its sightless eyes—could surely travel a long distance in a year.

"I'm sorry about your grandmother," I said.

Candice's face was expressionless. She didn't speak. Rain flowed down the rocks around her and into the ribbed wrinkles of scallop fossils like tears.

"What do you want me to call you now?" I asked. "I have to call you something. I can't just call you 'girl.' Everybody needs a name."

Candice shrugged and shivered and kept turning to peer into the woods. A gust of wind tugged the hood off her head. She was pale and looked exhausted, as if she hadn't slept all night.

"My auntie says I could be called by my middle name, but I don't like it," Candice said.

"What is it?" I asked.

"Mildred."

"That's a good name," I said.

"No, it's not. The boys will call me Mildew."

The tide started to lift the boat slightly, grinding it on the pebbles, slipping it in and out of the foamy water. The anchor chain clinked and rattled against the large rocks that were fractured into perfect rectangles. It tightened and slackened as the ocean tried to coax the boat away. I bent to tilt the propeller up off the rocks, first fiddling with the fussy latch and then hoisting the motor upwards, my boots shifting and slipping in the small stones, my hands red with cold. I thumped my elbow hard against the aluminum gunwale.

I straightened, rubbing the back of my arm where I'd knocked the boat, then turned to the empty spot where Candice once stood. She was gone.

"Hey!" I called out. "Hey! Stop! Wait!"

There was no answer.

For a minute I stood firmly planted in my spot on the shore. Images of what waited inside the woods flickered in my mind. Abstract impressions of twisted faces, hideous women with baskets of children, sinister beasts. I laughed at myself. Don't be a child, Molleigh, I thought. For crying out loud, it was a forest, a group of trees standing together, not some fantastical place found in stories and nightmares. Without thinking any further, I climbed over the rocks, parted the dripping curtains of cedar and stepped through the tangle of shrubs into the murky light of the rainforest. Like the closing of a window, the ragged branches sprang back and deadened the sounds of wind and rain behind me.

I held my breath. Slowly I looked around at the dim light between the trees, and I was struck by a strong sense of déjà vu—as though I'd been here before and knew better than to return. This was impossible, of course. Yet I couldn't shake the feeling that I shouldn't be here. Like I was a child doing something wrong by being in the woods. I looked behind me at the curtains of cedar where I had just entered and I wanted desperately to push them open again and throw myself back onto the shore. I pictured my uncomfortable furniture, the mould on the walls, how grey and dim the light was in every room, and desperately I wanted to go back home. All the way back home. To my apartment in Surrey where fully stocked stores were open all day and night and the only woods I ever had to enter were the displays of Christmas trees in the parking lot of the hardware store. But I couldn't leave Candice.

At first, I could see no sign of her. I listened closely for the snap of branches underfoot. Scanning all around, I caught a glimpse of a face. I flinched and looked away. I took a breath, then glimpsed the face again. It was only a chunk of a tree that had fallen long ago, the wood rotting away. Or was it? In the woods, it was easy to mistake figures for shadows and voices for wind and faces for bark. I peered at it once more. Two large knots spiralled into the oval shape of eyes. Deep lines arched over the ovals, straining upwards, like the eyebrows of somebody filled with dreadful surprise. Get a grip, I told myself. Nothing more than a chance face. Pareidolia. Like the man on the moon, or the face on Mars, or when people saw Jesus Christ in a piece of toast or a plate of spaghetti. The ordinary turned extraordinary.

Far ahead there was a hint of movement. It was Candice. She trod over layers of life and decay, over curling bracken ferns and the brown caps of mushrooms; over the rotten log homes of mice and martens and who knew what else. Weaving between tall trees, she disappeared and reappeared, ducking under cedars that reached for her with drooping boughs and foliage that hung like long, shredded sleeves.

"Wait!" I shouted.

But Candice didn't wait.

Pulling apart a suffocating web of tangled branches, I moved through the bushes. The patchwork of light and shadows, the never-ending layers of green, the repeating pattern of tree trunks and radiating branches—it all made me feel dizzy. I searched for something that looked unique, something easily spotted as a trail marker. Finding nothing distinctive enough, I considered etching an X into a tree trunk every twelve feet or so, and I tried this with my house key, but it only made a light scratch in the bark. I needed a knife. Was there one in the boat? I was certain there wasn't. A ribbon or some kind of tag attached to the branches, that would work. But I had neither of those things, either. There weren't even laces in my rubber boots, and even if there were, two was not enough. I needed several markers to ensure our safety. I knew I was wasting time trying to figure this out, yet there was no point in hurrying if we couldn't find our way back.

As I put the key into my pocket, I felt the hard cover of my small black sketchbook. I pulled it out and as I opened the book, a silverfish fled out of the binding and squirmed across the page in a rounded zigzag. It traversed the charcoal lines of Candice's nose, her long eye-lashes, the divot above her upper lip. I flicked the silverfish with my fingernail, sailing it high into the unknown. I then riffled through the pages, which were slightly larger in area than my palm. Dozens upon dozens of portraits flitted before my eyes like the stuttered images on an old-time film reel. I tore a page from the sketchbook and impaled it on a tree trunk at eye level. The splintered piece of branch went through Hannah Charlie's charcoaled mouth, turning the image into something violent and macabre.

I spotted fresh scuff marks in the needle-covered dirt; I headed in that direction, first pinning a sketch of Candice to another tree, trying this time to not maim her face. I then tried to call out, "Hello!" but it came out as barely more than a whisper. I froze with the thought of shouting loudly, of calling the attention of whatever might lurk nearby. I tried again, this time forcing my voice to pierce the air. The sound made my whole body tense. Still, I continued in this way, looking for signs of Candice, making myself call out "Hello!" and marking my path with portraits of my students.

After some time, I stopped for a moment to catch my breath and leaned against an old snag, smooth as bone. I looked up at the canopy of leaves and needles. At the sight of it, I saw myself as a child high in a tree, windblown leaves like the sound of rustling newspapers or the riffles of my sketchbook pages. I stared above my head for what seemed like an eternity, all the while feeling as though there were two worlds, the world in which we lived and that of the woods—separate and unknown.

I broke my gaze and moved my feet onward. Winding my way through a labyrinth of bark and moss, I yelled, "Hello?" The tapered ends of saplings whipped against my jacket, their tiny leaves whispering "wisha, wisha, wisha," sharing secrets, it seemed, as I passed. Like children on the playground sharing jokes with swear words and spreading gossip about who'd met boys or girls on their last trip to town.

"Hello?" I yelled again.

Overhead the sound of rain rose, and the wind shook the trees. As if holes had been punctured into Raven's Box of Daylight, shafts of silver came through the perforations and dappled the forest floor. The light was filled with mist as fine as chalk dust, beaten out of chalk brushes by children who would bang them together until a dozen lessons in English and a dozen lessons in Nuu-chah-nulth sprinkled onto the basketball court outside my classroom door.

I straddled a large cedar rotting on the ground and tried to climb over it. The bark crumbled under my touch. An entire nation of ants with shiny red beads for abdomens scattered from their broken home. They scurried across the tree trunk and over my yellow pants. I scrambled from the log and onto the soft and springy forest floor, brushing the ants off my legs and arms, shaking out my sleeves and my pant legs.

Ascending a small embankment, I walked into a large area where the cedar branches braided together, forming a thick tent above my head. It was darker here, and with little light slipping through the trees, the floor was bare of living foliage. As I stepped across the thick layer of cedar needles the colour of rust, the rain stopped. Leaning against a cedar, I pressed my ear against its rough bark and listened. At first I heard nothing. Then a sound moved through all the trees. It was a sound that was mine alone. *Molleigh.* I'd once read that everybody in the whole world had the same favourite sound: their own name. The sound picked me up and gave me a small pulse of relief. I stuck a portrait of Odelia Joe on a tree and headed in the sound's direction.

It rang out again: "Ms. Royston! Teacher! Teacher Molleigh!"

In the stillness of the forest, Candice's voice felt both electric and vulnerable as she tried different ways to catch my attention. Was it a sound of distress or excitement? I couldn't tell. I stood quietly for a moment. The air bristled with a peculiar resistance. Slowly I moved in the direction of Candice's voice, and I paused again for a brief instant when I thought I detected a faint whiff of death.

Was it only my mind playing tricks on my senses?

Yes, I told myself. A trick and nothing more.

In a small clearing surrounded by saplings and filled with skunk cabbage, I found Candice standing in a spot where a large cedar tree had long ago fallen to the ground in the middle of a sea of ferns. I stopped for a moment, then stepped toward her. Candice glanced at me as I approached but said nothing. It was just like Candice had told me. A beam of silver light streamed through a hole in the canopy where the cedar once stood. A colonnade of spruces had grown out of the cedar, their exposed roots grasping the cedar's trunk like fingers around a paddle. One of the fingers had poked through a cedar box overgrown with moss. It had grown through the bottom of the box and under the lid, which had then split apart and fallen to the ground.

As I stood beside Candice in silence and my eyes adjusted to the pearly light of the clearing, I first noticed the skull, the stark bone so clean of any flesh that it was impossible to envision the range of human expressions that had once adorned it. The rest of the skeleton was equally stark and clean, the bones collapsed from their joints, though some were still propped up against one another. There were signs of decay where insects and rain and bacteria and fungi had leached into the bones, gnawing away at the collagen. Next to the woman was a second tiny skeleton. I kept turning my head away in alarm only to look at it again. The sight of the dead, albeit only their bones remaining, was stirring. Jarring yet mesmerizing. But what shocked me most was how that spruce finger was lodged between the woman's thigh bones and how that finger had forced the lid of the box open, leaving the woman in the box with the baby staring straight up at the heavens.

Candice ducked down and took something out of the cedar box. She held her palm out and I saw something metal. Rusted. An old fishing hook.

Candice pointed at it. "This was for the afterbirth," she said. "It's supposed to be buried in the ground with it so the baby would get to be a good fisher. But if it wasn't buried, then the afterbirth wasn't buried neither and you can't do that because it was a part of the mother and it was alive and then it's not alive no more but it's still a part of her. Stuff like that can haunt you if you don't bury it. And this isn't right, neither. The baby should be in her arms. A baby should always be in her mother's arms."

Before I could stop her, Candice shoved the fishing hook into her pocket and stooped to adjust the small skeleton that was lodged face down beside the woman's rib cage. The baby's bones were loose and instantly collapsed into a heap in Candice's hands. Wrenching back, Candice's eyes flew wide open, her eyebrows arched in what looked like dreadful surprise.

It was a dreadful surprise, to see those bones fall. A moment ago, most of those bones still retained the vague shape of a tiny human being, and now they were a pile of rubble. A moment ago, I could imagine the soft, sweet-smelling bundle of life that once surrounded those bones, and now it was as though its memory had been dismembered. I felt a strong impulse to re-member the baby, to make the baby whole again.

Candice pulled a pair of pliers from the pocket of her hoodie and stepped to the other end of the box. To keep them from bouncing back again, she trampled on the fern fronds that arched over the sides and partly covered the woman and her baby. She examined the inside of the box closely, leaning over the woman's skull, the pliers poised in her grip.

"They're gone," she said. "Somebody took them."

"Took what?"

Candice looked straight at me. It was a look I had not seen in her yet, a kind of sunken stare like that of a dog on a scorching hot day, a stare of exhausted defeat, and it then occurred to me that from what I could tell, there was no treasure inside that box, no promise that Candice could make her mom like her better than her mom's boys.

I repeated softly, "Took what?"

"Her teeth," Candice said. "The silver one *and* the wood one. They're both gone."

The breath caught in my throat. I looked at the pliers in Candice's hand and their metal, serrated jaws seemed unnaturally violent. What darkness resided in Candice that she had come here with plans to desecrate the dead? That she could have been willing to steal the teeth right out of this woman's mouth?

"They're supposed to be here." Candice raised the pliers over her head and hurled them at the ground. "Now my mom will never come back home."

I ached for the girl. I ached to convince her that one day she wouldn't need to wish so desperately for a mother who lived in a tent on the beach with her boys. As I retrieved the pliers from the ferns and handed them to Candice, I said, "I know it might be hard to believe right now, but you can have a special life. You can. I can feel it in you."

Candice spoke with her jaw clenched shut. "I would have had a special life. If the teeth were still here." She wriggled the pliers back into her front pocket, then pulled out the photograph of her father. Staring down at the picture, she went quiet for a moment and then she said softly, "Oh, no."

"What is it?" I asked.

"Oh, no."

"What?"

"Oh, no. Oh, no." Candice touched her mouth.

I stepped around behind Candice to look at the photograph. Soaked by the rain, her father's face had separated from the paper mount, his eyes slid over to one corner, the emulsion dissolved, the features of his face in one sticky clump. Candice put her hand in her pocket and pulled the remaining shreds of his face out.

Candice's voice shook. "This was my favourite one. He was laughing in it like he was real happy. I shouldn't have brought him with me."

Rain crackled on the leaves above then stopped. Candice looked up at the canopy. As I looked too, I thought they must be looking for her by now. I wondered how they would call over the VHF for a girl with no name. Was Julian still hiding around the corner of the house, waiting and fretting that his cousin had upset the spirits, or had he finally woken up his father and told him where we had gone?

"We were sitting at the table sewing beads on my dance shawl," Candice said. "Grandma helped me put Indian money on the eagle's head and then we got a good idea to put stars on the shawl so we dumped a big jar of blue and silver beads all over the table and Grandma asked me what colour the beads were and I said, 'They're blue and silver, Grandma,' and she laughed like she was real happy and said, 'Like stars. Look, little bebba, we got the heavens on our table,' and I said, 'You're real nutty, Grandma,' and she said, 'Get me some water, little bebba, I got thirsty alls of a sudden,' and so I went into the kitchen and I got a glass of water and I turned off the tap, except the sound didn't stop, I could still hear water pouring but it wasn't water, it was all those stars falling off the table and they wouldn't stop falling."

It started to rain again, harder this time. Large beads of water knocked against the woman's hollow skull. Rain spilled into her gaping mouth and along the ridge of her broken teeth. It plummeted into the empty sockets of eyes haunted with the memory of seeing. It battered her bones and ran in rivulets down the tree root forever wedged between her thighs.

"I hope it didn't hurt to die," Candice said.

"I'm sure your grandmother died with grace," I said.

"What's that mean?"

I thought about this for a few moments before admitting, "I don't know for sure, actually. It just sounds good to me."

Candice raised her eyebrows.

"I think it means when you're given love," I said. "And compassion. And mercy. Whether you deserve it or not."

"I hope they died with grace, too," Candice said, looking at the box.

Nearby, a tiny bird spiralled up the tall trunk of an old snag. It disappeared into its nest behind the dead bark where it sang its song, *See-see-see-see-see-see*.

"Where can I get it from?" Candice asked.

"Get what?"

"You know, that thing you said."

I shook my head, still not understanding.

Candice sighed hard. "Grace."

"Oh," I said. "I'm not sure. Some people believe only God can give it. Other people say we can give it to each other."

Candice clutched at my sleeve. "Do you think we'll get haunted now? Do you think bad things will happen to us?" Her strained gaze upon my face looked as though she was pleading for the answer she wanted to hear. She clutched my sleeve even tighter. "Do you think it's true?"

"No," I said. "I don't think so, Grace."

Candice's face lit up for an instant. She smiled. A small, sad smile.

"I am Grace," she said.

*   *   *

Starting on our way back through the woods, I looked all around me. At first I thought it was a sense of being watched that prickled my skin. The forest was like that, I knew. In the forest, things kept a close eye on you. But that wasn't in fact what unsettled me. What was creeping up inside me was the sense of being lost. It was easy to get lost. Not only among the trees, but in your own mind too. I thought again about elder Candice's words outside the market that day in September, how when you get lost you go around and around in circles. That sometimes you pass over a part of another circle you've already been on, but you still keep going around anyhow. I could hear her voice in my head: "You got to get lost first because when you get lost you can only find your way back by looking real close and listening for everything. Everybody's got to get lost before they truly look and listen."

To my relief, we walked another ten feet before spotting a tree decorated with one of my small sketches. When we reached the tree, Grace leaned toward the portrait to get a close look. My cheeks flushed. I felt exposed. These drawings were my private work and the possibility of anybody appraising them had never occurred to me.

"Why is there a picture of Hannah on the tree?" Grace asked.

"I used it to mark the way back," I said.

"But where'd it come from?"

"My sketchbook." I took the little book with the black hardcover from my pocket and held it up. The spine was now cracked and collapsed in the absence of all those pages.

"You're real *utsiick*," Grace said, and I knew this meant "good."

I surveyed the woods until I spotted the next drawing a short distance away. I pointed toward it. Grace walked on, but I stayed back to retrieve the first picture from its branch. I hadn't noticed before how the moist air stirred the sweet and bitter fragrances of the forest—the pineapple smell of red cedar, the fresh citrus odour of fir, the smell of rotting wood, the rosemary scent of pine—and as I took in these fragrances, I wondered what to do with the drawings. I did not share Grace's concern about hauntings and bad things happening just because we had seen the woman in the box with the baby, but it nonetheless felt conspicuous to leave a trail of my presence here on this forbidden island. For this reason I considered taking them home and tossing them into the wood stove. Yet something about doing that felt uninspired. Nothing good ever came from destroying art. Taking hold of one corner of the sketch, I pinched it until my fingertips were white, but didn't pull on it. Without knowing why, I let go of it and walked away. Then I stopped, looked back at the paper on the tree once more, and reconsidered taking it. But it was a sublime thing to see, as if that tiny face was a beacon for those who find themselves lost in the dark forest.

So, I left it there.

"It's Hannah again," Grace said as I caught up to her. "Same as the other one, her eyes aren't done right. They look too—" Grace paused, apparently unable to find the right word. "She's more like this—" Grace scowled in imitation of Hannah. "You made her look like somebody who's nice to people."

I nodded but said nothing.

"Are they all pictures of Hannah?" Grace asked.

"No," I said.

Grace looked eager. "Are there ones of me?"

"Of course there are," I said.

For the next while, I followed Grace as she zigzagged from one portrait to the next. At each stop, Grace would state the child's name and offer a short commentary after close scrutiny.

"This one of Odelia must have taken forever." Grace sounded particularly impressed. Unlike most of the portraits, Odelia's eyes filled the page. "I can see every little sunbeam in her—what's this part of your eye called again?" Graced pointed at her eye and made a little circular motion.

"The iris," I said.

"Yeah, that's it," Grace said. "I can see every little sunbeam in her irises. They look like tiny flames. Or like a sunflower or something."

When we finally arrived at the picture of Hannah as the figure of Hope, I knew we were close to reaching our boats on the shore.

"This one is weird," Grace said. "Hannah is a tree."

I smiled, though something about the picture now disturbed me in a way it hadn't when I first created it. Now it appeared less like a depiction of hope and more like a startling metamorphosis. Kafkaesque. "The lines between her legs and the branches got smudged too much," I explained. "She's not a tree, she's just in a tree."

When Grace at last spotted a picture of herself, she rushed to it and plucked it off the branch. I could hear the sound of the waves against the shore, and I spotted the fallen tree with the chance face of dreadful surprise. The boats were through those curtains of foliage ahead.

Grace lifted her face to me quickly, as if she'd just remembered something. "You forgot to take your pictures with you. Don't you want them?"

I shook my head.

"Can I keep this one?" Grace asked.

"If you like," I said.

"Can you carry it for me? So it doesn't get wet?"

I held out my hand to take the picture, but Grace didn't pass it to me right away. She stared at it for a long time, touching it lightly with her index finger, the charcoal smudging her mouth and tugging her smile even wider. Small circles of white light like stars dotted the universe of her dark eyes. Those tiny constellations made Grace's charcoal gaze appear hopeful, as if everything bright and good and new in the world was ahead of her. Grace's own face, turned to me now, pulled down at the corners of her mouth and at the corners of her brows, and there was nothing close to light in her eyes as she handed me the picture for safekeeping.

*   *   *

On the way back across the water, Grace rode in the boat with me as we towed her dugout canoe. Not knowing what to do with her once we reached the village, I decided to take her to Sophie Florence's house. As we walked up the dock, Grace let out a small gasp. Stopping abruptly, she shoved her hand into her sweatshirt pocket and pulled out the fishing hook. "I forgot to put this back," she said. "You got to take it. I don't want anybody to know I got it." Grace reached into her pocket again and pointed the pliers at me. "These, too. Or Auntie Soph will see them."

I hesitated. I didn't feel comfortable colluding with a child behind Sophie Florence's back, especially when that child was also a student. But when I looked at her weary and frightened face, I didn't have the heart to refuse. I slipped the items into my rain jacket pocket. I then took out the picture of Grace and handed it to her in return as though we were carrying out an illicit trade.

Grace folded the picture into a tiny square and squeezed it in her fist.

"We can't tell anybody where we went," Grace said.

"Julian knew where you were going," I pointed out.

"But he don't know I got there. We can't say nothing." Grace shook her head thoughtfully and looked up at the dark clouds overhead. "We shouldn't have gone. The ancestors will be upset with us."

I tried to reassure her. "Everything will be fine."

But she had already started to walk away.

When we reached Sophie Florence's house, Grace opened the front door and cried out, "Auntie! Are you home? I took my canoe out and it got real wet and stormy but it's okay because Teacher found me when she was going to the store, so everything is alright—"

Sophie Florence came out of the kitchen and looked at Grace from head to toe.

"I just need warm clothes is all," Grace said matter-of-factly.

Sophie Florence's long hair was rolled up into a messy bun and her eyes looked puffy with exhaustion. She asked Grace, "What did you say you were doing?"

Grace turned and glanced at me.

It occurred to me then that I had not agreed to keep it a secret. Nor had I disagreed. The truth was that I didn't know how I'd handle things, and for now it was something I felt incapable of unravelling, as though the strands of what was right had woven around us and were now tangled and unyielding, not offering any clue about where to pull without tightening the knot. I wasn't ready to confess to something I couldn't yet fully grasp. Exactly what would I be confessing to? Yes, I had gone to an island I wasn't supposed to go to, but I had only done so to take care of a child. As for repercussions of hauntings and bad fortunes, these were the stories of Tawakin. They were not my stories to believe in. Still, a part of me worried about what Sophie Florence would say, and so I looked down at my boots and said nothing.

"Thank you for getting her back safely," Sophie Florence said to me. Then she looked at Grace. "Let's get you warm and dry and fed."

Shortly after I closed the door and had made my way down the path, Sophie Florence called out to me from her kitchen window. "Going to be a stormy one tonight," she said. "By tomorrow it will pass. A few of us ladies are going to Toomista tomorrow to spend some quiet time together after all that's happened. It's a terrible thing to lose an elder. We're going to look for glass balls. Come with us."

"Me?" I said, surprised by the invitation.

Sophie Florence laughed. "Be ready though. We trip and shove each other for glass balls. Sometimes we even wrestle."

8

By the time I had hiked alone back up the hill from the village, every corner and crevice was shadowed from the early evening light. My feet dragged with exhaustion. When I opened my door, the chicks greeted me from the living room with a symphony of peeping. I didn't even mind the noise. At least I was indoors and safe, sheltered from the elements, away from the darkness of the forest and back into the comfort of light.

After changing into dry clothes, I started a fire in the wood stove. On the kitchen table I set down the sketchbook, fishing hook and pliers in a neat row, as if the order would erase the strangeness of the day. Outside the window next to my seat at the table, the dark clouds gathered and rolled at every edge of the sky. Rain pelted the glass and the wind whistled through the broken lattice panels covering the hollow underbelly of my trailer. I opened my sketchbook and browsed through the handful of remaining portraits. Running my fingertip along the ragged edges of paper left over from the torn-out pages, I envisioned those portraits flapping around in a cold forest that would soon be pitch black.

How or why I had come to be so troubled by forests I couldn't say. My mother, not a lover of the outdoors, was strictly against me playing in the woods behind our street. So strictly in fact that the forbidden nature of the place intrigued me far more than my desire to build a lean-to or climb a tree. The first time I crept by myself into those woods

I stayed for only ten minutes, maybe less. I felt so guilty for disobeying my mother that I hardly had time to gather good sticks. Yet with each solo visit to the woods thereafter, my guilt eroded and soon I spent part of every spring and summer day there, fashioning bows and arrows, sweeping out the dirt floor of my tiny skew-whiff fort with the giant paintbrush I'd taken from home, climbing the tree that gave me a view of the surrounding world. But somewhere along the way, my childhood love of the natural woods was excised from my heart and replaced by an obsession with grim folklore and fairy tales.

A loud noise cut through the wind and the rain. A knocking. I peered out the window. Next to my trailer was the small shack the custodian had been transforming into a chicken coop. I could see the coop door swinging open and shut, open and shut. There was no latch yet on the door and I considered trekking out there and rigging something to stop it from swinging and slamming. I picked up the pliers, thinking I could jam the bevelled jaws under the bottom of the coop door. I snapped the jaws shut a few times, the harsh click-click-click of metal. A silver tooth. A wood tooth. Why would Grace risk being haunted for two teeth? The silver wouldn't be worth much. Was it some kind of dare among the kids? I looked out once more at the door swinging and slamming. I put down the pliers. The rain was falling even harder now, and I'd had enough of the outdoors for one day.

Somebody knocked on my trailer door.

"Just a minute," I called out.

When I answered the door, I thought somebody was standing to the right of my low porch, but it was just a craggly tree stump. The stump was as tall as a person with a little tuft of moss on the top, and it had often startled me when I left for work first thing in the mornings. Nobody else was there. I craned my neck around the door frame to see if it was children being silly or maybe Kevin Sam begging for the gym to be open, but there was nobody.

I went into the living room and fed the chicks and looked out the window. The light in the sky was vanishing. For some reason, I found myself thinking about the colony of ants I had thrown off my pants and sleeves after climbing over that rotten log, and I remembered a painting I did as a child of a whistling thorn tree, those African trees whose spiky appendages were turned into wind instruments by the ants that bored holes into them. To think of the equally intricate architecture that had been carved by the ants into that fallen cedar I climbed over today. How easy it was for me to come along and disrupt things.

The lights in the trailer flickered off and on.

I tensed for a moment, waiting to see if the power was going to shut off entirely. The last thing I wanted after today was to sit in nothing but the pale orange glow of the wood stove. I went to a kitchen drawer and got out a large flashlight and four candles plus a lighter. In the past month, the power had gone out a few times, and I had been warned that it would get more frequent as the autumn storms intensified.

Again someone knocked on the door.

I froze for a moment, feeling uneasy. You're getting spooked for nothing, I told myself. Probably just branches striking the trailer. I waited and listened. The knock came again, a distinct rapping of knuckles on my door. Hesitantly, I went once more to answer it, the light of the outside porch faintly visible through the crack around the door frame. I creaked the door open a few inches, and at that very moment, the power went off.

Startled by the sudden blackness, I slammed the door shut again. "Hello?" I called out. "Sorry to shut the door on you, I just couldn't see anything and it freaked me out." I tried to chuckle, but the growing nervousness in my voice cracked. "Joan, is that you?"

Nobody answered.

I put my ear to the cold door and strained to hear the sound of footsteps on my porch. I could hear nothing except the thin whistle of the wind through the sliver of space between the door and the frame. Who was there? Whoever it was, they hadn't moved from where they stood. Every plank of that old porch groaned loudly. There was no way a person could descend those steps without making noise. Was someone playing a prank on me? No, I couldn't imagine so. Who would choose to play pranks right after a death in the community?

Slowly, I backed away from the door. By the glow of the fire in the wood stove window, I found my way to the living room. Up the road, all the other teachers' trailers were also without light. I recalled the fact that there were no police in the community. Worse yet, I'd left my VHF radio on the kitchen counter with the battery dead. There was no charging it now.

These thoughts jolted me with panic. It didn't help matters that, despite it being nearly dark now, I could still make out the black outlines of the thrashing trees. Like beasts gone beserk in their madness and hunger, their movement outside my window was wild and frenzied, and I became starkly aware that the only thing separating me from the feral night was the thin window pane that quivered in front of me.

Once again there was a knock-knock-knock. This time it had the hollow sound of glass. It came from the kitchen window.

Every muscle in my body tightened. I didn't move. From my spot in the living room, I needed only to turn around to see the kitchen window next to the table. It was dark in the kitchen since I hadn't lit the candles yet, but there would be just enough light to make out a visage. Perhaps it was just Joan, I thought, knowing it made no sense that Joan would walk through the brambles to greet me at the window. I pressed my hand against my breastbone to brace myself and turned to look.

Nobody was there.

I heard footsteps coming around the outside corner of the trailer.

My breath caught in my throat. I moved past the window to stay out of view and peeked around the window frame for any sign of move-ment—an animal, the figure of a person, the shaky beam of a flashlight. There was nothing. Only darkness and the thrashing trees.

For what seemed like ages, I stood there at the window's edge lis-tening for footsteps. I couldn't stand there all night, or so I told myself. Slowly I became resigned to the idea that the knocking and the footsteps had been the storm throwing itself against my trailer. There was no other explanation. When I was convinced of this, or at least willing to pretend I was convinced, I left my stakeout at the window and lit the four candles, placing them around the kitchen and the living room.

I pulled down the blinds to cover the kitchen window, retrieved the sharpest filleting knife from the drawer and sat back down at the table.

As I sat there motionless, I spotted the dessicated carcass of a spider on the windowsill and it brought back a memory I hadn't thought of in years. When I was a child, there was a squished black beetle in the centre of Marvin Gardens on my Monopoly board. The outline of its wings soaked into the glossy pale green paper. I pictured the board lying on the cool concrete of Mr. Ellerson's garden shed, next to the strip of woods behind my neighbourhood. Surrounding the board was the usual gang: snotty-nosed George Ellerson, whose dad whipped him with a fishing rod; Bonnie Urquhart with her unwashed hair and hand-me-down pilled cardigans; Sharon Winnington, who lived alone with her widowed father and who was my best friend and a cheat in every game; and of course, me. Somebody else, another boy, hovered in my memory, but I could not bring to mind a name or a face. I could, however, remember the death of the beetle as if it were yesterday.

It happened in the summer of 1981. I was ten. We all huddled around the game, the sound of July rain on the roof, the stains of motor oil around us. We played according to the rules except for one thing: each child brought to the game all the money from their own Monopoly sets, and instead of paying the bank when we were taxed or penalized, we put everything into the centre and we bit our lips in unbearable anticipation whenever anybody came close to landing on Free Parking with its prize of winning that mountain of money.

It was George Ellerson's boot that killed the beetle. Not his actual boot, but his silver playing piece. He had rolled two fours on the dice, which I remembered clearly—strange I should remember such a small thing so clearly after all this time—and he was furious at missing Free Parking, landing instead on Kentucky Avenue where he had to pay me $250 for the rent of the two green houses on it. Because he had rolled doubles, George got to take two turns in a row. As he counted out his next move toward Marvin Gardens, he kept slamming his boot down on the board even though Bonnie snapped at him to cut it out on account of the houses and hotels getting rattled off their properties.

If I hadn't seen it with my own eyes I'd never have believed that the beetle ran under George's boot at the precise moment he struck it down onto the board, and if I was willing to consider that an insect could suffer existential angst, I would've sworn that it had thrown itself headfirst under that boot on purpose. There it stayed, its insides sprayed and sticky. None of us ever bothered to flick away the shell of its body. Eventually it decayed, leaving a kind of fossil-like black stain on Marvin Gardens, and whenever I now pictured that stain, I couldn't help but wonder why I hadn't done anything to prevent its unnecessary death. But that was ridiculous. The beetle was of no special consequence and if anything, the death was a small thrill, a spectacle for my amusement, and I'd marvelled at the bizarre misfortune of its tragic end. Not to mention the astonished look on George Ellerson's face. At that point in my life I was cavalier about death.

I heard footsteps again.

My heart sped up. The footsteps were louder this time and seemed to be coming from the gravel path outside my front door. There was a loud thump and a crunch of gravel, then a few more footsteps that faded into silence.

In the living room I blew out the candles so that I could see out the window better. From there, I would have had a view of the end of my path, where it intersected with the old logging road. But it was too dark to see much of anything. Still, I kept staring, waiting. Then I saw it. Barely. Something was lying on the ground, curled up. An animal? It had to be an animal. I watched for five minutes, maybe longer. It didn't move. Was it dead? Impossible to tell in the dark. I could hardly make out its black silhouette.

Turning my back to the window, I tried to pretend it wasn't there, whatever it was, and I considered whether I should go to bed early to put it out of my mind in the hopes that it would be gone when I awoke. But I knew that was impossible. How would I be able to sleep tonight with a strange thing outside my window? There was no fear like that of what was unknown.

I took my flashlight from the kitchen counter and headed to the door. I had no intention of exploring the thing up close, but I might be able to see what it was from my porch. Peering around the door frame, I directed the flashlight beam along the path. It was about thirty feet away, and the light that fell upon it was pale and mottled by the rain. I squinted to try to make out limbs and a head, but couldn't. The thing, which was coloured darkly, looked abstract to me, not anything recognizable. I took a step toward the porch stairs, and then a step down one of the stairs, and then another. Wetness soaked into my socks, and my entire body tensed as I inched closer, the thing's apparent lack of detail making me worried that I was mistaking it for nothing dangerous.

The closer I got, the more convinced I was that it was not a living creature. Or even a dead one. I had stepped right off the porch now, and the rain fell hard on me. About fifteen feet away from it, I stopped. I could see for certain what it was now. About the size of a steamer trunk, the large rock lay right in the middle of my path.

My stomach hollowed at the sight of it. How bizarre it was to see such a large rock appear all of a sudden. Yet it was only a rock, so harmless, just sitting there in my pathway. I shook the leftover adrenaline out of my hands. Once I felt calmer, I pointed the flashlight beam all around to look for any signs as to how the rock got there. Next to the other end of my trailer was a vertical wall of rock about twelve feet high, which led to the thick forest above, but that was too low and too far away. There was no way this rock splintered from that wall. And it hadn't been the sound of a rolling rock I heard. It had been footsteps. Maybe it toppled off the back of a pickup truck and the footsteps were from somebody—maybe Chase Charlie—getting out to see what fell. That was plausible. Except I hadn't heard the noisy sputter of his old truck.

I couldn't make sense of it. There was no reasonable explanation for the rock's presence. Impulsively, I shut off the flashlight. My arm fell to my side. Standing there in the darkness next to a large rock that had no business being there, I listened to the rain, its wetness drenching my skin. A profound feeling of lonely remorse overwhelmed me, a feeling of wanting to be anywhere but here, a feeling of wanting to disappear.

Bolting along the path, I turned up the logging road, marching so fast that the sound of my breath was like the roar of the ocean in my ears. From Joan's porch, I could see hints of candlelight through her window.

I knocked.

"I know it's pouring out," I said when she opened the door, "but I need to show you something. Get your rain gear on."

Joan gave me a puzzled look. "Okay," she said hesitantly. Then, as she twisted around to grab her rain jacket from the hook, she said, "Your clothes are soaked. Why aren't you wearing a jacket? Holy shit, Molleigh, you don't even have boots on. Are you drunk?"

I shook my head. "Just come see."

Once we had returned to my pathway, I pointed my flashlight at the rock. Joan did the same with her flashlight. I explained the noises I'd heard and how I couldn't figure out how the massive rock had ended up there.

When Joan didn't say anything, I looked over to see her hand covering her mouth. It was difficult to tell in the reflection of our flashlights, but her face looked as though it had lost a little colour.

"What?" I asked.

"Uh—" she started, then shook her head rapidly, as if she were having trouble gathering her thoughts. Then she clamped her hand over her mouth again for a moment. "Shit."

"What?" I asked again.

Joan moved her gaze to me without turning her head. "You know what they say about large rocks in unexpected places?"

"No, what do they say?"

Joan paused, then took a deep breath.

I got the distinct impression that she wasn't sure whether she should tell me or not. Impatiently, I pressed her, "What do they say?"

"That they're put there by a Sasquatch."

A small laugh erupted from my belly. It was a ludicrous suggestion.

Joan ignored this. "Sasquatch will place big rocks in the middle of roads, or on top of unusual places. Just to let people know they're around. A kind of calling card."

I scoffed, though I did wonder what else could move a rock that size. "Let's just say that's what happened here," I said, playing along. "Then the question becomes: Why would any creature bother to do that—in my path?"

Joan panned her flashlight around, looking behind her and even up on the roof of my trailer, which put all my nerves back on edge. She said, "Some people say that Sasquatch are tricksters. Tricksters are always messing around with shit. So why not leave a big rock where it shouldn't be?"

"You don't actually think it was a Sasquatch, do you?"

"No," Joan said, though she sounded unsure. "But do you know who will actually think it?"

"Who?"

Joan motioned her head toward the village. "Most everyone down that hill. And who knows. Maybe they're right. Maybe they see more than we do here. They'd know better than us, right? We have no connection to this land and its history."

"I suppose," I said, "but I just can't believe that a Sasquatch—"

Joan pointed her flashlight beam straight into my face. I craned my neck to avoid the glare. "You don't believe? You sure? You don't seem sure. The world is full of strangeness," she said in a mockingly spooky tone. "But chances are, this happened naturally. From that rock face back there, for example."

"I already considered that," I said. "But there's no way a rock from there could gain enough momentum to wind up here."

"Maybe not. But what if it somehow ricocheted across the boughs of those big cedars and then bounced off your roof?" Joan took a few steps backward to check the top of the trailer more thoroughly. "Hmm, no sign of denting. Could be a prank, you know."

"Who would go to all this trouble just to prank me?" I asked.

"Any reason a student might be trying to get back at you for something?"

I thought of Hannah. "How could an eleven-year-old move a rock like that?"

"One of the teenagers?" Joan suggested. "You haven't opened the gym for them since the first week you started."

"No way," I said. "Kevin's the only one who asks, and he's way too polite for this. I don't think it's a prank. I mean, I know it's large, but I can simply walk around this. What kind of prank is putting a rock in my path?"

"The kind of prank someone might pull if they believe in Sasquatch," Joan said. "If they wanted you to worry that a trickster was bothering you for some reason."

For some reason. The words echoed in my ears. Could I tell Joan about finding the woman this afternoon? I figured she would be discreet about the whole thing, and probably she would support the choices I made that day to help Grace. Though who could know for sure? Really, there was something else to my uncertainty about telling Joan. Stinginess. It was an experience that felt uniquely mine, the private sort of experience you wish to hoard, if only for the fact that the telling of it would demystify it.

I looked at Joan, and despite my hesitation about telling her, I had to. I had to tell Joan and I had to tell Sophie Florence. I had to explain before they heard it elsewhere. I didn't want Sophie Florence to think I had disregarded her warning about the island and the woman without good reason. And I didn't want Joan to think that I was different than her, that I didn't understand things like *isaak*.

"Today I saw the woman in the box with the baby," I blurted.

Both our flashlights still pointed at the large rock. The rain pinged off the roof and off Joan's rain jacket, and several moments passed before she replied. "You're not allowed on that island," she said sternly.

"I know."

"Then why would you do that? You know how serious this is, right?"

"Yes," I lied. I knew it was serious, but Joan's tone worried me. She made it sound even more grave than I had imagined.

"You cannot tell anyone," she said, then she repeated it slowly: "You cannot tell anyone."

I felt a pressure on my chest. "I have to tell."

"You can't."

"I have to," I said. "My drawings are on the trees."

"Your drawings are on the trees? What does that even mean?"

"I stuck pages from my sketchbook on the trees so I wouldn't get lost," I explained. "I left them there."

Joan said, "Oh, I see. Well, don't worry about that. No one goes there. Ever. People don't even pull their boat up to the shore."

"But what if a kayaker who doesn't know better goes camping in there and takes the drawings to the market and says, 'Hey, I found the strangest thing on Fossil Island,'" I asked.

"It's October," Joan said dismissively. "Your drawings will disintegrate in the rain long before any kayaker comes here next spring. Don't worry about the drawings. Just do not tell anyone."

"I have to," I said once more. "I went there with a student."

"What?" Joan gasped. "Who?"

"Grace."

Joan grimaced. "Who?"

I whispered, "Candice."

Joan threw her hand back. "Shit, Molleigh."

"I had to. I had to follow her," I said, pleading my case. "She was in a half-dugout canoe and it was getting stormy and I couldn't stop her. I tried. I couldn't just leave her alone."

"What if—" Joan stopped and squinted thoughtfully. She pointed her flashlight beam at the rock. "What if this is here because—" She stopped again, seemingly hesitant to finish. "What if this is here because you saw the woman in the box with the baby?"

I tilted my head skeptically.

"Just saying." Joan raised both hands in a sign of surrender. "*Numak.* Bad things happen when you disturb the dead."

"So you think I'm cursed now?" I asked in disbelief.

As she turned to head home, Joan said once more, this time without the mocking tone, "The world is full of strangeness."

Once I was inside my trailer again and changed into dry clothes, I found myself too wired to consider bed, even though the power was still out and anything I did would have to be by candlelight. As I put more wood into the stove, I considered that there was only one possible answer to the mystery of the rock because there was only one person in Tawakin with a truck to move a rock that big. Chase Charlie. Was he still upset at me for kicking Hannah out of class when I had promised I wouldn't? Or was it a warning to keep my promise to stay? I couldn't believe that someone like Chase would resort to such an odd gesture, and besides that, we were on good terms when he left my classroom. Then again, Joan did say that he was *very protective* of his daughter.

Hannah. I remembered Odelia's claim that Hannah was cursed and that was why she was hiding her hands, and for a brief moment I felt jarred by the possibility that Hannah had also gone to the woman in the box with the baby. Then I quickly reminded myself that while I would never disparage such things as *numak* publicly, in private I could never bring myself to consider the possibility. Strange things happening from finding old bones? Curses? No. The mummy's curse, the curse of the Hope diamond, famously cursed spiral staircases that you never use if you wanted to live a long life. Figments of people's imaginations. People who believed in curses and hauntings from past generations—those were people eager to make sense of a senseless world. People who needed to bring order to chaos. That was not me. It wasn't. Seeing the extraordinary in the ordinary? Yes, okay. That was only a matter of perspective. But misconstruing coincidences and mishaps? Could I buy into that? No.

Outside, in the pitch blackness of the night, the rain on my roof punctuated my thoughts with a discordant rhythm as I walked around the living room in a state of unreality. The whole thing was incomprehensible in a way that agitated me, and the strangeness of it made me want to feel some measure of control. I had to do something. I found the roll of packing tape in the drawer and carried out the stack of moving boxes I kept folded flat in the broom closet. I wasn't entirely sure what my plan was, and I was hardly going to pack up all my things in the flickering shadows of candlelight, but what I needed right then was to feel like I was in charge of something.

Was it a good idea to hide my visit to the woman in the box with the baby from Sophie Florence? If she were to hear about it from someone else, would they explain that I was only there to make sure Grace stayed safe? Who knows how the story might get twisted if I wasn't the one to set things straight. I needed to tell Sophie Florence. Tomorrow I would find a quiet moment alone with her and I would explain everything. She would understand, I was sure of it. And she was the heart of the community. If she forgave me for visiting the woman in the box with the baby, then everyone else would, too.

After twenty minutes I had taped into shape eight large cardboard boxes that lay scattered and empty around my living room floor. The integrity of some of the boxes was questionable. The ocean spray over the gunwale of Chase's fishing trawler on the day of my arrival had soaked the boxes beyond reuse. The seams were soft and would surely not hold.

A small smile lifted my face as I blew out the candles and used the flashlight to guide my way to bed. How hard Chase had laughed at the wharf when he saw that I hadn't packed my things inside plastic totes. "Cardboard? On the West Coast? That's a real good sign," he said. "Only people that never plan on leaving Tawakin bring their stuff in cardboard."

9

As Sophie Florence had predicted, the storm had passed by morning and the sun played peek-a-boo through the clouds. I drank my coffee standing in the living room among the empty boxes, all of which looked even more pitiful in the light. From my spot at the window, I tilted my head in consideration of the rock. Except for its size, there was nothing interesting about it. Though its presence was no less strange than it was last night, I felt lighter about it now. Mornings always eased the oppression of nighttime and all its dread.

I took one last gulp then slipped on my jacket and boots and went outside to take a closer look. When I compared it to the colouring of the rock face next to my trailer, it was clear that these were two different types of rock. The rock face had a tint of orange to it, and there was no evidence of fresh fracture lines anywhere on the wall. Nor were there any smaller pieces along the path or the road. If it had tumbled accidentally off Chase's pickup from the road, there would be other fractured chips from its fall. A sign of scuffing on the gravel road at least. Something that heavy couldn't crash and roll off the road without leaving a mark in the dirt. And if Chase had put it there on purpose, which I now thought was an unlikely hypothesis, there would have been tire tracks from where he'd driven onto my path.

I hiked down the gravel road on my way to wrestle glass balls from other women. I was always on high alert when heading down the hill, watching for cougars in the cedar boughs above and black bears in the dark brambled arches below. At first nothing was visible from the road except the trees and the brambles and the large warts of granite that dotted the hillside. Then I noticed it: high above my head was a fresh divot in the rocky slope. I could tell it was fresh because it was coloured much darker than the rest of the stone and it wasn't covered with any of the moss or lichen that otherwise veiled every inch of the slope. It was also about the size of the rock in front of my trailer. What were the chances that the rock had fractured and fallen just as Chase Charlie drove by with his pickup truck? And what were the chances that it fell perfectly into the truck bed and then toppled off the bed and onto my path? The odds were extremely low. But anything was possible.

Somewhere in the village a chainsaw started up.

From where I stood, I could see a vast expanse of the ocean, and I let my mind soak in the serenity of the water. I moved my gaze across the distant horizon from where those prized Japanese fishing floats drifted toward the shores. Near the bottom of the hill, I approached the yard of a small brown house where six-year-old Tara Frank sat on a trampoline. She stared at me. Her eyes looked remorseful. Or maybe shy. I said hello, but Tara didn't utter a word. I asked why she was not bouncing. Tara blinked at me. I looked at the front door of the house, at the eagle and the penis and the pot leaf crudely spray painted in blue and black. Then I waved goodbye, and Tara fell over sideways as if instantly asleep, or dead, her eyes closed, the trampoline rebounding ever so slightly.

Down at the dock, the four women waited in a small skiff. Sophie Florence was seated in the back next to the motor. Strands of her hair, most of it tied back, swirled in the wind like curlicues of ink. She didn't say hello or how are you today, she only pointed at an empty seat on the skiff.

I squeezed myself onto the middle of the bench between Gina Joe and Margaret Sam. Lizzie Joe sat on a triangle of wood where the bow came to a point. Our weight settled the hull deep in the water. Shoulder pressed against shoulder, the four of us sat facing the stern

The Morning Bell Brings the Broken Hearted

while Sophie Florence started the motor and twisted the throttle to warm up the engine, blue and grey smoke puffing out.

I reflected on my decision to tell Sophie Florence about my visit to Fossil Island, but the thought of telling her in front of the other women made me nervous. I couldn't be sure how they would see things, though wouldn't it be important to the women that I helped a child? They would surely overlook any transgression that occurred in the process. Still, I felt more comfortable waiting until I was alone with Sophie Florence.

"Nice day. Finally, no rain. Tide's pretty low," I said, raising my voice over the sputtering motor. "You can see the bottom," by which I meant the juice bottles, the broken chair, the bicycle, the garden spade, the electric frying pan. Also two diapers that hovered a few feet below the oil-sheened surface, and the shiners that darted between them. I looked at Sophie Florence. "How is she today?"

"She is resting in the house with my brothers," Sophie Florence said. "When I get back today, we will get her ready to leave."

"She's leaving? Where?" I asked.

Sophie Florence stuck out her bottom lip, which she always did whenever she was thinking carefully. "Foster home in Port Hardy."

"Can't she stay with you?" I could hear the hint of panic in my voice. "Or someone else? There must be someone here she could live with."

Sophie Florence nodded slowly and gave the throttle another twist. "I'm going to ask for her to live with me, but there'll be lots of meetings about it before she's brought back to us."

My stomach knotted at the idea of Grace being shipped off to a stranger's home. How heartless to make a young girl grieve alone, so far away from all her aunties and uncles and cousins. So far away from her home.

"When is she leaving?" I asked.

"Tuesday," Sophie Florence said.

I frowned. The day after tomorrow. I couldn't imagine that Grace would be at school on Monday, given the circumstances. Turning to look at Sophie Florence's house on the ridge behind us, I decided that I would come down the hill after school tomorrow to say goodbye to Grace. A temporary goodbye, that's all it would be, for there was no way Sophie Florence wouldn't be seen as a fit caregiver for Grace. I would see Grace back in my classroom again, I would.

Sophie Florence steered away from the dock and toward the mouth of the cove, which separated the Tawakin Reserve from Mitchell Island, the narrow island scarcely big enough to shelter the reserve from the Pacific Ocean. We sat in silence, jostling from side to side as we moved slowly through the passage. On one side was a tall sea stack, and beside that, a small outcrop of sharp black boulders with a few trees. In the middle of this outcrop somebody had driven a wood cross, about three feet tall, into the ground. It tilted toward the village.

Halfway through the passage the motor stalled. Sophie Florence untangled long ribbons of kelp from the propeller and yanked at the starter cord, rocking the skiff so that the briny water nearly cascaded over the gunwale. We crashed against one another as the skiff wobbled and drifted alongside rocks and mounds of purple starfish.

"You got a man yet?" Lizzie asked.

I twisted my head around and looked sideways at Lizzie. "Me?"

Lizzie raised her eyebrows, yes.

"A man? You mean back home?" I asked.

Lizzie wrinkled her nose, no.

I thought for a moment. In the distance, the cove sparkled like a blue plate of broken glass in the morning sun. I asked, "You mean from here?" And then, after more silence, "Well, no. I only moved here a month ago."

"Well! What's taking you so long?"

There was a wild eruption of noise, whoops and cackles. The women threw their heads back and slapped their thighs. Their otherwise stern-looking faces opened and lifted into gaping laughter.

I pulled my head back in surprise, having assumed that the trip to Toomista would be a solemn one in the aftermath of Candice's death.

"Real nutty, sister!" Sophie Florence shrieked. Her glasses went lopsided as she wiped away the wet corners of her eyes.

"*Haw-ess!* Gina said, clutching her belly. "You'll scare Magoo away!"

Gina had called me this since I first arrived in Tawakin, and each time she did, I pictured the nearsighted cartoon character, wealthy and bald, with streaks of stubbornness and good luck. I wished Gina wouldn't call me that, but I was determined to fit into the community, so I hadn't protested despite the fact that I didn't want a nickname. Little walls of words defining and confining who I was without my permission.

I looked at Sophie Florence. "Why does she always call me that?"

Sophie Florence flapped her hand dismissively in Gina's direction. "That's just what she calls all the new teachers."

The motor started again and we picked up speed, moving along the remote coastline and across the swells of open ocean toward a triangle of small islands: Waas, Rubant, Toomista.

"How long you going to stay here for?" Gina asked me.

I stumbled to speak. I didn't know the answer to this question, of course, and how could I ever confess to any of these women that all these days spent in the classroom with their nieces and nephews, and with their grandsons and granddaughters, had left me feeling like I was going to start wearing away. "I don't know," I said.

Gina scoffed. "One year? Two years? Half a year? Three months?"

"Certainly longer than three months," I lied. I was not certain.

"How much longer?"

My voice turned thin. "I'm not sure."

"See? There you go," said Gina. "What's the point in me learning names? None of you ever stay for long enough."

"Maybe I will," I said, feeling challenged.

"Don't matter," Gina said. "You all leave eventually."

I turned my face away from the women. I didn't know how to respond to Gina's last statement because I knew it was true. I pictured those empty boxes in my living room and thought of the promise Chase was holding on to and how I didn't think I could keep it. Even if things had gone better for me, Gina would still be right. I would not stay in Tawakin forever.

"But you have to find a glass ball before you can leave," Margaret smiled.

"And if we're there when you do, you better beat us to it," Lizzie added.

"Good luck. We're pretty good at finding them. Have you seen how many we all have? We have baskets full of them in our houses," Gina said, and I detected the teasing in her voice.

Sophie Florence slowed the boat to a crawl when we reached Waas Island. Through a shallow channel of water between the island and a tall sea stack, we moved carefully over a sand bar. Sophie Florence pointed at a cave in a low cliff on the southwest shore. Most of the cave's black mouth was covered by piles of driftwood.

"There are lots of bones in that cave. Enemies from a battle long ago," Sophie Florence told me. "Like Fossil Island, it's also forbidden. Don't ever go on that island."

My stomach hollowed at the mention of Fossil Island. I nodded.

Gina laughed. "Remember when Chase Charlie went in there? What was he—twelve?"

"Fifteen." Sophie Florence turned the boat slightly.

"Boy, the trouble he got in!" Gina said.

"Did he ever!" Lizzie said.

Gina posed as if she were pointing a rifle. "Hunted his first *muwach* and nailed the skull to his shed."

"He hunted a deer on that island?" I asked.

Lizzie wrinkled her nose. "He hunted a *muwach* and nailed the skull to his shed because he went in the cave."

"Once the flesh was done rotting off it," Margaret said, "he knew it was time to feed the community. Then he hosted a dinner for everyone and gave away his first *muwach* and said his apology."

I let out a long whistle. "A whole community dinner? That's a lot for one kid to do."

"But you got to do it like that," Sophie Florence said. "You don't got to hunt a *muwach*, but you got to host a dinner for the community. Like I told you, ancestors get upset by stuff like that, disrespecting the dead. It can cause a lot of trouble for the whole village."

"Remember why he went in there?" Lizzie asked.

The other women laughed.

Gina said, "Real nutty kid, he was."

"To find Truth." Sophie Florence nodded with a chuckle.

"The truth about what?" I asked.

Lizzie flapped her hand at me. "No. Truth, like with a capital."

"A person named Truth," Gina added.

I winced in confusion. "Who's that?"

"Some lady, I don't know," Sophie Florence said, chuckling louder now. She seemed tickled by the whole story. "One time Chase's older brother Ronnie told him that he'd gone into the cave when he was Chase's age. And he told Chase about this woman who lived in there. Told him that she lives in there painting shadows on the walls by firelight and that she's real ugly, uglier than the Basket Lady. Her teeth yellow and splintered like wood."

"Her dress ripped up and covered with soot," Lizzie said.

"Her hair dirty and tangled," Margaret said.

"Her skin crumpled like a lunch bag," Gina said.

I grimaced. "Why would Chase ever want to find somebody like that?"

"Ronnie had told him that when you go in there," Lizzie said, "you can feel things moving past the fire but you can't see them, you can only see the shadows painted on the wall."

Gina stroked her chin. "Ronnie was just messing with Chase. Big brothers. Real mischief, hey?"

Sophie Florence smirked at Gina and agreed, "Real mischief. Ronnie was a clever one. He said that when he found the woman, she told him that she looks different to each person, and that when he left the cave, she said to him: 'If you tell anybody about me, tell them that I have shiny hair and skin as smooth as a drum. Tell them that I am young and beautiful.' And then she changed her mind. She said, 'Tell them I am a man. Strong like an oak tree. A tall, old man with one of those long beards. Tell them that,' she said."

"Then she said to Ronnie," Lizzie added, "'Or don't tell them anything. It don't matter. I look different to each person anyway.' That's why Chase got so curious."

Gina nodded. "Besides that, he wanted to do what his big brother done."

"So I guess Ronnie hosted a dinner when he was young, too?" I asked.

Sophie Florence wrinkled her nose. "Nobody knew Ronnie had ever gone in there until Chase did. Not long after, Ronnie took his own life."

The women went silent.

I felt a stream of regret wind its way from them to me. I searched for something to say in sympathy, something to acknowledge their loss even though it happened many years ago. The wind picked up as the boat exited the narrow channel and entered a wider area of water between the three islands. To our left was Rubant Island where the village buried their loved ones, and straight ahead was Toomista, with its small cluster of abandoned houses looking grey and battered and lonely on the field above the shore. Finally I said, "He sounds like he was a very interesting character, Ronnie. What an imagination."

Sophie Florence nodded. "He was a storyteller."

"Must have been," I said. "That's quite a story for Chase to believe."

Sophie Florence shrugged. "Who doesn't believe a good story?"

"We laugh about it now," Gina said, "but Ronnie shouldn't have told it to Chase."

"It was a mean trick," Margaret agreed. "Ronnie knew that Chase wanted to believe in something special."

"He did. So bad," Lizzie said.

"So bad he never even thought it was just a trick," Margaret said.

"I think he would have believed it even if he knew it was a trick," Lizzie said. "We all want to be tricked by a story, don't we? We don't even care if we know it's a trick—if it's a story we want to believe. It can be good for the heart."

Sophie Florence nodded. Then she sighed and said, "Except for some stories. Some stories put the heart in danger."

To this all the women lifted their eyebrows high in agreement.

10

On the beach of Toomista Island there was sand, driftwood, grass, a spine of rock, snakes of kelp. Beyond that was the endless ocean, the wind, the firmament and the circular current of our prized glass balls. About fifty steps from the shore where we anchored the skiff and waded through the knee-high tide with plastic containers of food in our arms, there were the four abandoned houses nestled in the tall grass on the elevated field. Wood-slatted relics—some standing upright, some slanted and crumpled—with grey clapboard and dark, cavernous windows of broken glass.

We climbed the short embankment to the field and set the food on the ground beside a small fire pit that had been dug out of the grass and circled with large stones.

"Come on, let's get her things," Sophie Florence said.

I stayed next to the fire pit and watched the women walk toward the dilapidated house to our left. Glancing back at me, Gina motioned that I should come as well. I followed them through the thick, long grass, but when we reached the house, I wished to go no farther. The house had rotted in places, as wood does after years of torrential rain, and I suspected that the outside stairs up to the main door on the second floor were incapable of supporting our weight. The whole place appeared waterlogged and perforated along its seams.

At the top of the stairs, Sophie Florence walked through the doorless entrance, setting her foot carefully on the kitchen linoleum, which blistered and curled away from the soft plywood underneath. She stooped to pick up a VHS tape. A long ribbon of dark grey tape hung out of the top. I watched from the doorway, wincing with every step Sophie Florence took. While the outside stairs had remained intact, I was convinced the floor couldn't withstand our collective weight. As the women piled into the kitchen, I expected one of them to disappear at any moment with a thunderous crash. Next to the kitchen, the living room floor was in even worse shape, a tattered honeycomb. Rotten patches of black holes leading to the depths of the basement below. Where the floor was solid, it was cluttered with various electronics—a stereo receiver, a VHS player, an old TV with a bent antenna.

Sophie Florence put the VHS tape on the counter beside a stack of wet newspapers as plump as pillows and started to upright things: the rusted toaster, a jar of what looked like peanut butter and a blender splattered with something pink and hard as enamel, impervious to the rain that must have fallen through the holes in the ceiling. The other women started to do the same, and as I stepped gingerly into the kitchen, I was unsure what was happening, why they were tidying a house filled with forgotten things.

"Come help," Sophie Florence instructed me. "Might seem point-less now, looking at the condition of this place, but it just feels right to straighten up the house a little for her."

I tiptoed across the floor and looked for something to do. I emptied a rain-filled coffee pot into the sink, where the water washed away the kinked coils of dead spiders.

"We had to move off Toomista ten years ago because there were too many of us and the water well wasn't big enough," Sophie Florence explained. "A couple families kept living here for a little while after that, but not many. Eventually everyone moved off the island to be with the community in the village."

Sophie Florence sniffed an empty Smirnoff bottle and stuffed it through a hole in the floor. It got stuck halfway, so she stomped on the glass neck until it disappeared and shattered in the dark basement below.

Next to the sink there was a dirty plate with a knife and fork on top. As I picked up a leftover bite of petrified meat and dropped it through a hole in the floor, I wondered, in spite of what Sophie Florence had said about the water well, why everything had been left so abruptly.

In between cleaning, the women opened and shut all the cupboards, stretching up on their toes to wipe their hands across the shelves as if searching for something. Sophie Florence went into the living room and walked across the beams, hopping clumsily over the holes until she reached the other side. I peeked around the edge of the wall.

"Is there something we're looking for?" I asked Sophie Florence.

Sophie Florence lifted her eyebrows. "Her things."

"Whose things?"

"This used to be her house," Sophie Florence said.

"Right over there was where she saw the hairy *puukmis* when she was a girl. Remember that story, Gina?" Lizzie Joe stood next to the living room window and pointed to a spot on the field. A few pointed shards of glass were all that remained of the window, sticking out like large incisors.

Gina lifted the flap of a soggy cardboard box and it came right off in her hand. She peeked inside before answering. "Her sister dared her to go out in the dark. She was a brave one—I'd never have gone out there at night."

"Remember how she used to argue with Nurse Bernadette about it?" Margaret said. "Nurse Bernadette would tell her to be careful about her diet because of her diabetes, especially since it had already made her blind, but she'd flap her hand at Nurse and say it wasn't from the diabetes, it was from the hairy *puukmis*, that they got eyes as bright as diamonds and if you look right at them, you go blind, and how she wished she'd never listened to her nutty sister. Then Nurse would try to explain that she got the timing of her story all wrong, that that story was from too long ago to be the reason. She just kept on laughing at Nurse. Every time."

Sophie Florence returned from a room in the back with a cedar box in her arms. "I got it. Most of it was in here, but I found a few other pieces on the windowsills. The roof is good back there so the stuff is damp, but not soaked."

When the women returned to the field, they all gathered wood and kindling from the adjacent forest and set it next to the fire pit. Sophie Florence went to the edge of the forest once more and retrieved four cedar branches. She placed two of the branches in the fire pit and lit them with a match. Then she reached into the box and set a beautiful cedar hat onto the small flames.

I was startled to see a handcrafted object destroyed. It didn't take an expert to see the incredible skill needed to weave the intricate pattern. When it didn't catch right away, the moisture in the cedar strips smoking, I privately willed it to defy the flames. Nothing good ever came from destroying art, I thought, and I pictured those sketches in the forest on Fossil Island, doomed to disintegrate in the rain. At least that was a natural weathering. This, on the other hand, seemed a terrible shame, all that work come to nothing. Soon the cedar strips were dry enough to ignite. I grimaced as the hat crackled with flame, though the fragrance of the burning cedar was almost as beautiful as the hat itself.

Margaret moved some other branches from the pile and added them to the fire. Then she took a beaded eagle feather out of the box and placed that on the top. The plastic beads melted instantly under the heat. Lizzie lifted a large square of folded black fabric out of the box. She felt around for its corners and lifted them high above her head, letting the fabric fall open like a curtain in front of her. Fringed with silky red tassels, the dance shawl was decorated with a sequined eagle.

"Gorgeous," Sophie Florence whispered.

"She made the most beautiful shawls," Gina said.

There were patches of mildew visible on the black fabric, but it was otherwise an elegant sight. Lizzie rolled it up around her forearms and dropped it onto the flames.

"Why are we burning these incredible things?" I asked.

"It is our way of giving her stuff back to her," Sophie Florence said. "We burn two cedar branches to start the ceremony, burn her things, then burn two more cedar branches. Then we roast some hotdogs."

"We'll have a bigger ceremony for her things in the village," Gina said, "but we wanted to get the stuff from her old house right away."

"I get that the water well was too small for all the families here," I said, "but why were all these things—" I looked at the fire then motioned at the house "—and all those things in there, why was everything left here like that?"

"Ha," Gina said, "bet where you're from, you can just pick up the phone and hire a truck. Or when your old mattress is ready for the dump, you just put it out on the curb. You know how hard it is to move things around here? They took what they wanted with them."

I turned my gaze back to the fire. "I'm surprised these things weren't wanted."

"They were. She treasured these things." Sophie Florence poked at the fire with a long stick. "She made that shawl with her grandmother when she returned from residential school. And she beaded that eagle feather back then, too. All of it. She left this stuff here where she thought it belonged. In the house she called home."

After the box was emptied, we roasted hotdogs. Margaret peeled off the Tupperware lids and passed out the paper plates. The wind blew across the field, flapping our plates off our laps as we drank coffee from the steel thermoses and ate potato salad and meaty gooseneck barnacles, which slipped out of their shells like socks from boots.

A short while later we went to Rubant Island. It was right next to Toomista Island, so close you could almost leap over the dividing sleeve of shallow water. Nevertheless, we took the skiff over, then hiked through a narrow stretch of trees and into a clearing where the overgrown grass was as high as our knees. A giant totem pole stood guard over the rows of crosses. I followed the women as they looked at the burial plots. The hands of time had scrubbed some of the names from the crosses, but the women each brought strips of stories of fallen sisters and brothers and husbands and children, and they weaved them together, quietly under their breath. Stories of singing and dancing, of filling jars with jams, of drumming and laughing and eating fish head soup, of hanging and burning and falling from great heights, of drinking and shooting and drowning in cold darkness.

I listened to the women, hearing only ragged snippets in their whispers. Some of the burial plots were surrounded by picket fences adorned with mementos and sun-faded, plastic-covered photographs. A teddy bear, its fur disintegrated and discoloured from years of rain and hail, sat on the grave of a baby, *Alesha Sam*. A motorbike with a racing plate on the handlebars—number 42—leaned against a young man's freshly painted fence. *Kyle Joe*. A cross of popsicle sticks decorated with yarn, the type of handicraft children make at summer camp, dangled over the plot of a fourteen-year-old boy. *Shane Henry*.

"Where is—" I stopped, unsure how to ask where little Candice's father was buried without uttering her old name or her new name, which might have remained something between us. I didn't even know her father's name. Stephen? Chris? I was certain Grace had mentioned it to me once or twice, but I couldn't remember. I should have remembered.

It made me wonder about the woman in the box with the baby, too—why she was not here on Rubant Island. Though I felt a strong urge to ask, I worried doing so was wrong. Worse yet, if I asked, would my voice, my face, or the simple asking of the question itself, make it plainly obvious to the women that I had visited the woman and the baby?

Instead, I searched the names for Ronnie Charlie, and when I couldn't find it anywhere, I asked the women which burial plot was his.

"He's not here," Sophie Florence said. "He was buried near his mother's home farther up the coast. His mother moved up there to live alone so she could be near the spot where her oldest son, Stan, had died the year before. Sometimes we boat up there to bring her fresh fruit and a box of tea bags."

I was dazed to hear of a second brother's death, and I pictured Chase Charlie, in his greasy green ball cap that covered his eyes, and tried to imagine what things were like for him to lose not one but two brothers. A pressure began to rise within me like an incoming tide. I could feel it surging, swirling, washing over me. How could I break my promise to Chase by leaving Tawakin before the end of the school year now that I knew this about his life?

Sophie Florence pointed at a spot on the ground and explained to me, "This is where she'll be buried when the body is returned. The children won't go to school if she is returned on a weekday. They'll have to stay inside with the curtains closed."

I nodded absently, my thoughts still fixed on Grace and her father and on the brothers and on all the other young deaths that lined this place. After a few moments, I stared at Sophie Florence and asked, "How can you carry so many sorrows?"

She looked at me. Then she stuck out her bottom lip and raised her face to the sky in what seemed to be deep thought. Finally she said, "With many hands and large baskets."

Gina and Lizzie covered their mouths. At first I thought it was out of sorrow, or perhaps a somber realization, a sudden awareness of the weight they carried. Margaret burst out laughing, and I then saw that Gina and Lizzie tried to conceal their giggling.

Lizzie said, "She's teasing you. About the baskets full of glass balls we all got."

"And you don't have any," Gina said.

"But I do," I said. "Somebody left one on my windowsill."

"That's not even the same," said Gina.

"It's not the glass balls we appreciate," said Sophie Florence. "After a ball breaks from its fishing net, it can spin in the same ocean currents for years. It's their long journey we treasure."

"So you got to find one on the shore," said Gina, "not on your windowsill."

"But watch out," Margaret said. "Gina will wrestle you for it."

As we walked through the silky grass back to the beach, I thought again about all the dead buried so young under the meadow and I wondered how I could ever win a glass ball from women with hearts of this musculature. Meanwhile Margaret kept laughing about the baskets of glass balls and the tricks the women played on each other.

Sometimes they planted light bulbs, she explained to me, the fat kinds that illuminate vanity mirrors, halfway into the sand. The bulbs glinted in the sun just like their precious balls. It was a clever trick, but I hoped they wouldn't ever play it on me.

On the beach there were driftwood logs, smooth as suede. We sat and licked cream off tarts and ate blackberry pie from the pan.

"More *chumiss*?" Lizzie held out the pie pan.

It was what the women called this sweet part of the meal. It was a Nuu-chah-nulth word for that which is very satisfying. It was to be well fed. I took a fingertip of cream from Lizzie's pie pan, and I heard the word in the wind and in the waves—*chumisssssssssssss*—and the sound rubbed against my deepest longings.

*   *   *

When we finally hiked to the west side of the island to search for whatever the ocean had delivered, we shared shreds of dried salmon from a plastic baggie. The salmon, Sophie Florence said, came from her smokehouse. I imagined the women huddled together in the evenings to fold the fish over cedar sticks while marvelling at the growth of little ones, clucking their tongues at troubles in the village, planning small celebrations of life. I felt the urge to join their work in the smokehouse someday, to be a part of the community in that way, a strip connected to a larger woven pattern. But I imagined these women worked hard and fast for long hours and I worried I'd be clumsy with a knife and that I'd split wood too slowly to keep the smoke thick. But maybe I could learn, and if I did, and if I stayed, what a great thing it would be, a far better thing than the solitary life of an apartment where there is no marvelling, no celebrating, no sharing.

Along the way to the other side of the island, Margaret spotted one half of a large abalone shell in the rocks. It was the shape and size of an ear. While the outside of the shell was rough, striated and dull, the inside was a smooth iridescent swirl of deep blues and greens, with veins of rich purple and glinting silver.

"This one's real good for beading," Margaret said.

"Real good, sister," Lizzie agreed.

"You put beads in it?" I asked.

"No. Or else you couldn't see the beautiful part," Margaret said. She put the shell, rough side down, inside my hand. "This one's got a good shape for beading. See? I'm going to bead a nice cover for the ugly part."

Soon we rounded the corner to a place where the beach unfolded like velvet.

Lizzie started to tell a story. "Two men working on a fish farm over there," she said and pointed vaguely to the south, "make a bet. The first one to find a glass ball got all his cooking and clothes washing done by the other man until the end of summer."

Gina asked, "Could they even cook, or nah?"

"Pfft!" Lizzie said. "Nah! Not even!"

They laughed and climbed the steps of basalt that intersected the sand.

"So anyways," she went on, "one of the men gets up real early one morning and takes a cup of coffee down to the beach to watch the sun come up. And the light got brighter and brighter and when it did, he started to see like a bright circle of light bouncing on the water. So he gets all excited and takes off his shoes and rolls up his work pants and starts going to get the glass ball that's floating in the tide. And it's not a small one neither. But it's still quite a ways away and the water is too cold, so he has to wait. All of a sudden there's a loud *bang!* Just like that. And there's this big splash and little pieces of glass floating all over the place. So he turns around and sees the other man on the rocks all smiling like that. With a shotgun in his hand. And that man says, 'If I can't have it, neither of us will.'"

"Ay-ha!" the women cried out, chuckling.

We ducked under an arch of rock and passed through the wind-splintered branches of an old snag. Everywhere the sand was wet and strewn with seaweed. Their eyes fluttered madly, and I realized that the women were now searching for round green glints in the sun.

We navigated through the dispersed crowds of moon snails and wrinkled clam shells, giggling and uttering unintelligible sounds of anticipation. Tiny fragments of beach glass were scattered in the sand like an unfinished mosaic of blues and greens and whites. These fragments, with their pale glints, played tricks on my mind. Everywhere I looked, I felt the impulse to run for glass balls that weren't there.

Sophie Florence squeaked out a noise and started to run toward an outcrop in the distance. The hurly-burly began with squealing and shouting. We nudged each other as our hips waddled into a clumsy sprint, and soon there was shoving and tripping. Our soft bodies bounced against one another, and the gentle folds of our girth applauded us as we raced, our breath cut short by laughter. Lizzie and Margaret were thrown to the sand and sacrificed like virgins tossed into volcanoes. My eyes watched the rock growing nearer, not the rocks under my feet, and I caught my toe and fell to the ground as Sophie Florence and Gina raced ahead.

I slouched alone in the sand, disappointed that I had missed my first glass ball. By the time the women returned, I had finished picking grit from the cut on my knee. The women were breathless and joyful, bursting at the seams while I was crestfallen. They sat around the place where I had stumbled and they sprinkled a plastic baggie of sugar on some type of plant stems, which they ate. Occasionally I glanced out at the outcrop of rocks in the ocean, where oystercatchers poked their bright orange beaks into the crevices.

After some time passed, Sophie Florence held out the glass ball she'd won. It was small and green and etched with the scars of its long journey.

"If you can't have it," she told me, "none of us will."

Cradling the gift in my hand, I imagined the basket I would get to carry my first glass ball. My deepest longings stirred once again, as though some hidden part of me begged to be let loose.

"Thank you," I said.

Gina shook her head. "You say, *klecko*."

"*Klecko*," I said.

Together we sat there in the sand and sifted our hands through the broken coral and pebbles and anemone tentacles, searching for small shells in silence. I moved my hand through the bits of shells and dried seaweed but did not pay attention to any of it. My head was reeling between thoughts of Fossil Island and thoughts of that graveyard. I wanted to tell the women, all of them, that I had seen the woman in the box with the baby. I felt guilty that I had not confessed this fact, especially when they had shared so much with me today, yet the thought of telling them brought even greater guilt. And then there was that graveyard. I could not stop thinking about it. How could the children in my classroom learn anything when they lived in a world with so many tragedies? How could they recite their multiplication tables, or practise spelling words, or learn the difference between there, their and they're when they carried these stories?

"What can I possibly offer them?" I muttered.

"Who?" Sophie Florence didn't look up.

"My students."

The wind picked up the top layer of sand and sprayed it over our legs. Gina brushed her legs clean and stated the obvious. "An education."

"But how can I do that when—"

"Just be there," Gina added.

"That's not enough," I said. "Any Magoo can be there."

"*Really* be there." Gina picked up a thin white tooth of a shell.

"And love them," Sophie Florence said.

"But you got to stay long enough to love them," Gina insisted.

I felt the stain of guilt, and for the first time it dawned on me that perhaps I should never have come to this place if I had not been prepared to commit long enough to give them what they needed from me. "There's too much I can't understand," I said.

"Sure you can," said Sophie Florence.

I gripped a fistful of sand and felt its grittiness against my palm. "My mother died when I was a teen. And a boy from my neighbourhood." I jutted my chin in the direction of the graveyard. "But I've never known this."

"But you can understand it," Sophie Florence said. "Even just a little."

"I don't think I can."

Sophie Florence smiled. "If you listen to them, listen to them closely, listen to them with your heart ready to be changed by what you hear—the bad and the good—you can understand enough. And if you love them, truly love them—not for who you think they should be but just as they are—and you do all that while truly believing in them, in their ability to learn as much as any child, you will make a difference."

Lizzie tossed a small, smooth stone playfully at my leg. "Don't lose hope in them."

11

After I returned from Toomista on Sunday evening, Joan had helped me move the brooder into my classroom. The weekend, with all its explorations, had exhausted my body and spirit. Introducing the chicks to our school days was as much for me as the children, and for that reason, I gave the students a break from our usual routine on Monday morning. I sat with a book on the Read-Aloud Rug, the children gathering around me in a quick and orderly manner, eager to be closer to the brooder. Normally they'd pick at the carpet, pull at their T-shirts with their teeth, pinch one another sometimes, whisper complaints and accusations that rubbed between them. Not one child stirred that morning, all eyes fixed on the yellow balls of fuzz. When the chicks tumbled over one another, a few of the children let out small gasps of joyful surprise. At that moment, to my delight, it seemed as though nothing could induce discontentment in them.

From my seat in a small chair at the end of the carpet, I asked the class, "Do you know why I put the chickens here beside the Read-Aloud Rug?"

The children wrinkled their noses.

"Because chickens love a great story," I said.

"For real?" Odelia asked.

"For real," I said. "That's in fact why the chicken crossed the road. Because the library was on the other side."

"Bull," Hannah said, her sleeves still covering her hands.

I smiled, put on my special reading glasses and opened the novel I'd been reading to the class. "I'll prove it. You watch what happens when I read."

In preparation for the arrival of the chickens, I had started reading a story called *The Chicken Doesn't Skate*. In the book, Milo's classmates named the baby chicken he brought to school Henrietta. My students also named their chickens Henrietta. All fifteen of them. Henrietta #1, Henrietta #2, Henrietta #3 and so on. Today I read the part when everybody came to believe that Henrietta was a good luck charm for the school hockey team. Partway through the scene, I nudged the base of the plastic pool with my foot. This sent the chicks into a flurry of movement and noise.

"They like this part of the story!" Odelia exclaimed.

"Teacher hit the pool with her foot," Hannah said. "I seen her."

"No, she didn't," Kenny said. "It was the story."

"Yeah, it was the story," Odelia said.

"You're stupid if you believe that," Hannah said.

"It was so the story. And I'm not stupid," Odelia said. "That's why stories are called make-believe, right Teacher? Because they make you believe."

After storytime, as the children headed back to their desks, Hannah asked me if she could use the washroom. I looked out the window beside the classroom door. Through it I could see a circle of orange construction paper taped to the window of the primary classroom across the hallway. A secret signal from Joan, which meant one of the younger girls was in the washroom. Hannah was not supposed to be alone with the younger children.

"No, not right this minute," I said.

"Geez, Teacher!" Hannah said and stomped her foot. "Maybe I'll have to pee right here and maybe it'll go all over your stupid sandals!"

* * *

During lunchtime, while all the other kids went down the hill to their homes for something to eat, Odelia and Kenny stayed in the classroom to draw pictures that they could then hang on the top of the chicken wire as a kind of household decoration. From my desk, I could see that Odelia was drawing a variety of flowers, which was what she always drew or painted in her free time at school. But Odelia's flowers were unlike the flowers children at her age of ten usually drew. Even by that age, most children stop drawing things as they truly appear. If only they would look closely and trust their own ways of seeing. Instead, they have already learned to resort to the safe practice of drawing objects as the inaccurate symbols they've become inside minds fearful of making mistakes. People's heads turn into circles. The sun acquires spokes. Flowers become round petals with round discs in the centre on top of poker-straight stems with two leaves.

Not Odelia's. Although her drawings and paintings lacked a certain finesse, she showed herself to be somebody who examined the world with a microscopic lens. To begin with, she noticed that the world contained more than daisies and roses. She drew black-eyed Susans, baby's breath, asters, blazing stars and bleeding hearts, geraniums, trumpet vines, rain lilies, snapdragons, magnolias and marigolds. Not only did she depict the features of these botanical species with accuracy, she also understood perspective. She twisted the lines of leaves as they twist in the real world. She foreshortened petals at the front of flowers. Odelia sensed that in this world there were positive and negative spaces, there were vantage points from which you could see the world as it really existed, as well as vanishing points where things were made increasingly small and irrelevant until they finally disappeared altogether.

"You know the silver one?" Odelia said to Kenny, tapping her front tooth, as she looked up from her picture.

I perked up. Children rarely feel the need to lower their voices around adults who are working. Since I sat at my desk preparing for the afternoon's science block, neither Odelia nor Kenny paid any attention to my presence. Looking away from Odelia, I pretended to concentrate on my lesson plans.

Odelia said, "He says it belongs to Lucifer. You know who that is, right?"

Kenny shook his head.

Odelia swung her long, black hair over her shoulder, the bottom half of her tangled tresses coloured purple. "The Devil," she said.

Kenny took a gurgling suck on the straw of his juice box. "What devil?"

"*The* Devil," Odelia said, wide-eyed. "Satan."

"Get out of here," Kenny said.

"It's true, I heard the whole story," Odelia said.

Kenny winced at Odelia in disbelief. "How'd she get the Devil's tooth?"

"A long time ago," Odelia said as she coloured, "there was this garden and it was paradise and there were all sorts of animals and stuff, and two people, you know those two, the ones who wore leaves on their private parts."

Kenny nodded. "Adam and Eve."

"Yes, except before they wore leaves they were naked all the time because they didn't even care that they were naked or nothing. They had as much food as they wanted on account of all these fruit trees everywhere. They'd just reach up and grab whatever they wanted and eat it, except there was this one tree in the middle of the garden that they weren't supposed to eat because God told them not to eat it. They would die or something."

"Poisonous, I bet." Kenny rummaged in the pencil crayon tub until he found the right colour of green.

"No, it was powerful fruit that would make Adam and Eve just like God and God didn't want them to be just like God. That's what the snake said to Eve. The snake said if she ate that fruit she wasn't supposed to eat, her eyes would open up and she'd know all kinds of stuff she didn't know before."

"I'd eat it," Kenny said. "Wouldn't you?"

"You know who that snake was? It was just a snake, but it was possessed by Satan. Before all this stuff happened, the snake wasn't all slithery like it is now. It probably had legs or something. God punished it for helping to get Eve to eat that fruit, which God was really mad about, and so God made it crawl with its belly on the ground. That's how come snakes are like that. Anyways, after Eve ate the fruit, she went and told Adam that he should eat it too, so he did. Then they got in really big trouble for doing that and God gave them a bunch of punishments."

"Like what?" Kenny sounded worried.

"Like they had to leave the garden and because Eve was the one who first wrecked everything she got extra punishments, which is total bull because at least Eve was tricked by Satan, who is real powerful, but Adam just sort of said, sure whatever, as soon as Eve said here, eat this fruit we're not supposed to eat. Anyway, that's the part that's in the Bible, but it's not the whole story."

Kenny stared at Odelia.

Odelia continued, "Eve was crazy mad. She was all, this ain't fair, me getting blamed like this. So you know what she did? She went looking for that snake, and one day she found it curled around a branch sleeping. She took a rock and pounded it in the head until she thought she'd killed it."

As both children fell into a moment of silent concentration on their drawings, I wondered where Odelia got this version of the Eden story. Television, most likely. Then I thought about the worn building that served as the church in the village. Although there was no pastor or clergy of any type in the community, a handful of people apparently gathered every Sunday morning and took turns delivering a sermon or reading a passage out of the Bible. I had never attended myself, but perhaps that was where she'd heard it.

"Because it had been possessed by Satan," Odelia said, "the snake had a silver tongue and silver teeth, because silver is Satan's favourite. When Eve smashed the snake's head, one of its silver teeth fell out onto the ground. And this was a big snake, nothing like we got now, not even like those boa constrictors that can swallow a whole pig. This snake was bigger than that and it had huge teeth. Hey! Did I tell you Grandpa is coming home?"

"Grandpa Ray?" Kenny asked.

Odelia's Grandpa Ray was in fact her great uncle, Sophie Florence's brother. I had learned that in Tawakin, uncles were called grandfathers, aunts were grandmothers, grandmothers and grandfathers were often but not always mothers and fathers, and all cousins were brothers and sisters.

Odelia nodded at Kenny. "He's bringing me something special for my flower collection," she said. "Brighter than anything I ever seen before. That's what he said. I can't wait to see it. I'll paint you a picture of it."

There was another long pause of selecting pencil crayons and colouring. Now and then, the chicks made a noise that prompted both children to turn to the brooder and smile.

"That tooth just sat there for thousands of years," Odelia said, "until some guy was digging up old stuff under the ground and he found it. Everybody in his family kept passing the tooth down to their children and their children's children and their children's children's children and their children's children's children's—"

Kenny held up his hand. "Okay, I get it."

Odelia shrugged. "Then it ended up in her mouth."

"Wasn't it too big for her mouth?" Kenny asked.

"I think they made a tooth out of the big one just for her," Odelia said.

"Oh." Kenny broke a hard cookie into shards on the table, sweeping the crumbs with the back of his hand onto the floor. "When that guy found the tooth, how come he knew it was the Devil's?"

"Because it has special powers," Odelia said.

"Does that mean she had special powers, too?" Kenny asked.

"She must have," Odelia said.

Kenny winced again. "Then how come she ended up in that box?"

"Don't know. Maybe it didn't work right for her," Odelia said. "But if you got the tooth, you can get anything you want."

Odelia stood up from the table and attached her three drawings to the top of the chicken wire with a paperclip, facing inward so that the chickens could appreciate her art. I peered over a wall of binders on my desk. The first drawing looked like a castle surrounded by delphiniums. The second one looked like a brick wall covered in climbing roses. The third one looked like something by Hieronymus Bosch. At first, it appeared to be a garden of earthly delights, so lush it was in foliage and strange colours. But as I peered more closely, I saw that it depicted a bird's-eye view of a woman in a rectangular box with a baby, a sea of ferns and skunk cabbage surrounding them, the roots of a tree drawn not like metaphorical fingers, but as actual fingers poking up between the woman's thighs and around the large cedar trunk that lay on the ground, a beam of silver light descending from the sky.

Had Odelia been to the woman in the box with the baby? Her drawing made it seem likely, but then again Odelia could have created this picture after listening to the same detailed description Grace had told me the morning she brought me one of her mother's letters. I asked Odelia. "That was quite a story. Where did you hear it?"

Odelia flashed me a look of surprise, as if she'd just remembered I was there.

"That's not exactly how the story goes," I said.

Odelia stuck out her bottom lip the same way as her grandmother Sophie Florence.

When she didn't answer, I went to the chicken brooder and pointed to the picture of the woman in the box with the baby. "Tell me about this drawing."

Odelia stared at me. Then, saying nothing more, she selected a red pencil crayon and started to draw on a fresh sheet of paper. Avoiding my gaze, Kenny also selected a pencil crayon and turned his attention to the paper in front of him. The children in Tawakin had an uncanny ability to refuse to speak if they didn't want to. I knew from firsthand experience that they had the capacity and the will to stand in front of my desk for an eternity in silence while I waited for an answer. I could never outlast that kind of determination, even on my most patient days.

That afternoon, the class went to the library to use the computers. The school library was in a portable across the field, which was still damp with a light rain, so I changed out of my classroom sandals, the

The Morning Bell Brings the Broken Hearted

ones with the teal stones, and into my rubber boots. Hannah stayed behind with Sophie Florence in the office to finish her writing. She had three more days on her suspension from using the school computers after I caught her during the first week of school searching the Internet for *sexxi boobs, koks, vajinah*. The only reason why this suspension hadn't upset Chase, who came to the school to meet with me and Mr. Chapman, was because Hannah blamed her grandmother. Hannah often blamed her grandmother, Loretta Joe, for her behaviour, claiming that her grandmother's meanness made her do bad things, and Chase seemed more than willing to accept Hannah's punishment as soon as the finger was pointed at his mother-in-law.

There was a job posting for a teacher's assistant in my class, specifically to support Hannah, but so far no one in the village had applied for it. Nobody was willing to work with Hannah, and it was impossible to recruit somebody from outside of Tawakin since the pay was not enough to compensate for the eight-hour roundtrip journeys to get groceries beyond the slim pickings at the Tawakin Market or to see a dentist. Not to mention there was nowhere for outside support staff to live. I had to use whatever resources I could find, and thank goodness for Sophie Florence.

When I returned at the end of the afternoon, the bell had rung to dismiss the students. All the other classes were gone, and so was Hannah. My sandals with the teal stones were also gone. I looked everywhere in the classroom, on top of the cupboards, in the wastebaskets, in Hannah's desk. They were nowhere to be found. I searched the other children's desks, too. In Grace's desk, I found an envelope. It was padded thick with paper and unsealed. Inside were the five letters Grace had written to her mother, those stories Grace had told herself. It could never be underestimated, I thought, this need for people to connect to one another. I put the letters back inside Grace's desk and went to find Sophie Florence.

"You leaving work soon?" I asked from the doorway of the office. "Thought I'd walk down the hill with you to see her before she leaves tomorrow."

Sophie Florence crammed a file halfway into the drawer. "She's gone."

My stomach sank. "Gone? But you said tomorrow."

"They came early," Sophie Florence said. "She left this morning."

I frowned, blindsided by the possibility that I wasn't as central to Grace's life as I had assumed. Why else hadn't Sophie Florence told me that Grace was leaving early? I wanted to ask but didn't have the courage.

Sophie Florence pointed at a piece of paper on her desk. I picked it up and read Hannah's composition assignment.

I do stuff for my Grandma. I get her coffee. My Grandma loves me lots too like the mom of Mucous Boy. I know it becuz my Grandma gave me new sandells. They got blu roks on the top. Thank you Grandma for the new sandells.

Something snapped inside me. Clutching Hannah's composition tightly, as if it was the only evidence I had, I marched out of the school and headed toward the village in pursuit of my sandals. How dare she? How dare she steal my things? Stuff from the classroom was one thing. But my personal belongings? This was the thanks I got for being patient with her? This was the thanks I got for bringing some order to her chaos? For doing everything in my power to keep her at school every day. Had Hannah really ever said anything admiring or warmhearted about me like Chase claimed? Had she really cried that I had kicked her out of the classroom? I felt like knocking on Chase's door and asking him why I should promise to stay when this was the thanks I got? I stopped on the road and took a deep breath. She was a child. But I didn't know if I could stand it anymore.

12

As I walked down the hill, I thought about how I had also been a thief as a child. In my bedroom I had a small school desk with an inkwell that my mother picked up at a yard sale. One winter morning I stole a bottle of my mother's iron gall ink and poured it into the desk's well. Eventually my mother asked if I'd seen the bottle anywhere. Even though my bedroom walls, my pillow, the doorknob and the handles on my dresser were all smudged with faint black fingerprints and the black heels of my hands, I insisted that I hadn't seen the ink. I couldn't recollect my mother ever calling me out on this, though that made sense to me.

When I reached the bottom of the hill, a group of children leapt into action as soon as they spotted me, wrapping themselves around my legs and arms. The younger children in Tawakin did not hug lightly. Rather, they squeezed and held on with all their might. It made me uncomfortable, this intrusion into my personal space, the physical contact, particularly how they moved wherever I moved, scuttling alongside me. Suckerfish on a white whale.

"Come to the dock! Everybody's at the dock!" they exclaimed.

When we turned the corner, I saw that the dock was cluttered with bicycles and sea urchins. Along the wood railing, the adults sat on the edge between the rope cleats. In the air was the briny fragrance of the sea urchins, some of which were in buckets, some dumped on the dock in spiky hills of purple and red. The adults, whose plump cheeks were slicked with a glossy sheen, looked at me as I walked up the dock and nodded. Empty chambers of cracked urchins surrounded my feet. All of the adults held sticks and screwdrivers except for two women who smoked.

As the children ran to the piles of urchins, Patty hopped down from her seat on the dock railing and approached me, pointing her finger at me. "You know how excited Hannah was for chess club? It was all she talked about every day she come home from school in September. Then that racist principal starts the club and doesn't even teach her chess. He teaches her checkers. She don't want to play checkers. She wants to play chess."

"I'm sure he plans to teach them soon," I said.

Patty laughed, and it sounded bitter. "He ain't ever going to teach them. That's what he told Hannah. Said she probably won't understand the game. That it's too complicated for some people. Some people. Some people like *us*? That's what I asked him. I went up to the school the other day and asked him. Hannah come home after chess club crying about it."

Even though this was now the second report of Hannah crying, and even though she was an eleven-year-old girl, it was still difficult for me to imagine.

"She said he thinks she's too dumb to learn it," Patty said.

"I'm sure Mr. Chapman doesn't think that," I said.

Patty demanded to know: "You calling my daughter a liar?"

"Sometimes kids mistake what someone meant," I reasoned.

"Hannah doesn't get mistaken like that," Patty said. "Hannah is sharp. She sees every expression, every twitch of an eye, every movement. She hears every voice that puts us down. You are her teacher, so I know you know that about her."

"Yes," I said.

And I knew it was true. Since the first day of school, Hannah had kept a constant lookout for any weaknesses in me, any signs that I might be faltering. This was one of Hannah's most acute abilities: she could pinpoint the faintest hint of fear or falseness with precision. Shaky voices, voices heavy with fake bravado, sweaty palms, averting eyes, widened eyes, fidgeting, shifting weight, quick movements, awkward jokes, sarcasm, shallow breathing, condescending voices, false smiles, false words. Nothing escaped Hannah. Fear and falsehoods were, to Hannah, like baked salmon or fish head soup: something she could smell immediately, even from a distance. More than that, it was delectable to her. It fuelled her. It was instinctual, a detection honed after years of rejection and alienation, and it was her only source of power. As I scrambled each day to defuse her detonations, to disconnect her deadly wires, Hannah checked to see if my hands were steady.

"You never answered me," Patty said.

"About what?"

Patty narrowed her eyes. "Are you calling my daughter a liar?"

"No," I said.

"Better not be," Patty said. "And that principal better not give me no bullshit excuses about him thinking she has learning issues. Racist bullshit. You all look at me and you think right away: 'Oh, she's an Indian so she must have been drinking lots. She's an Indian, so her kid must have fetal alcohol.'"

I remained silent, not knowing how to respond.

"If that's what you think, you're no better than that stupid principal and his stupid fucking chess club," Patty said. "You tell that principal he needs to watch himself. He wouldn't be the first principal we've kicked out of Tawakin."

The moment Patty started to march up the dock toward the village, the children returned to encircle me again. Some of the older children also surrounded me. The adults watched and giggled as the children held out urchins to me. The children bounced and squealed and begged.

"Eat it eat it eat it eat it eat it eat it eat it eat it eat it eat it eat it."

Standing the closest to me was Hannah. Unsmiling, she came upon me like a spectre and she entered the small orbit of my face without warning. I wondered if she had overheard her mother's accusations. There was an urchin cradled in the sleeve that covered

Hannah's hand, and it was cracked wide open. The insides were a swirl of liquid and black organs, specks of seaweed, gritty bits of sand. Without draining any of this, Hannah pried her meaty lips into the hole and tilted her head back. The other children uttered sounds of disgust. I watched, repelled, as Hannah sucked at it all. The noise was desperate, like air gobbled in suffocation. Excretions of something gelatinous spurted out the sides and onto her cheeks. With her finger, Hannah scraped the gonads at the bottom of the shell and slipped them into her mouth. She dragged the back of her hand across her face and tossed the hollow globe into the ocean where it floated above a submerged tricycle and dozens of coffee filters that bobbed below the surface like jellyfish.

A small boy named Kelly, hopping from foot to foot, dropped a purple urchin into my hand. Salt water trickled into the creases of my palm.

"Are the spines poisonous?" I asked.

Several adults crinkled their noses, no.

"We offer you that *tucip* to thank you for teaching our children," Lizzie Joe said as she strolled onto the dock and sat with the other women. She giggled and her shoulders lifted up to her ears.

"So you got to eat it because it's a gift, Magoo," Gina said.

I had learned from Sophie Florence that there was no word for welcome in Nuu-chah-nulth. It was shown by giving food. And when it was offered, you must accept. Since then I had tried rock stickers, chitons, geoducks, gooseneck barnacles and one fish eyeball. But those had been cooked. Those had been cleaned. And those had not been pulsing with dark viscera.

Chase Charlie strolled up the dock and pushed his green ball cap back off his forehead. "Who was being real mischief last night?"

"What you talking about?" Gina asked.

"All that knocking," Chase said. "You hear it?"

"On my door," somebody said. "Three times last night. Nobody there."

"Yep, on mine too," somebody else said. "Middle of the night. Got up to answer it. Nobody there."

"Better not be them kids," Gina said.

"Better be them kids," Lizzie said, chuckling.

"Because if it ain't—" Margaret stopped with a shudder.

I felt a sense of relief that I wasn't the only one visited by spirits, though I still didn't believe that spirits were in fact to blame. But what if it were true? What if that rock in my pathway and the knocking of doors were done by something otherworldly? What if? Things unseen, toying with mundane objects. I felt a brief shiver of wonder and bewilderment, but it faded quickly as it occurred to me that if things were happening down the hill, whether they were otherworldly or only believed to be so, then the rock in my path might put the spotlight on me in a way I did not wish for.

Around me, more people from the village started coming and going, taking away their share of urchins. Some of the children stood and watched me, waiting, while others sat on the dock. Small armies of dogs marched among the bicycles. Ernie Frank was seated in his docked boat with another woman who looked just like him. From time to time he and the woman would look at me with what seemed like anticipation. At the other side of the dock, I could hear teasing voices and then something encouraging and then a torrent of laughter.

Hannah pulled her lip back like a horse, and she laughed, too.

I stared intently at Hannah, wanting to say something sharp in return, something to erase her smugness. On Hannah's back was the knapsack she carried everywhere. It was filled with surprises, mostly stolen. Candy, fridge magnets, braided bracelets, tarnished rings, batteries, beads, broken cigarettes. I had heard that she gave these surprises away as gifts to other children, to relatives, to strangers who flew there in floatplanes to catch big fish. Tokens to obligate reciprocity, to delay inevitable rejection, to coerce love.

Then I noticed Hannah's feet. And Hannah noticed me noticing. We both looked at the sandals, two sizes past Hannah's toes. Teal stones on the leather straps. Sure, I could have demanded them back right then. I could have made her take responsibility. But there would likely be an inconsolable outburst. Swearing. Rage screaming. You could never tell with Hannah. She would then shout that it's her grandmother's fault—"She's so mean to me!"—and I would find my sandals one day washed ashore or up in a cedar tree.

"If I eat this urchin," I said, "I get those sandals."

Before Hannah could answer, Loretta Joe, Hannah's grandmother, approached me from the end of the dock. The children unstuck themselves from me and scattered. The Joe family was the most powerful family in the village, and Loretta Joe was its matriarchal boss. The outpost nurse, Bernadette Perkal, once whispered to me that Loretta Joe was "a cold tide who decided which sands of truth and which shells of lies spread across our shores," and ever since, I had done my best to go unnoticed by the woman.

Pointing at Hannah, Loretta asked me. "Did you know she steals?"

I wanted to say, "Yes, now that you mention it, there's a calculator, two magnifying glasses, a box of chalk, and a brand new skipping rope missing from my classroom. Plus a certain pair of sandals."

But Loretta's face was bursting to continue. "Have you heard about the people whose skin turns to tree bark?"

I shook my head and crept backwards a couple of steps until a blood-red urchin ruptured under my shoe with a loud crack.

Loretta narrowed her eyes at the broken urchin. "I should probably tell you sometime. Shouldn't I, granddaughter? Shouldn't I tell your teacher about how we send away people who are evil to other people, how we send them away from the village and how their skin turns to bark and their arms into branches until they are stuck living as a tree all alone? Shouldn't I?"

Hannah spun away from her grandmother and tucked her covered hands into her armpits. As her grandmother marched back up the dock, Hannah said, "Geez, Teacher. Fine. Eat the stupid urchin."

The urchin's spines, which protected the creature from predators, were hard yet brittle. A few snapped off as I plunged the screwdriver into the shell, prying it into the mouth, breaking the small circle of five teeth. Around and around I worked the screwdriver until there was a hole the size of an egg yolk. At the sight of those membranes and digested waste, ovaries and other organs, I felt myself faltering. Everybody watched and waited for me. What could I do now but go on?

I rimmed my lips around the hole and poured the salty liquid and its slippery contents into my mouth. It splashed against the roof of my mouth and I forced it down. My eyes watered. There was a tightening at the back of my throat. My face contorted with retching. The hopping boy named Kelly pointed at the roe still inside the shell, shaped like orange tongues, and told me that I was supposed to eat those. When I tried to scrape them out, Kelly sighed and told me that I was going to rip them doing it like that, and he pulled them out for me.

"You have to be real gentle," Kelly said.

I swallowed the slippery mass. To my surprise, it tasted like melon.

There was laughter, some applause from the adults, and then more laughter.

"You weren't supposed to eat the whole thing," said Lizzie.

"I wasn't?" I asked.

"No," Lizzie said, screwing up her nose. "Just the roe. But not all that other gunk. That stuff is real gross."

Hannah was walking away already, but she turned back once to smirk at me. She had tricked me into eating the whole thing, and she didn't care that she had to swallow the same dark viscera in order to pull off the trick. Her face told me it was worth it to her.

Hannah crossed the grass to the dirt road. She was barefooted.

Somewhere behind me one of the adults asked, "What's she wearing that ugly shirt for all the time?"

"Been wearing it every day to school," Gina replied.

"Bet it's spray paint on her hands again," somebody else said.

"She's probably been putting more of those nasty pictures on people's houses," another person suggested.

"For sure," Gina agreed. "She needs a good lesson, that one."

Good lessons, I recalled from Nan Lily and elder Candice, always happen over food. As you take in the food, and the salt water and the dark viscera, you take in the lesson. You digest what you've learned. It becomes a part of you.

I picked up my sandals and headed home.

*   *   *

That evening from my kitchen, I heard kids screaming playfully across the logging road. I looked out my window and spotted Mr. Chapman corralling a group of kids into the gym. I was impressed at Mr. Chapman's generosity—that he was willing to spend his evening giving the kids extra time to play like that. Then I remembered how Patty had accused him of discriminating against Hannah at chess club. I still had a difficult time believing it. Then again, I had only ever seen Mr. Chapman talk with the students when there were other adults around. Who knew how he behaved when unwatched? I had to see for myself.

I waited until I figured the kids were fully engaged in whatever gym games they were playing, then I headed across the road. The gym door was propped open a crack with a wedge of wood. I stood next to it, off to the side slightly to avoid being seen. Inside there were twelve or so kids of varying ages, including Odelia and Kenny, but no Hannah. I could hear Mr. Chapman explaining the rules of Simon Says as he stood in front of the group. It was a tiny gym, about half the size of a basketball court, which meant that the kids took up most of the floor space when they spread out to play the game.

I watched as Mr. Chapman went through a sequence of motions, the kids laughing at his occasional silliness—like when he stuck out his tongue ("I didn't say 'Simon Says', Kenny!") or when he flapped his arms like a chicken. The kids laughed and squealed as they reacted to Mr. Chapman's movements, slumping their shoulders dramatically if they lost the game and had to sit on the bench. At the end of each round, the kids begged Mr. Chapman to play again, which he generously agreed to each time. After the tenth round, just as I was about to leave, I heard Mr. Chapman say, "Simon says, 'Believe in yourself!'"

I peered through the crack of the door and then through each of the two little door windows, trying to see everyone's reaction to this. The children looked all around, as if trying to see if any of them had understood how to respond with movement to his instruction. Odelia scrunched her eyebrows at Kenny.

Mr. Chapman pointed at Odelia and asked, "Odelia, do you believe in yourself?"

She stood still for a while, then finally nodded her head a little.

He then pointed at Kenny and asked the same thing. Kenny also nodded. Soon the younger children jumped from one foot to the other, pointing their fingers at the ceiling in a playful dance, exclaiming, "I believe in myself, I believe in myself!"

I could feel the energy vibrating from the kids, and I concluded that Patty had misinterpreted Mr. Chapman's words and his intentions. Patty was a bitter person, there was no doubt in my mind about that, and bitter people were often prone to describing the world to match their own pessimism.

I stayed for a while longer, watching the children's movements closely. At home I had started a fresh, new sketchbook, and with drawing in mind, I studied how the children arched themselves back then sprung themselves forward as they jumped the way Mr. Chapman had jumped, their feet lifting then stomping to the floor again. I tried to see only their movements free of distracting details like contours, shadows and highlights, tones. I tried to see them each as a single unit of energy. A single unit of movement. I tried to feel them, too, because it was a fallacy to think of drawing as an act of merely seeing. All the senses played a role in how an observation translated into a drawing. Silk would always be drawn differently by the artist who had never had the chance to feel its feathery smoothness.

"Don't draw what the boy looks like, don't even try to make him appear at all like himself," I remembered my mother once telling me. "Draw what it is he is doing, Molleigh. Don't think of him as a boy. Think of him as motion. He is movement."

There were certain rules that my mother followed more religiously than her actual religion, and many of those came from Kimon Nicolaïdes. For as long as I could remember, my mother kept a tattered copy of Kimon Nicolaïdes's *The Natural Way to Draw* on the side table next to her cold tea and the half-smoked Matinée Kings bent and broken in the ashtray. On lazy Saturday mornings, my mother would lie on her side, stretched out on the couch, her head propped on one hand, her other hand pressing Nicolaïdes's book open. Perched atop the bony hill of my mother's hip, I would listen as I gazed out the window at the newspaper boy pulling his wagon along the empty sidewalk.

My mother would read a page from the book out loud. Any page. Wherever the spine fell open. Sometimes it was Nicolaïdes's thoughts on contours and the human sense of touch. Or his insights into the nature of draped clothing and how it moved as one with the flesh. Other times, his instructions for how to capture gestures on the page. Now and then my mother revisited the introduction, and I would giggle at Nicolaïdes's assumption that as we practised our own drawings, we would naturally be working with a nude model.

"Let your pencil go wherever his movement takes it," my mother continued. That particular Saturday morning, we both sat on our knees looking out the window with our sketchbooks resting on the back of the couch. "But do not capture his edges. Quick studies of gesture are not about the details of the figure. His clothes, his light blond hair, his skinny ten-year-old body—none of that matters. Like Nicolaïdes says, gesture has no definite edges. No precise shape. No set form. It's motion through space. The only way you can capture his movement is to feel it in your own body."

I tried to feel the boy's movements in my own body, tried to feel in my own muscles and tendons how he stooped to grasp a rolled-up newspaper, how he arched his body back then sprung himself forward as he flung the paper onto the doorstep across the road. I worked hard to capture the tiny hesitation in his gestures, like the physical equivalent of an almost imperceptible speech tic. Many times he'd drop a newspaper and shake his head as if admonishing himself. I trapped this onto the page, too, the stoop of doubt in his spine and how it gave the impression of sighing even though I couldn't possibly observe his breathing from that distance. One thing was clear about my gesture drawing: even at age ten I detected his lack of confidence.

"Do you feel as though you are doing whatever he is doing?" My mother asked this as she worked feverishly to scratch out her quick study of the boy. "If you do not feel his movement deep inside you, you cannot understand what you are seeing. Remember what Nicolaïdes said? If you don't feel what the boy feels, your drawing is nothing more than a map or a plan."

The aim of these quick studies was to get the gesture onto the page in a matter of seconds, in a way that suggested, however roughly, every part of the body that contributed to the gesture. I found it exciting. Liberating. And my mother had a way of making the study of a newspaper boy's gestures feel more important than anything else in the world.

"Action and expression," my mother said. "We are capturing life itself."

✳   ✳   ✳

It had turned dark by the time I left the gym. On the quick walk back home, I thought of what Loretta had said about those who turned to bark and I couldn't help but feel the trees around me in a new way. I envisioned every branch as the reincarnation of an arm, the trunks a fusion of two legs, the bark hardened and skin cracked. How painfully alone a person would feel to be trapped in the form of a tree, rooted to the same spot for a century or more, the rings of your years marking rainy seasons and dry seasons, seasons of early growth and seasons of late growth, scars from forest fires and the scourges of pests, all the while each new ring reminding you of the time that has passed since you were cast away from humanity. Except for those days when the wind would rush between your branches and send you into a frenzied dance, you would be immobile, not even able to pace your cage in cramped circles.

When I turned down the path to my trailer, I halted suddenly and stared in disbelief at the tall tree stump next to my porch, its outlines backlit by the small lamp next to the door. The stump was a foot taller than me and about the width of a large dinner plate. On top of the stump was another large rock. Like the other rock, this one was also the size of a steamer trunk. Unlike the other rock, which still blocked my path, this one had a more uniform geometry, a naturally occurring rectangular shape with smooth flat sides. It was its flatness that allowed such a large rock to balance on top of the narrow stump. I gazed unblinking at it. My breath, strained and shallow, filled my ears with its airy din. What a feat of strength it must have taken to get something of that size atop a stump that was at least six and a half feet tall. Surely it couldn't remain there. It couldn't. I considered how much the thing weighed. Five hundred, maybe six hundred pounds. Such a thing could topple and kill a person.

Who would do this? Who *could* do this? Somebody had done this while I was in the gym. But how? Surely it took machinery of some sort to lift and place the rock. I was only across the road—I would have heard a truck. Or maybe several men did this, all lifting in tandem. Why would anybody bother? Was it meant as a prank, as Joan said? If so, I didn't get it. But wait. I paused for a moment to clear my mind. What if this wasn't done as a prank but as a warning? Or, not so much a warning but an attempt to scare me off? To make me believe that a trickster of a creature was leaving me calling cards in the hope that I would then leave Tawakin in fear. Was that it? Did somebody not want me here? If so, why on Earth would anybody hate me that much already? As far as I could tell, I'd made a reasonably good start with the kids. For crying out loud, I was the first teacher in Tawakin to keep Hannah Charlie in a classroom for longer than two weeks. I was doing a good job. I knew I was. Wasn't I?

"Holy shit—" Joan said when I dragged her away from her book to see the second stone. "Holy shit."

"Yes," I said.

Joan's voice was full of awe. "I've never seen anything like this."

"I can't figure out how anyone got it up on that stump," I said.

"Should we try to push it off? You know, in case it topples onto you one day."

"We could try. It might be up too high for us," I said.

"We could use a pole of some sort. A hockey stick?"

"Don't think we'll get enough surface force on it that way," I said. "Really, I don't think you and I can do it."

"The school truck has that small crane on the back for when John moves the fuel tanks around. We could try that," Joan suggested.

I stared at Joan, lost in thought. I had forgotten about the small crane on the back of the school's pickup truck. I had not spoken often to John, the school custodian and maintenance guy, but he had always been friendly. "You don't think John did this, do you?"

"No way," Joan said. "John isn't a prankster. And he keeps to himself."

Hesitantly, I said, "Do you think there's any chance—" I paused, thinking of how little I knew about the high school teachers, "—that it was another teacher?"

"Couldn't have been," Joan said. "Timothy and Diane helped me pick up a load of textbooks from the dock a few weeks ago and I had to drive because neither of them knew how to drive a standard. And all the support staff from down the hill aren't allowed to use the school truck."

"I don't know what to think," I said.

"I think you better be prepared," Joan said.

"For what? Another stone?"

"For everyone in the village freaking out if they see these here," Joan said. "Luckily only a few people come up the hill and your pathway is blocked a bit by that tree, so it's possible that nobody notices. But if they do, then you'll have a Sasquatch problem to explain."

Later that night, I climbed into bed and stared into the darkness. I could feel the presence of those rocks outside my bedroom window, but I felt small and timid for letting them occupy my thoughts when

Grace was right now in some stranger's home feeling lonely and far away. Without her favourite photograph of her father. Was the foster family kind enough? Did they know that her name had been put away for a year? Or that her favourite sandwiches were crunchy peanut butter with honey? I ached with the thought of it. In just one month, I had taught these children far longer than my heart could bear. I thought of that graveyard on Rubant and I rolled my eyes. Get over yourself, Molleigh. Yet, still. How could I be expected to prepare lesson plans and mark math tests when there were much larger things to cope with, when so much of my energy was spent on student outbursts, on their anxieties and their emotional struggles? In a place with no resources, I was seeing now that my days would be spent playing counsellor, psychologist, social worker and then, and only then, finally being a teacher, and where would that get any of them?

As I slipped into sleep, sounds from the VHF radio on my kitchen counter floated into my bedroom.

"We're getting the knocking on our doors again."

"Us too, Uncle."

"Anybody know if it's kids doing it?"

"Where's Hannah Charlie? She at home or wandering the village?"

"She's at home."

"Them sounds ain't the kids."

"It's freaking us out."

"Two pictures fell off our wall right in front of my face for no good reason."

"My chair moved to the other side of the room when I wasn't looking."

"Somebody did something bad."

"Somebody must have done something real bad."

It was me, I thought drowsily, drifting in and out of slumber, I am the one who did something real bad.

I could feel the panic rise in my chest, threatening to snap me wide awake again. Despite how many years it had been since my mother had died, I yearned for her laugh to enter my dreams and make me less afraid. Not afraid like when you think you hear a creak on the staircase of your empty house at night. Or when you walk out to the edge of the high diving board and stand over the chlorine-blue water. It was a fear of things more primal. Of being utterly alone. Of being rejected. Of failing. But none of these things were what frightened me most. What frightened me most was dying and becoming nothing. All for nothing.

13

"Sometimes all your choices are stolen. I was stolen." The Language and Culture teacher, a woman named Dawn Jimmy, announced this to my class the next day. "Many years ago, I was stolen from my village when I was a child and taken to a building far away from home. Four stories high, it was the tallest building I ever seen. It had rows and rows of large windows to catch the sun, but the inside of the building was always so dark. I cried every night for my home, for my mother and father, for a supper of salmon or an ocean swim with my brothers and sisters. It was like I'd been stolen by the Basket Lady, except there was no cedar basket. Only a dark broom closet. And whitewashed woodwork with red spots as thick as shreds of *muwach* liver. I was made to speak words I didn't understand back then, and some days I had to mop up those red spots after the boys were hit with hickory sticks, and some days I had to strip the wax off the floors instead of learning my school lessons. What was my choice except to move the mop around the floor, outlining animal shapes with the soapy water as I named my world in the silence of my own head. *Muwach, kakawin, mamulthni*: deer, killer whale, white person. When I finally came back home, I wasn't ever the same. None of us were ever the same. Don't talk. Don't trust. Don't feel. That's all we learned at that school. But you know what, children? You cannot heal what you don't feel."

For Language and Culture class that afternoon, Joan's primary students had joined my students on the Read-Aloud Rug in my classroom.

It was a special arrangement so that the students could all start to prepare for the small school potlatch in eight weeks. It wasn't a true potlatch that followed all the proper protocols. Normally, the school would not be allowed to hold such an event. However, the Tawakin elders had given the school permission to have what they called a "learning potlatch" as part of the students' curriculum. It was a warm-up to the much larger potlatch in spring, when the school would host the other schools in the district. How all those students would fit onto the local water taxis, I couldn't imagine.

Some of the children listened patiently to Dawn, while others didn't pay any attention whatsoever. In fact several of the older students did everything in their power to make it known they were not listening. Loud, dramatic sighs of boredom. Bodies flopped sideways onto the carpet. Eyes rolled to the ceiling. It was not the subject matter they resisted. Once before I had watched them listen closely to the residential school stories. It was Dawn Jimmy they resisted. It was the first thing Dawn had told me when we met. Although Dawn was Nuu-chah-nulth, she was originally from farther down the coast. The fact that she'd married a Tawakin man and had lived here for decades did not temper the prejudice she faced from certain families, who thought it wasn't right that somebody with a different dialect should dare to teach language to their children. Like most prejudices, this one had been inherited by many of the children.

Joan stood next to me in the corner by the door and whispered, "You should know, these potlatches are going to eat up big chunks of our days from now on. They'll need to spend time making crafts to give away, as well as practising their dancing and drumming. Plus the students who are chosen to invite people from the village will have to practise their invitation speeches in Nuu-chah-nulth and then they'll have to go door to door reciting their speeches."

"How much time?" I asked quietly.

"Hours. And hours," Joan said. "Every day. Some days the whole afternoon will be spent on preparations."

"But only for the next eight weeks, right?" I asked.

Joan shook her head. "For this first school one, yes. But then we'll start preparing for the big spring potlatch sometime in February. From then on, be ready to throw away your lesson plans at the drop of a hat. Many of the practises are spontaneous. You won't always know what your day is going to look like."

"But what about their other learning?" I asked. "These kids are already behind grade level in their reading and writing. As a school, maybe we should be rethinking this."

Joan laughed. "You know potlatches used to be banned, right?"

"Of course I know," I said.

"So you want to suggest they can't have a potlatch?" Joan smirked playfully. "Is that really how you want to be remembered here? The white outsider who tried to ban the school potlatch?"

"Okay, okay." I smiled. "I don't want to mix politics with teaching."

"Everything about teaching is political," Joan said matter-of-factly.

In the far corner on the Read-Aloud Rug, the children were singing the Nuu-chah-nulth alphabet. How easy it was, I thought, to claim that I supported the integration of First Nations language and culture into the classroom. It made me anxious to think of how much less time I'd have to teach reading, writing, math, science. Those were the things I was responsible for. Which was more important at school? Academics to bolster their success outside Tawakin? Or cultural activities, after years of having them stripped away from their lives? I didn't know how to untangle such a question. But I did know that I wasn't the one to answer it.

"The only thing worse than the teachers who come in and shun the practice of culture in the classroom are the white saviours." Joan gave me a funny look.

"Who, me? You're not saying I'm a white saviour, are you?"

Joan shrugged. "Aren't we both?"

"Speak for yourself. I'm just here to teach them. I'm not here to save anybody."

Joan gave one of her students a stern look and motioned with her hand that he should turn back around. She whispered to me,

"Don't you think it's a little problematic? Teachers like us coming in to teach them?"

"So no teacher like us can ever come here and teach without being a white saviour?" I asked. "Surely it's possible to be something other than that."

"Sometimes I think we can. Other times I feel less sure," Joan said thoughtfully. "But Nurse Bernadette told me once that all outsiders who come to work in Tawakin fall into one of three categories: there are the Users, who come because they needed a job to get a better job somewhere else, the Runners, who come here to get away and hide from something else, and the Savers, who come here to feel good about rescuing the First Nations people."

"I don't think I'm any of those," I said.

Joan cocked an eyebrow. "Oh? Why did you come here, then?"

"For starters, I wanted to go somewhere I was really needed. I know how hard it is for these tiny, remote communities to recruit teachers."

"And?" Joan asked.

There was the lack of jobs in the city but instead I said, "And I wanted the adventure of it," which I thought was also true.

"Then aren't you a user?" Joan asked. "You came to their traditional territory for an adventure."

"But they needed a teacher."

"True, getting a teacher serves their needs. But adventure serves your needs," Joan said. "The whole thing is mutually beneficial and problematic. Teachers like you and I may have a fruitful relationship with our students. But it will always be a flawed relationship. If only for the fact that none of us stay."

*　　*　　*

After school that day, I sat at my desk and mulled over the words: white saviour. The term left me feeling ensnared. Like a nickname, a wall of words that limited who I was and who I could become. I felt damned if

I did. Damned if I didn't. Even so, I found myself wondering honestly about my perception of my students. Did I see them as beings who needed saving? Did I hold ideas of deficiency? Did I privately believe that my students couldn't ever achieve academically because they came from broken homes, broken cultures? The racism of low expectations: was that something I harboured deep inside me?

Mr. Chapman strolled in with a smile. "Thought I'd come have a look at those chickens."

"Yes, of course," I said.

Leaning over the brooder with his hands clasped behind his back, he said, "We are postponing Meet the Teacher Night by one week out of respect for the death in the community. We'll hold it once the body has been buried."

I went to the sink and rinsed out the margarine containers the class had used that afternoon for a science experiment on hot and cold solutions.

Still bent over the brooder, he twisted his head in my direction. "The body is returning to the community next Friday to be buried on Saturday. Don't expect any kids at school on Friday, they'll be kept inside once the body arrives."

I shut off the water faucet.

Mr. Chapman straightened and cast his eyes around the room. "My classroom in Bodder was a rectangular metal box that had been hauled onto the corner of the school grounds next to the soccer field because there was no room for us inside the main building. The carpet was worn bare. The fluorescent lights buzzed all day long. It smelled of old shoes. A portable. Funny word, that, since none of the kids in it were ever going anywhere."

I checked Mr. Chapman's face to see if he meant it as a joke. I couldn't tell. Joke or not, his comment about the kids in Bodder not going anywhere seemed so unlike his usual optimism.

From the top of the chicken wire Mr. Chapman unclipped Odelia's drawing of the woman in the box with the baby. A corner of his mouth twitched into what seemed to be a smile, but only for a brief second. He ran his index finger over the drawing, perhaps either to feel its texture or trace its lines.

Staring at the picture he said, "There was this kindergarten teacher in Bodder named Barbara Robinson. She had become a local fixture in the school after marrying the owner of the Super A grocery store. My first week there she told me that the anger in the school was as thick as fog and that I'd been given the most difficult class she'd seen in over twenty years. She told me that every weekend my students would try to break into my house and steal my things and every Monday morning they'd smile at me and tell me to fuck right off."

I stacked the margarine tubs into a neat tower. "Did they?"

"Did they what?"

"Break into your house and steal your things?"

He squinted his eyes for a moment. "I don't remember."

"You don't remember?" I asked, surprised.

"No, but I do remember the one morning a young moose calf got itself trapped on the soccer field. The snow was deep there and it couldn't find its way back out the fence." He continued to touch Odelia's picture as though he were a blind man attempting to detect the nature of the thing. "We stopped our math lesson and we all gathered at the windows and we watched the calf throw itself headfirst into the fence. It did this over and over and over. The fence rattled and clanged, rattled and clanged."

I uttered a noise of sympathy as I picked up a small dish towel.

With a snap of his fingers, Mr. Chapman then spoke with the sudden certainty of somebody who had uncovered a hidden truth. "You know what the North does?"

Shaking my head, I dried my hands on the towel.

"It numbs people," he said.

I recalled his descriptions of ice, rock, scour-pad vegetation, those bleak tessellations of white and grey. "Maybe people become the land they live on."

"Not true," he said. "People become the stories they hear over and over."

Tiny chick feet scratched across the sawdust. Mr. Chapman clipped the picture back onto the top of the wire then bent and scooped a chick into his hand. The small creature chirped frantically and turned in lost circles.

"The kids," he said, "acted like that moose was the funniest thing they'd ever seen. They couldn't stop pointing and laughing. Tears of laughter. And when the blood started to come, they laughed even harder. After a while the calf collapsed, and they begged me to put on their boots and go see it up close. We all marched to the spot where the thing had died. Bright red stains in the snow. We stood there for probably ten minutes, maybe more, just staring at the animal. Nobody was laughing by that point. Finally, Sonya Littlehead looked at me and said: 'See? Even—'"

Mr. Chapman stopped abruptly and stayed silent for a long while.

"Even what?" I asked.

He cleared his throat. "She said, 'See? Even the moose commit suicide here.'"

I stared at him, dumbfounded by the casual despair in Sonya Littlehead's words.

Jutting his chin forward, Mr. Chapman blew on the chick like it was a dandelion and its yellow fluff would drift into the air. He continued, "I later took that day to be a premonition. You see, the next week I went to Louise's Store. It was a tiny store along the Bodder Highway. I'd gone there to buy a dozen Hershey's chocolate bars for a math lesson on fractions. I'd already bought all the Hershey's from the only other store in Bodder, the Super A, which was once the Super Value until Tom Robinson bought it and changed the name by removing four letters, and since he couldn't be bothered to repaint or otherwise update anything else, the bright wood in the shape of the old letters was a godawful reminder that nothing ever really changed in that dismal place. Let me tell you though, Louise's Store was even more dismal. Two rows of shelves and an old pool table lit by a hanging lamp. When the lamp heated up, the nicotine would run down the metal shade in dark lines the colour of mustard. It's where my eleven-year-old students hung out and smoked cigarettes and joked that cousins are for practising."

I winced.

"That morning the store was empty, and as I was leaving, she told me that if she or anybody else died and was brought back to town to be buried, the children would remain inside. Evil spirits have been known to gather around unburied bodies since time immemorial. Children's souls, she told me, are easily taken by the spirits on account of their souls being soft and loose. The only way to protect them was to keep them inside with the curtains shut, or with a piece of charcoal."

"Charcoal?" I hung the towel back on the rack.

"That's what they believe up there. Louise then warned me to carry a piece of charcoal outside if she or anybody else died. But it wasn't anybody else who died. It was Louise. Three days later. Suicide."

"Oh." I frowned. "That's terrible. But why would you have to carry charcoal outside? You're not a child."

"I wondered that, too, why she'd told me this thing about charcoal since I'm an adult and my soul isn't soft or loose. Anyway, I stopped at the door and asked Louise this, if she thought my soul wasn't completely solid yet, but she just smiled and exhaled a thick tendril of cigarette smoke between her two front teeth."

"So you never found out what she meant?" I asked, intrigued.

Mr. Chapman shook his head. "I still think about it often, wondering. Such a strange thing to say. Sometimes you just don't know whether strange things like that are nonsense or if they have meaning."

I nodded.

"You must be wondering the same about your stones," he said.

I turned my wide eyes full on Mr. Chapman's face and said nothing. I tried to respond, but I stammered on my words. "I—they—they just appeared—I—I don't know who would do that—"

"It's a very strange thing, I agree. You need to be documenting all the details," Mr. Chapman said. "In case this turns out to be connected to a student. After all, what if this escalates to something worse? And you have no idea who might do this?"

"Apparently I should consider that it might be a Sasquatch," I said.

Mr. Chapman swiped his hand through the air. "Hogwash. Mumbo jumbo superstition. Just like all the rubbish going around the village of spirits making stuff happen. This worry about bad things coming and bad luck coming and blah blah blah. You know what brings bad luck? Superstition." Tilting his head to one side, he squinted his eyes in what seemed to be playful suspicion. "You don't believe that—about a Sasquatch, do you?"

I wanted to say no, I didn't believe that. But his particular use of the word superstition, how he said it with what sounded like disdain, left a sour taste in my mouth. It was one thing to not share the community's beliefs, but quite another to discard them as superstition.

I shook my head to let him know that no, I didn't believe it was a Sasquatch that had placed those stones. Then I added something that surprised me. "But I think I need to believe in the possibility."

*   *   *

That night as I tried to draw in my new sketchbook, I found myself distracted by Mr. Chapman's moose story. The image of bright red blood on stark white snow, a calf's life ended because it forgot the way back out of the fence and was desperate to escape. And Sonya Littlehead's comment—it shifted something inside of me.

Turning the pages of my sketchbook, I looked at the few portraits I had finished recently, noting that I had imposed the same wishful seeing onto their faces. How could I want them to hope so fervently for themselves when I was not willing to keep the hope myself? I pictured all those sketches on Fossil Island and I thought: Molleigh, you fool. My sketches—what empty illusions. The naïve work of somebody who merely wished a world from the comfort of their kitchen. What had that art reviewer said about that showing in Seattle years ago? That I needed to learn how to see, that's what he said. That I was an artist who wouldn't create anything of real interest until I stopped shielding my gaze from all the nuances of life.

What vanity, to think that I could simply transform them with a charcoal line curved a particular way, or that I could fill them with hope by artfully pouring it into them with a few carefully chosen words, or that I could connect with them by shaking their hands each morning. True, I'd been doing my best with them in the classroom, giving them my attention and energy, and I'd thought that was enough. Yet I ended up in the middle of that cold, wet forest, trading my comfort and my nascent hopes for what? Giant calling cards from Sasquatches?

That was it, I decided. Tonight was my last night of sketches. I put the sketchbook back underneath the glass ball on the windowsill and I vowed to not open it again until I had learned to see, which might not be an easy thing because just as I had feared, the boundary between my personal and professional life was blurring. If I wasn't careful, it might soon scarcely exist at all. Maybe it couldn't exist. Maybe in a place like Tawakin, the only way to make a difference, the only way to matter, the only way to inspire hope was to immerse yourself, your whole self, so deeply, so fully into the students' that there'd be no boundary. No divide between Molleigh and Ms. Royston. How could there be any other way? What agent of change anywhere in the world managed to make a real difference by dipping only their toe into the water? A whole-body baptism by ice water, that's what it took, your head submerged, every muscle shocked by cold, lungs seized by panic. You could not merely think about the water or talk about the water or draw the water. You could not merely think about the children or talk about the children or draw the children. You could not simply dream something other than reality. You had to plunge into cold depths. You had to throw your whole heart into it. You had to walk with them into the middle of the dark forest.

Now I was glad that I had left those sketches on the trees of Fossil Island, because when I pictured them there, it felt like a commitment. As if to say: I was here, I am still here, and I will walk with you into the middle of dark forests. If only to be present with you.

14

It was Saturday morning, drizzly and cool, when Hannah showed up at my house. Of all the kids who had ever shown up at my house, Hannah was the only one to knock on my door. One evening in early September, I heard voices in my kitchen as I unpacked boxes in my bedroom. Next thing I knew, Kenny, Julian and Odelia stood in the doorway of my bedroom next to a pile of bras and underwear I'd just sorted from my things. That was awkward enough, but I was thankful that was all they saw in my bedroom. Stunned by what I thought was boldness, walking into my house like that, I stared at them, speechless. I soon learned that entering a home in that way was commonplace in Tawakin, and I quickly got into the habit of locking the door every minute of the day.

I closed my laptop to see who was there. Hannah stood on the porch, holding a long axe, her now filthy sleeves covering her hands.

"Hannah," I said with surprise. I glanced down at the axe. "Do you need something?"

Hannah stared at me but said nothing.

"Have you been chopping wood?" I asked.

Hannah wrinkled her nose, no.

"Are you going to chop wood?" I asked.

Hannah still said nothing.

I thought for a moment. "Are you wanting to chop my wood?"

Hannah raised her eyebrows, yes.

After several hours, Hannah had split and stacked enough wood to keep my stove burning for a good two months. From the window, I watched her now and then. Hannah was a conscientious worker, calm and focused and persevering. Even with her sleeves covering her hands, Hannah was skilled with an axe.

When Hannah finished, I took a mug of hot chocolate and fifty dollars out to her. Hannah smiled and, for the first time ever, thanked me—proudly, clearly, politely.

We stood next to the porch. I glanced sidelong at each of the large rocks and wondered why Hannah hadn't mentioned them.

"So, are you saving up for something special?" I asked.

Hannah took a sip of her hot chocolate, holding the mug with both of her covered hands. "Dirt bike."

"Have you made a lot of money chopping wood?" I asked.

"Nobody will let me."

After Sophie Florence told me the story of Hannah being kept in the cold water by her cousins, I had asked her why Hannah had been bullied since such a young age and why people yelled at her from their windows to go away.

"People's anger coming out sideways," Sophie Florence had said. "People undercutting each other. Someone starts to do well for themselves and gets pulled down. People say to them, 'Oh, you think you're better than us now? You just know all that *mamulthni* stuff now.' Or the complaints about bloodlines. None of that happened before status cards told us we weren't an Indian without one. Now people say, 'Who the hell do you think you are? You aren't even from this community, you're from a village down the coast, how'd you get a job here?'"

I nodded and waited for her to explain what this had to do with Hannah.

"It didn't help that Hannah was a difficult child from the time she was a toddler," Sophie Florence said. "I think it gave people an excuse to take things out on her. As if she deserved it anyway. But I don't think it even started out being about Hannah."

"How did it start, then?" I asked.

Sophie Florence gave this some consideration. Then she said, "I can't say for sure. Some family feud, probably. Families fighting over something from twenty years ago and the children don't know why. The children get caught in the middle."

Rain started to fall on Hannah and me, popping and crackling on the waxy leaves above our heads. I suggested we head indoors.

"In there?" Hannah asked, nodding at the trailer.

"Yes, before we get too wet."

"I can come into your house?"

"We'll play chess," I said. "Do you know how?"

Hannah wrinkled her nose.

"I'll teach you," I said.

"In your house?"

"Yes, Hannah. In my house."

Inside, I put out a plate of cookies and a short stack of white napkins. I topped up our hot chocolates. After getting the chess board from the drawer, I showed Hannah where to place the pieces and how each piece moved. Hannah caught onto the game quickly. She was calculating, tactical, and after only three games she beat me in twelve moves. The whole time she sat with a posture more relaxed than I had ever seen before. Although she kept her hands in those sleeves, her body appeared more open and welcoming than usual, and her face, too, which looked perhaps as peaceful as Hannah Charlie could look, with an occasional smile lifting her cheeks.

"You been hearing any screams in the woods?" Hannah asked, sliding a pawn to the next square.

"What do you mean, screams?"

"A loud scream. Kind of a growl-scream. You been hearing that?"

"No, have you?" I took hold of my bishop.

Hannah wrinkled her nose.

I examined the board once more. "Then why did you ask?"

"Them big rocks out there."

I fell back against my chair. Them big rocks. How odd that she took this long to mention them. It gave me the impression that Hannah wasn't especially surprised by their presence. Scream-roars in the woods. Had I heard anything like a scream? No, and I didn't care to think about it. Changing my mind, I let go of the bishop and castled my king instead. "Your move."

"*Aalth-maa-koa*," Hannah stated.

"What?" I shook my head. "What's that?"

"What moved your rocks," Hannah said. "*Aalth-maa-koa.*"

"I don't know what that is," I said.

"You know. Like a Sasquatch." Studying the pieces, Hannah slid her rook horizontally and snatched up my bishop.

I moved my queen out of harm's way and looked at Hannah.

"There's an island just past Toomista. It's real small. Hardly anybody goes there ever. It's my own special place. There's a clearing of fallen totem poles past a whale rib on a driftwood log. I heard one crying in the woods there one time."

I took a long look at Hannah's covered hands.

Hannah moved them out of sight under the table.

"What's wrong with your hands, Hannah? You can tell me."

"You better move your king, Teacher," she said, "or you're going to lose again."

I looked down at the board and placed my king one square over.

For the rest of the game, we played mostly in silence, except this time I noticed Hannah stealing quick glimpses of my face. I might have assumed this had something to do with the game itself, that Hannah was perhaps trying to read my next few steps on the board, were it not for the palpable tension in Hannah's glances. Was it because I'd questioned her hands? Then again, it was the same nervous energy I had felt emanating from her since the first day of school. Was she wondering when this bubble was going to burst? Was she anxiously waiting for the moment when I would reject her and tell her to go away? Of course, that possibility was only ever a figment of her imagination, but perceived reality *was* reality in the eyes of the beholder. As she quickly stole another glimpse, it dawned on me that students like Hannah did not merely look at me and think, I see you. They looked at me and thought, I see you seeing me and how connected or not that feels. It was as Dawn Jimmy had told me: the generational legacy of residential school. Don't talk. Don't trust. Don't feel.

Hannah moved her bishop diagonally and put my king into checkmate.

"You're very good at chess, Hannah. Very good," I gushed. "Not surprising considering how smart you are."

Slumping back in her chair, Hannah pulled her arms into her body. She shoved her covered hands in between her knees and tilted her face down.

I tried to coax her into the compliment. "You should feel proud."

Hannah's eyes went vacant as she stared at the board.

Setting a row of black pawns along my side of the board for the next game, I felt a severing of any connection we might have made only minutes earlier. What else could I do? I was trying to connect with Hannah in the only way I knew how. Face to face. Eye contact. The sort of "great job!" enthusiasm that I myself had grown accustomed to since my own childhood.

Hannah turned her head and looked at the living room, visible through a wide opening in the wall. "My dad says you promised to stay here and teach."

"Uh—" I felt blindsided. It never occurred to me that Chase would tell Hannah. Impulsively, I said, "Yeah, I guess I did."

"Then how come you got all those boxes in there?" Hannah asked.

I thought quickly. "I'm still unpacking."

"But most of them are tipped on their sides empty," Hannah pointed out, her tone growing more aggressive, accusatory.

I nodded. How could I admit that I had only said the promise was true because I didn't want this moment to end, that I was scared Hannah would erupt out of her peacefulness, her pleasantness if I even hesitated to say it was true. Except there were my sagging boxes, ready for packing, and any moment now this connection between us would be gone, the promise dismissed by Hannah as yet another lie, just like all the other lies that everyone told all the time.

Unexpectedly Hannah dropped it. Instead she turned back to the chess board and asked, "You ever hear about a wood tooth?"

I halted my pawn mid-air. "No."

Hannah looked at my hovering pawn. "You gonna make a move?"

"Tell me about it. The wood tooth." I set the pawn down on the board.

"Probably a dumb story anyways," Hannah shrugged.

"That's okay. Tell me," I said.

"It's a tooth made of wood," Hannah said, staring at the board. "It's supposed to have special powers, but I'm not stupid enough to believe that."

"What kind of powers?"

"When you have it, it's like you become a whole new person. You get to start over. Not become a baby again, not like that. But it is kind of like getting born again. Except more like the person you were sort of just disappears. You get to forget about who you were. You get to be whoever you want."

"Be whoever you want? You get to pick a person you want to be?"

Hannah scowled at me. "You don't get to become Tupac or Dr. Dre or anything like that. But you get to choose the kind of person you become."

"I see," I said. "So if you wanted to become prime minister of Canada, you could if you had that wood tooth?"

"Yeah," Hannah said. "But who would choose something as lame as that?"

I laughed. "What would you choose?"

Hannah stared at the board for a long while in silence.

At the start of the school year, I asked each student to share their future plans in a short writing exercise. If any students didn't want to write it, they were welcome to share it verbally with me. Only one child, Odelia, managed to articulate any vision for her future. Artist. The others drew a blank, so it didn't surprise me now that Hannah didn't know what to say. In an effort to scaffold their understanding, I had brainstormed a list of vocations on the chalkboard. Quickly I ascertained that the children had a narrow awareness of occupations and little curiosity or interest in any of them, which was less to do with apathy and more to do with how unknown the wider world of work was to them, beyond fishing and logging and working in the school or the Nation office. Studies showed that children with a vision for their future eventually experienced greater happiness and success, whatever that meant, than those children who did not have a vision. It didn't matter what the vision was—all that mattered was that they had one for themselves.

"You believe it?" Hannah asked. "That a wood tooth could do that?"

"Not sure," I said. "It does seem hard to believe."

Hannah looked disappointed. "Yeah, that's what I thought."

"You ever hear about a silver tooth?" I asked.

Hannah narrowed her eyes at me. "How come you know about that? You're not supposed to know. Only a few of us are supposed to know."

"Then why did you tell me about the wood tooth?"

Hannah glanced out the window. "I wanted to see if you believed it."

"Why only a few people?"

Hannah shrugged. "Just because."

"Tawakin people?"

"No. Kids."

"Only children get to hear about the teeth?" I asked.

"Only a few special children."

"Who told you this?"

"I can't say."

"Why can't you say?"

"Don't tell nobody I told you."

"What's the difference?" I asked.

"The difference is I'll get in big trouble if you tell," Hannah said.

"No. What's the difference between the wood tooth and the silver tooth?"

Hannah smirked. "One's made of wood. The other silver."

I smirked back. "Yes, thank you for that explanation. I am so much the wiser now. You know what I mean. Do the teeth have different powers?"

"Like I said, the wood one gives you the power to be whoever you want. But the silver one gives you the power to get whatever you want." Hannah checked my face and asked me once more. "You believe it?"

"No," I said. "I just can't believe it. A silver tooth from the Devil—"

"And a wood tooth from a cross."

I stared at Hannah, blinking. A wood tooth from a cross. From the tilting cross stuck in the ground on the little rocky island next to the village? Or from *the* cross? Hannah stared back at me, and if she shared the same feeling of awe, it didn't show on her face. Rather, she seemed to be waiting to continue the game as if she'd said nothing extraordinary at all. I looked at the board. There was no move I could make now. With my index finger, I reached out, tipped my king onto its side and dropped my white napkin onto the board in surrender.

*   *   *

The next morning I got ready to go for a run up the road past the Mossy Spot, a hidden clearing where a thick carpet of sphagnum moss covered a large swath of ground. The children liked to go there and bounce on the moss, which was as springy as a tight trampoline. I had been an avid runner prior to arriving in Tawakin, and I missed my daily runs, often too nervous to encounter a bear or, worse yet, a cougar. But I'd rigged an outfit that, while not making me invincible to wildlife, would hopefully make me less appealing. It was raining lightly, so I wore my bright yellow rain jacket. In the breast pocket I put my phone, which was useless in Tawakin as a phone but invaluable as a source of noise. Instead of using headphones, I plugged a tiny portable speaker into the phone and blasted my music as loud as it would go. On my back I hung a rubber Halloween mask, and although the mask depicted a bloodied monster, its features were human enough to convince any cougar stalking behind me that I was in fact watching it closely. As a last-ditch measure, I slipped a canister of bear spray and a hunting knife with a five-inch blade—still in its leather sheath but with the safety strap unbuttoned—into my other jacket pocket.

Walking outside past the rocks, I felt a moment of hesitation as usual. Running along the logging road with the forest on either side of me was challenging enough. But now the thought of unknown creatures and their scream-roars in the woods gnawed at me. I had figured out a loop that traversed the most open areas around the school, allowing me to skirt the forest as far from it as possible. When I reached the gravel road, I headed up the hill toward the other teachers' houses. Something orange on the side of my trailer caught my eye. Turning, I stood face to face with a giant portrait of myself.

It was spray-painted in bright, almost neon orange, and it was about eight feet high and six feet wide. It was crudely painted with a simple backwards *L* for a nose, two squashed circles for eyes, a rectangular mouth with big square gnashing teeth, top and bottom rows clenched together, and a ponytail of long, straight hair. The only reason I knew it was supposed to be me, besides the fact that somebody had taken the trouble to spray-paint it on my trailer, was the pair of cat-eye reading glasses that had been added to my face. Across my forehead was a single word, all capitals: *BITCH*.

It was a Hannah Charlie original, of that I had no doubt. Yesterday we had connected in a way that I had started to believe was not possible. It wasn't that we'd had a particularly personal conversation, but we had shared a space peacefully, and we had each chosen to simply be present with one another. And that, at least for now, was more than enough for me. Yet looking at the Tawakin street art on my trailer, I realized it had been too much for Hannah.

I now knew my relationship with her would be an endless pendulum between me being accepted and being rejected. When it came to Hannah, I had rarely acted, only ever reacted, and sometimes with anger, though I felt no shame in showing a bad temper occasionally. Not only because it was a natural thing, to be frustrated or furious with Hannah, but because I wanted to show her that anger did not equal hate. Hannah knew how much I was tolerating, I believed this, and she also knew that I was the first one to tolerate it. Yet she clearly worried that I would turn on her like everybody else, and as such, couldn't stop her impulse to reject me before I could do the same to her.

I remembered saying once to her in the middle of September:

"Hannah, your behaviour doesn't have to be your destiny."

"Fuck you."

Funny enough, the longer I gazed upon the hideous version of myself, the more the optimism swelled inside me. Hannah had hope. This picture was proof of that. Something inside the tall, angry girl had ignited, or she wouldn't have bothered to do this. She wouldn't have taken the time and effort to push me away like this, which in itself was an act of caring. She cared more than her angry and apathetic façade suggested. Something in her heart could be coaxed out. But what would happen to that hope if I left?

15

Nearly every adult from the village crowded the cemetery in the woods on Rubant Island Saturday afternoon. Today was the burial of Grace's grandmother. The blind woman who loved shapes and knitting and telling tall tales. Silver and blue beads that looked like the heavens, she had loved those too. A memorial potlatch would be held in her honour in a year, Sophie Florence had explained. But no formal memorial service today. Just the burial. And many speeches, long and impromptu.

Standing next to Joan and Sophie Florence, I surveyed the crowd. Mr. Chapman, who must have caught a boat ride with someone else, was just across the grass from us, chatting with a small circle of men. There was a stout man with a bad limp and what were probably the initials of his former lovers tattooed in blue ink on his fingers, a tall, bald man who continually tugged at his beltless jeans, and a man wearing a cedar hat who kept loudly exhaling with a puff of his cheeks.

"Mr. Chapman seems to be fitting into the community well," Joan commented to Sophie Florence.

"Mmmmmm," Sophie Florence hummed, as if she needed to consider it more thoroughly before agreeing. "Could be."

Just then, an uproar of laughter came from the far side of the clearing where a large group gathered in a ragged circle. Elsewhere, people chatted and chuckled, all of them dressed in long Adidas shorts and sweatpants and oversized T-shirts with unzipped jackets over top. I could feel little sorrow in the air.

"They're following the old teachings," Sophie Florence said, as if reading my mind. "This is why we put pictures away. So we don't pity ourselves. Leaving their pictures out can get them stuck here, unable to cross over. When you leave a picture out, you keep looking at the picture and you start missing them and crying for them, then they hear you and come to see you, and they see how much you're missing them. When they see that, they start missing you, too. Then they might try to take you with them. That's when people get sick or have a bad accident. So you can't just say, 'rest in peace,' and not act like you mean it. You have to show it by letting them go. Not by pitying yourself."

The grass around the burial plots had been neatly mowed since I had been there with the women, and I commented on this fact to Sophie Florence.

"Hannah," Sophie Florence said. "She boated a lawnmower over on Thursday all by herself and got the grass ready. Nobody even asked her to do it."

Behind them, Sophie Florence's brother Ray was talking loudly about the present he brought back for his granddaughter, Odelia. "Got her the most amazing flowers she will have ever seen," he explained to a small group of people. "Can't wait for the look on her face. They go best with good music. None of that rap shit, neither. We'll start with Beethoven's Symphony no. 5 in C Minor, followed by Vivaldi's *Four Seasons*, then we'll finish with Strauss's *The Blue Danube*."

I turned to sneak a peek at this great-uncle of Odelia's who was so well-versed in classical music, but just as I glanced at the thin man with the stringy silver ponytail, someone made a loud request for quiet so that Nan Lily could say the opening prayer.

As I continued to survey the crowd, I thought it didn't look good that Joan and I were the only two teachers there from the school. The high school teachers, Diane Rickman and Timothy Ness, chose to skip the burial in favour of a short kayak excursion, claiming they didn't really know the elder anyhow, so what was the point? Joan and I had knocked on their doors in the morning and tried to convince them that their presence would show support for the community. Joan informed both teachers that the village keeps a mental inventory of *seen faces*, those teachers who regularly ventured down the hill or across the water for community events. "People are already complaining that they never see you two down the hill," she warned them. "You're setting yourself up for a professional and social death."

It didn't take a genius to recognize how essential it was for the school to keep good relations with the community. Knowing this, Joan and I had taken the school boat to Rubant Island, careful to follow the instructions we'd been given. Before leaving the dock, we watched the men load the casket onto the boat. They put the casket onto the boat feet first, then they spun it in a clockwise circle once so the spirit couldn't find its way home. Eventually Joan and I followed the procession of boats, everybody expected to remain behind the boat with the casket.

I fixed my eyes upon the casket that rested in the grass next to the rectangular hole sliced deep into the soil. The body had arrived in Tawakin the day before, and people had taken turns sitting with it in the ramshackle church all day and night. It was eerie to think of the elder's corpse in a box down the hill, and I'd had a fitful sleep. By morning, I was still thinking about the body down the hill and the evil spirits that were known to gather around unburied bodies. Was my soul soft and loose like a child's, or was it hard and fixed in place like an adult's? This was what I obsessed over while drinking my morning coffee. I took a willow charcoal stick out of the clamshell on the kitchen windowsill and dropped it into the pocket of my rain jacket. Now, as I stared at the casket on the grass, I slipped my hand into that pocket and rolled the stick gently between my fingers.

The presence of the body had kept all the children inside. Not one kid had come to school on Friday and there were no children in the crowd now. When Joan and I boated past the village, the curtains in every house had been closed tight, the children kept away from the windows. No pregnant women here either, Sophie Florence added when I commented on this to Joan. How sad it seemed to me that

Grace couldn't be here for her own grandmother's funeral. But even if she was still in Tawakin, she wouldn't have been allowed to risk being stolen away by spirits. Instead she'd been stolen away by policies made up in offices far from here. Culture, I thought, should eat policies for breakfast.

As Nan Lily finished the opening prayer, my mind cast back to my own confinement at home, after the death of the boy from my neighbourhood. Most children in that era of four television channels and no video games would have been despondent to be locked indoors, especially in the warmth of summer and especially when all the other brunette children could be heard outside playing hide-and-go-seek and road hockey. For the most part, I was indeed disappointed, but the time spent with my mother was equally if not more magical. Mostly we painted together, and I could still remember every strange landscape I created during my quarantine—how they consisted of lush foliage and botanical species and creatures mysterious to me. Around that time I'd started to read what I could find about African wildlife, diaries from great treks across the savannah, a library book on my favourite animal—the giraffe—by Anne Innis Dagg, field guides on African trees. I memorized the trunks and branches of the fever tree, the baobab tree, those upside-down giants who lived forever, the sausage tree with its massive oblong fruits that could knock a passerby out cold, the quiver tree, the whistling thorn. I used a starter set of acrylics and brushes with cheap bristles and some canvas that my mother and I stretched over frames we'd made out of scraps of wood. I painted the bleakest images of suburbia I could invent: empty parking lots with weeds in the broken cracks of asphalt, blue and rusted garbage dumpsters, long coupe and sedan cars from the late 1970s, early 1980s, usually a brown Oldsmobile with a broken tail light. Growing out of the dumpsters I painted a variety of African trees, and across the asphalt I painted translucent wild grasslands. Giraffes drove the brown Oldsmobiles that parked and waited in the empty lots, their necks curving out of the open windows. At the time, my mother told me that every writer, every artist revealed in their work the things in life that devoured them. Why

Africa dominated my childhood art, I did not know. Likewise, I did not know why things so lush and beautiful, tangled in vibrant clusters and coloured emerald, bronze and gold, were always layered over an underpainting of dirty greys and dusty blacks and the decay of rust, or why I depicted life inside blue dumpsters and brown sedans.

One day I asked my mother if she could hang my African paintings in the hallway next to her paintings of relatives I had never met. Together we constructed simple wood frames, which I painted carefully in glossy black, but when it came time to hang the paintings, my mother admitted she could not bring herself to look at them every day. There was just too much going on in the world for such pictures, a statement about my paintings that had perplexed me at the time and still did whenever I thought about it. In terms of the world, I knew she meant the peculiar metamorphosis of our neighbourhood. It was as if our piece of the suburbs had gone to bed a boy and awoke in the morning to find it was a huge insect. A beetle on Marvin Gardens.

If you were shown the fragments of television reports from that summer of 1981 and told that those shattered souls were the grieving parents—the parents of five victims with five more to come after our neighbourbood was changed forever—and if you were to hear the rumours around the neighbourhood that the Beast was now targeting not just teens but younger children, perhaps children with blond hair like the boy, you might understand why I was not allowed out of the house. There had been things in the newspaper, too, which at first my mother pored over every evening with a nervous intensity. But at some point the newspapers stopped coming, that I remembered clearly. That and the fact that I was high up in my favourite tree overlooking the woods and the parking lot behind Safeway when I heard the news that a child from our neighbourhood had been stolen away.

It was also around this time that my mother flipped all five of my paintings around so that they leaned backwards on the floor against the wall, their bright colours hidden from sight. To this day I can remember how hurt and disappointed I felt that she didn't want to look at them, especially when our shared love of art was our greatest bond. Then again, it was easy to see this rejection as part of her unravelling. It always struck me how differently my mother had reacted than the other parents in the neighbourhood. Not only because I could see my friends going to school each day during the last two weeks before summer holidays, but because of how often I would catch my mother watching me from the corner of her eye as we each read or drew a picture. As if I were a cipher she needed to crack, despite the fact that I always had the strong sense, a gut feeling, that it was she who knew something secret.

While Ernie Frank launched into a long speech about Grace's grandmother, I thought about my mother's untimely death when I was only eighteen. A blood clot in her lung, that was what had killed her. How many times had my mother read Alice Munro's short story "Royal Beatings," only to point out that she'd never die of a blood clot in her lung like Rose's mother because now she knew from the story that it would feel like a boiled egg in her chest. "With the shell left on," I would add, having heard the story a dozen times. It went without saying that Alice Munro was a masterful writer. I always figured that in that one paragraph, however, her descriptive powers had missed the mark. Because never had my mother complained about any farm products lodged in her chest. Or was it possible that my mother, despite how many times she'd read the story, forgot to take note of her similar sensation? Or maybe she did remember and did feel it, and still did nothing.

After my mother's death, I started to search the world for signs. Not of anything in particular, just small moments of serendipity, insignificant coincidences, a chance meeting with an old friend, the sun's rays beaming straight from the heavens though thick clouds, a butterfly on my mother's birthday. Anything that felt like a knowing in my heart. In that grieving phase of my life, I took in the world in a new and purposeful and intensified way, a Kodachrome way, believing my senses could help me make sense of things. But they couldn't.

Two women finished sharing memories of Grace's grandmother, then the casket was lowered into the ground. I glanced at the pile of fresh soil next to the burial plot. Once that soil covered the casket, the evil spirits that gather around unburied bodies would be gone. My hand had remained inside my pocket the entire time. Clutched between my fingers, half the charcoal was now crushed to dust.

"Look!" Margaret Sam pointed to a trail in the woods.

Through the path's opening, a small strip of the beach on Toomista Island, across the finger of water, was visible. Standing there on the black rocks were three large wolves. Motionless, they stared at all of us.

Sophie Florence gasped.

"Will they come over here? Should we leave?" I asked.

"To see a wolf is one of the greatest gifts," Sophie Florence said. "It means that you are open, spiritually. They're not here to harm us. They're here to protect us."

"From what?" Joan asked.

Sophie Florence stuck out her bottom lip. "The upset spirits. All those strange things happening in the village."

"Anybody got a gun in their boat?" A man's voice called out.

"Don't shoot them! They're our protectors!" Somebody else argued.

Another man laughed. "You won't be saying that when one of them sinks its teeth into your belly."

One of the wolves turned its head toward the expanse of ocean to the west and then sauntered off, the two other wolves following its lead. With their departure, the people took their own departures from the clearing. As the crowd dissipated and boat motors were revved to life down at the shore, I felt a finger tap on my shoulder. It was Ernie Frank. With a tug of my jacket sleeve, he pulled me off to the side where nobody could hear him.

"When there is a darkness inside somebody," he said, "it can make them do bad things. And when somebody does really bad things, we vote to send them away."

I thought of the people whose skin turns to bark.

"One of my cousins," he said, "had a darkness inside him, and he did some bad things to his daughter. We voted to send him away."

"Where did he go?"

Ernie stared at me. "It's you," he said.

"What?"

"My sister seen it when you came to the dock for *tucip*. An aura."

"I don't understand," I said.

"It's you," Ernie repeated. "You're the one with the darkness."

"Me? But I—"

"It's you," Ernie said again. "I can feel your dark energy right now. Sharp as broken glass."

"It can't be me," I said, my voice thin. "I do not have a darkness."

Ernie gave me a gentle look. He insisted. "I can feel it."

"Makes me sound like I'm evil," I said.

"It's not like that at all," Ernie said.

I waited for him to say more, but he walked past me toward the shore.

I took a moment to gather my senses. I refused to believe it. It couldn't be. I didn't have a darkness inside me. I'd have felt it if I did. Wouldn't I? Maybe the darkness Ernie's sister saw in me did not belong to me at all. Maybe it belonged to the woman in the box with the baby. That would explain it. Like when soot coats your skin and hair after a long bonfire, I must have been coated with a layer of death. But that was a ridiculous notion, and I knew it. Ernie had sensed the dark energy in the school kitchen before Grace's grandmother had died. Before I had followed Grace to the woman.

The darkness was not from the woman in the box with the baby.

It was from me.

16

Since Grace had left Tawakin, I had lost my enthusiasm for writing period. Aside from art, writing was my favourite thing to teach. Every week I delivered small lessons on grammar and spelling and prose and poetry structures, but those things came second to nurturing their imaginations and views of the world. Building the children's confidence in their own voices felt like the most meaningful work I'd ever done in my life. To see the joy and pride on their faces when I read their pieces, my eyes widening, begging them for more: "You've got me on pins and needles! I can hardly wait to see what happens next!" Yet none of that was the same without Grace.

For today's writing period, I gave the students time to continue working on their personal narratives. With some prodding, most of the students buckled down and got creating, scratching out sentences with their pencils and pens. Except Hannah. Given that it was a victory to get Hannah to write about anything at all, I suggested that she only had to write one sentence for today. About something she liked to do for fun. Anything.

"I like to play basketball," Hannah said, rubbing her covered hands between the thighs of her jeans.

"Good, then write about that," I said.

"Nah, I'm just gonna go play basketball instead."

"It's not time for basketball. It's time for writing," I said.

"Fuck writing."

I stood in front of her desk and realized that inside me there were different versions of myself. There was the teacher I wanted to be. There was the teacher I probably was. And there was the teacher I was afraid of becoming. I looked down at Hannah. She stared straight up into my eyes and barked like a sea lion. I didn't move. If I followed Hannah's Safety Plan, which instructed me in most cases to ignore Hannah as if she were a stain on the carpet, I would now avoid eye contact and step away from her personal space immediately, or risk escalating matters. But I'd recently come to believe that Hannah's noises were triggered by an anxiety that craved relief. I set both hands on Hannah's desk, leaned over her upturned face, and barked back. All the sounds of rustling paper and scratching pencils and pens stopped. I barked again, louder, holding my gaze on Hannah's surprised face, waiting for her to make the next move.

"I can write about anything I like?" Hannah asked.

"Anything."

"Well, go away," Hannah said. "I can't write shit if you're going to stand there."

As I checked on the other children, Hannah hunched over her notebook, scraping her covered hands against the edges of her desk. She stopped and wrote down a word. Tugging the front of her large shirt to her nose, she sniffed it, and wrote another word. After a few moments, she wrote another word, and then drilled the pen nib into her hand, scraping it across her skin hidden under her sleeve. I thought I saw a dark circle spread on the cuffs that covered Hannah's knuckles. Hannah shoved her hands under her desk when I returned. I picked up her notebook. There was only one sentence on the page. It said:

I like to rape.

At lunch, Hannah and some of the other students played on the computers in the library. I watched Hannah from the table where I sat with a stack of the students' writing. All the feelings of hope I had when I first gazed upon the graffiti picture of myself on my trailer faded away. I shuffled the notebooks around, pretending to assess the contents of each, when it was Hannah's sentence alone that bound my attention. I read it, looked away and read it again, hoping for some magical transformation. But the words stayed in their place, the letters, shaky and malformed, deviating above and below the lines, standing like little walls erected to house immense brutality. I knew it had to be reported, Hannah's sentence, but what would it mean for her? Everything that happened at the school made its way down to the village somehow, and that sentence would support people's horrible treatment of her. And yet, what if the sentence was true? Was it possible that Hannah had done this to someone already? If not, was the sentence a forewarning? I stared at the period that marked the end of Hannah's sentence—that big, round scribble of ink—and suddenly I saw it as a knot tied with the bitter end of rope.

*   *   *

By nearly the end of lunch, as I continued to puzzle over Hannah's vicious sentence, Hannah's mother, Patty, burst through the library door holding a soggy brown paper bag. Patty's hair hung heavy with rain. She shook the water off the front of her large sweatshirt and scanned the room for Hannah.

"You forgot your lunch, Hannah," she said. Her voice was loud, battering.

"I don't want your fucking lunch."

"Hannah, come get your lunch," Patty said.

Hannah turned up the volume on her computer. A music video played on the screen. The other children stared at their own computers, the sounds of screeches and crashes and laser pulses emanating from their games. A few children snapped fat-foamed headphones over their ears.

Patty lumbered across the room toward Hannah. The lunch bag started to rip along the wet creases as she swung it back and forth. Her voice was even louder now. "It's a salmon-and-pickle sandwich. You told me you like pickles. So I gave you damn pickles."

Hannah sneered. "I said I don't want it. You eat it, you big, fat whale."

"Why you got to talk to me like that for?" Patty held the lunch bag out to Hannah, but when Hannah wouldn't even turn to look at her, Patty set it down on the table beside the computer.

Hannah knocked the bag to the floor with the back of her covered hand and said, "We're not allowed food in the library."

"What is that? Is that blood?" Patty looked down at Hannah's cuffs. She grabbed Hannah's wrist and slid up the sleeve. "Sweet Jesus, Hannah. What the hell is wrong with your hand?" Then Patty turned to me and screamed, "Why didn't you tell me about this? What is wrong with you? What is wrong with this school?"

I wanted to protest, to explain that I'd asked Chase about her hands, but Patty was too preoccupied. She stuck out Hannah's hand for me to see. It was covered with tracks of blue ink where she'd dragged the pen nib across her skin. She'd scratched so deep her knuckles had bled. Red bumps and tiny grey tunnels covered the back of her hand. Before I had a chance to say anything to Patty, Hannah jumped up, flipping her chair to the floor and kicking it. Her eyes watered. She stuck her middle finger up at everybody in the room as they all stared at her.

"Fuckers! Haters!" Hannah shouted.

The bell rang to end lunch, and there was a sudden scraping of chairs and shuffling of feet. The children rushed out of the library, taking the long way around to avoid Hannah.

"What's wrong with her hands?" Patty demanded again.

"Hannah," I said as Hannah started to rip posters off the wall.

"Leave me alone," Hannah spat as she spoke. She ran out into the hallway and shouted at me. "Redneck bitch!"

"Hannah," I called after her, "why don't we go talk somewhere?"

"Why don't you go fuck yourself?"

Out the window, I watched Hannah storm across the field.

"You are all useless," Patty seethed at me. She spun around and headed out the library door, calling back, "You and that principal. You both better watch your backs."

That evening I went onto the Internet and researched sexual assault by young girls. Every search phrase resulted in articles and statistics of sexual assault against young girls. There were also cases of grown women committing sexual assault, but there was nothing about children committing sexual assault against other children. Certainly not where the girl was the perpetrator. Mentions of sexual harassment by young girls, yes. The posting of pictures on social media, sexual comments, the starting of sexual rumours, touching, grabbing, sexting. But nothing on rape. I figured there must be documented cases somewhere. But I uncovered nothing.

Was Hannah acting out sexually because she herself had been assaulted? It would explain a lot about her behaviour. And there was the matter of the orange circle Joan would tape to her classroom window whenever one of the primary grade girls went to the washroom. At the beginning of the school year, Joan and I met with Mr. Chapman and a counsellor, a woman named Katerina who regularly flew in on the mail plane to meet with local clients, both adults and children. Very little was said to me about why Hannah wasn't allowed alone with the younger children, and when I asked for more information, Katerina explained that she could say nothing more due to confidentiality issues. At one point, Katerina and Mr. Chapman excused themselves from my classroom in order to have a murmured yet heated debate in the hallway over how much to divulge to the teaching staff, Katerina insisting on protecting the privacy of her counselling sessions. I overheard Mr. Chapman say to Katerina, "How can we do our jobs with only half-truths?"

Shutting my laptop screen, I leaned back in my chair and considered my options. Was this a matter of contacting Child Protection Services? The RCMP? I could bring it to Mr. Chapman. Maybe consult Joan first. I knew there were protocols but I didn't know where this fit. I had never expected to encounter an eleven-year-old girl who confesses her desire to rape. Yet here I was, and I couldn't help but think of what was at stake for Hannah. She was just a child, a fact that could easily be forgotten, and I didn't want to spoil the small gains the girl had made. But what if I failed to keep other children safe, all for the sake of protecting Hannah? The bottom line, I decided, was that I didn't have enough information yet. I needed to find out more before making my decision about the sentence. I needed more time.

Just then, Buttons made an appearance on the VHF radio. My handheld radio on the counter clicked repeatedly. Somebody must have been waiting for the exact moment the clicking stopped, because a woman's voice interjected with perfect timing. "Damn you, Buttons!" the woman said. I didn't recognize her voice, so demanding. "Who are you? Tell us who you are, you coward! Quit your hiding!"

After dinner, I could hear a faint *boom-boom-boom* sound from across the road. Rhythmic and pulsing, the sound of rawhide drums was soon accompanied by the singing of men's voices. Quads and dirt bikes and Chase Charlie's pickup truck cluttered the sides of the gravel road. Across the road, children ran in and out of the gym doors. It was dance night, everybody practising for the school potlatch, which meant that the floor would be covered in white flour for my block of physical education first thing in the morning. The dancers danced without shoes or socks, the flour reducing the friction under their sliding and twisting feet.

In my bedroom closet were several boxes I had yet to unpack. I put four of the boxes on my bed and pulled the flaps open. In the first three boxes were items I'd brought for the classroom. A rock tumbler with all the different grits of polishing sands, a dozen owl pellets wrapped in aluminum foil with a set of miniature dissecting tools, rocket-building equipment. My students would love this stuff. Maybe I could try again after that first disaster with the gyroscope. I smiled at the thought, then sighed. I was just so tired, mentally and physically and emotionally. I had no energy to introduce such projects, and who could think of such fun anyway with that sentence burning in my mind?

In the last box I found what I was looking for. On top of a stack of books was my paperback copy of *Foucault's Pendulum*. Despite my failure to get very far into the novel years ago, I was willing to give it another try. What could take my mind off everything better than a story about medieval Knights Templar and a hoax?

I took *Foucault's Pendulum* to the kitchen table. As I riffled through the pages, the binding snapped open to where I'd discovered the painting of Hope on the Jordanian stamp. Although the stamp was no longer there, its faint impression was still on the page, a barely visible hint of colour impressed over rows of words. Everything in this world left a ghostly resonance. The stamp upon Eco's clever sentences, the letters removed by Tom Robinson from the Super A in Bodder, the scallop fossils on the shores, the black stain of the beetle on Marvin Gardens. The imprint of things upon life. Things gone but never erased.

17

That night I dreamed I was a tree man.

The village voted to kick me out for harming a child. While it was unclear what I had done to deserve banishment, the people of Tawakin held a meeting in the community centre on the shore, where the wind shook the windows until the glass cracked. They cast their votes, and I was forced to leave in a small boat.

Alone I headed south along the tremendous stretch of coastline, unsure where I was going. The nearest town was so far away: half-hour by boat, the next two hours by car along the logging road, then another hour down the highway. But in my dream I didn't have a car. Slowly I boated over the dark depths of water, wondering and wandering.

Eventually, I pulled into a small inlet and stepped onto shore. The boat, still running and not anchored, floated aimlessly away from me toward the middle of the water. Behind me, cedars and firs covered the mountain that ascended steeply from the shore. I climbed until I reached a high bluff overlooking the ocean. All the way to the distant horizon the Pacific rippled unbroken by land, except for the occasional outcrops of black rock populated by howling sea lions. I breathed deeply. The salt air scraped my insides. I felt it exfoliating the failures that lined my inner surfaces. The wind brushed hard against my cheeks and my hands. I removed my shirt and my pants to let the wind scour my whole body until my skin felt new again. Looking down, I remembered how much smaller and smoother my legs were when I was ten, and I thought it strange how I ever came to be this woman. I felt a stain on my soul, and so I waited for rain. I waited all morning and all afternoon and into the evening for the rain to come and cleanse my spirit.

It never came.

At dusk the clouds split apart and the indigo sky opened up to me. From here, along the edges of the world, I felt the line to God was clear and direct: there was no static, no bad signal, no other voices hogging the space. It was my voice I heard in my dream, and my voice alone speaking straight into God's ear. First I begged for forgiveness. Then I begged for redemption. I begged for the rain to come and wash the mark off my soul. I even begged for mercy though I believed I deserved none. Again I waited for something to happen—for rainfall, for a sign in the sky, for a divine tingle in my bones—and when nothing happened, I began to wonder if I was moving through life unnoticed by God. As the sky turned black I heard the wind whisper, and its words entered my ear and moved through my naked body.

I felt the hardening first in my marrow, and then in my muscles, starting at my toes and spreading up through my legs, my torso, my chest, my neck and finally my face. I struggled to breathe. I held out my hands and watched my skin turn into bark. Slowly my heart transformed into wood and my body stiffened. The wind swayed the branches that were my arms and toppled the rootless trunk that was my body. I plummeted over the bluff into the cold Pacific below and drifted toward the village all night long, staring up at the dark sky, seeing nothing except faint sparkles behind the thin clouds. Things moved past me and lurked beneath me, large bodies whose deep sonar sounds bounced off my bark skin. Sometimes I churned for over an hour inside an estuary, or I tangled in a kelp bed, or I snagged on a rocky outcrop. By morning I was cold and exhausted. For a short while it was as though I fell asleep inside my dream, and later I awoke to the face of a woman. The woman leaned over a stack of cardboard boxes from the deck of a boat, and as she stared at the two large knots that were my eyes, I could see in her face that she too was searching for something at the edges of the world.

*　　*　　*

I awoke to the sound of footsteps crunching up the road the next morning. Sitting upright in my bed, I could see Joan walking slowly past my trailer. Her face and her clothes were smudged black. She looked like a coal miner returning from a long shift, the whites of her eyes glowing against the contrast of her stained skin. Through the tops of the trees, the sun smouldered its deep amber flame at the edges of the sky. Quickly I pulled the window open and called for Joan, who stopped and looked around, dazed, until she spotted my head peeking out. Joan stared at me with the haunted eyes of somebody who had just seen demons.

"Wait there!" I called out.

Outside, I went to Joan, who hadn't moved from her spot on the road.

"What's the matter? What happened?" I asked.

Joan's voice sounded hoarse and lifeless. "There was a fire."

"Oh my god. Where?"

When Joan didn't answer, I guided her by the shoulders into the kitchen where I made a strong cup of instant coffee, the way she liked it. Black with a pinch of cinnamon. Meanwhile I remained silent, giving her a chance to gather her strength and her senses.

Joan spoke in a raspy whisper. "It was Sophie Florence's house."

I dropped into the chair opposite Joan.

"We tried," Joan said.

"Did anybody—?" I couldn't bring myself to ask.

Joan stared into her cup of coffee.

Fetching a towel from the bathroom, I dampened it with warm water and set it next to Joan in case she wished to clean off the soot that rimmed her eyelids. Up close I could see that the glowing whites of Joan's eyes were red with irritation.

"They were trapped. The roof collapsed. We couldn't get to them."

I gripped the edge of the table. My head rushed with questions I was too scared to ask. Was Odelia safe? Sophie Florence?

"All her brothers—" Joan took a deep, shaking breath. "They're gone."

I cupped my hand over my mouth. I didn't know any of Sophie Florence's brothers. I didn't know their names or what they looked like except for Ray and his musical appreciation for Beethoven, Vivaldi and Strauss.

"Odelia?" I uttered.

"Odelia was in the house with her uncles," Joan said.

My breath caught in my throat.

"She got out on her own. But her hands—" Joan scrubbed the damp towel over her face. "Her hands are burned. The doorknob, I think, when she hurried out of the house. Sophie Florence was playing bingo at the centre when the fire started."

"She's okay?"

"She's devastated," Joan said.

I went to the sink and dumped out my coffee. After several minutes of staring vacantly into the drain, I lifted my head and took a stick of charcoal out of the clamshell on the windowsill. I circled the tip into my palm until black dust adhered to my skin. I should have been thinking more of those poor men, of Sophie Florence's loss, of Odelia's loss, but for some reason all I could think about was how Odelia needed her hands for her art. Art was her refuge. It was how she made sense of the world around her. It was the thing that brought her joy. Turning on the faucet, I washed away the charcoal dust and dried my hand on a dish towel. A faint smudge of black remained on the towel and my hand.

"She's at the hospital?" I asked.

"Second-degree burns. Nurse was able to treat her at the outpost." Joan took a gulp of coffee. "It started just past eleven. That's when people started calling for help over the radio."

I remembered turning my VHF off because of Buttons.

"We knocked on your door. Loud."

Joan's tone had an edge to it. Was she accusing me of something? It wasn't as if I ignored her knocking on purpose. Was that what she thought? I had gone to bed early listening to ambient nature sounds on my small headphones. Roaring waves, chirping robins, babbling brooks. I couldn't be blamed for that, could I? I couldn't be blamed for falling into a deep sleep.

"We?" I asked.

"Me, Tim, Diane and Mr. Chapman," Joan said. "We even shouted for you outside your bedroom window."

My cheeks burned with shame that I had slept soundly in my cozy bed while everybody battled flames and tragedy. I plucked bits of beach glass out of the clamshell. "How did it start?"

"Who knows. Lots of theories, for sure. Some people are saying—" Joan stopped abruptly.

"What?" I asked. "Some people are saying what?"

Joan placed both palms flat on the table as if she were steadying herself. "Some people are saying it was Hannah."

"No. I don't believe that," I said, vigorously shaking my head.

"What's that old African proverb?" Joan's voice was clearing up with coffee. "A child not embraced by the village will burn it down to feel its warmth."

"No," I was still shaking my head. "People are desperate to make sense of things, that's all. Hannah wouldn't set fire to somebody's house. She wouldn't. I just know she wouldn't."

But I wasn't that naïve. I didn't know what Hannah might do. Nobody knew what Hannah might do. On the counter I placed the bits of smooth beach glass into a tiny blue and green mosaic house. I fidgeted with the arrangement, my hands shaky and restless.

"Other people are saying that Ray and his brothers hadn't put away their pictures of Grace's grandmother," Joan said. "And that if they were crying too much over her death, maybe she came back and took them with her on her journey."

I added a triangular fragment of white glass as a roof.

"But most people are blaming the spirits around the village," Joan added.

With my fingertip, I nudged the edges of the tiny glass mosaic house. Its cracks spread open, so I nudged it from the other side but the cracks spread in the other direction. I used both hands to pinch the construction tightly, but the pieces didn't fit flush. I turned to Joan, who had grown quiet again.

Joan gave me a look of doubt.

"What?" I asked softly.

"Look, I'm not saying for sure that I believe in this stuff, but if they're right, if there are spirits upset with the village—" Joan took a deep breath, her shoulders lifting high. Then she flapped her hand. "Never mind. I'm just exhausted is all. I can't think straight."

"No, tell me," I said. "If they're right, then what?"

"Then the spirits seem to also be upset with you."

Nodding slowly, I shoved the pieces of the glass house apart. Down the hill, doors had been knocked on by no one. Pictures had been bumped off walls by things unseen. Chairs had slid across rooms for invisible guests. And up the hill, two giant stones had appeared in front of my place. Not in front of Joan's place. Not Timothy's place. Not Mr. Chapman's place. Only my place. I brushed the glass house off the counter into my cupped palm, then sprinkled the pieces back into the clamshell along with the pea-sized shells and the grains of sand and the tiny pebbles, and it all reminded me of Loretta Joe, the cold tide who decided which sands of truth and which shells of lies spread across the shores. When Loretta Joe had asked Hannah if she should tell me about the people who were sent away to turn into trees, I had assumed Loretta was speaking about Hannah. But what if it had actually been about me? After all, Ernie said that the dark energy, sharp as broken glass, was coming from me. Certainly I hadn't made things better by not getting out of bed to assist the community during their greatest hour of need.

"It seems they are upset with me," I admitted, and this time I meant it.

*   *   *

After Joan left for home to shower and sleep, I turned on some music. Strauss's *The Blue Danube*. Beethoven's Symphony no. 5 in C Minor.

Vivaldi's *Four Seasons*. Wanting to tune out the world around me, I turned the speakers as loud as they would go. The four-note opening motif by Beethoven—that ominous da-da-da-duhhh with the fermata calling for an indefinite hold of the last note—reverberated off the grey walls and filled the empty spaces of my home. The sound of fate captured in four simple notes.

I went to the bathroom and ran the shower. In the mirror I looked at the glassy shadow of myself and I caught a fleeting glimpse of my purpose in life—that it was to serve others, and that I was failing miserably, only ever managing to serve myself even when I fooled myself into believing it was otherwise. I stepped into the icy cold shower, hoping to wash away this darkness that Ernie and his sister had seen in me. In the other room, the music changed to Vivaldi's *Four Seasons*. While I loved the punctuated drama of Beethoven's piece, I felt more drawn to the story that Vivaldi told of the seasons on Earth, the seasons of life. I shivered and listened to how the violins and cellos played in a way that sounded like flowing creeks and singing birds and I felt inside the music. Inside the music like this, I believed that since I could never know for certain if I was the one who caused the events in the village, I could never know whether my leaving would serve others or if my staying would serve others. Inside the music like this, I felt myself splitting into two different women. One woman was despair. One woman was hope. Two women at odds. Forever irreconcilable. For what could hope possibly ever say to change despair's mind? I knew how much Hannah needed me right now, and Grace too, when she returned, and I felt a connection to them both. Inside the music like this, I understood that I needed to stay and help Odelia, and for the first time since arriving in Tawakin, I understood how I could matter—and that it required that I not dwell on whether I did.

18

After the fire destroyed their house, Sophie Florence and Odelia moved into the old church beside the beach. Not a church with stained glass windows and pews. The walls were made of wood planks the colour of dried mud and the handful of people who came to worship used the same folding chairs for praying as for playing bingo. Except for those chairs, some old plates and pots in the tiny kitchen, and the Bibles stacked against the wall, the church was empty when they moved there. Everybody brought something: clothes, blankets, food, family photographs, towels, toothbrushes and an old mattress, which Sophie Florence put in the corner so they weren't in the way on Sunday mornings.

"That smells wonderful," I said. I stood with Odelia beside the church kitchen one afternoon while Sophie Florence slid bread pans out of the hot oven. "Doesn't it, Odelia?"

After the fire, Odelia took some time off school. To make sure that she didn't fall too far behind, I went down the hill every day after school to bring her the math lessons she missed. She was in discomfort, of course, but she was managing well and with the ointment she was given, she was healing and there was likely to be little scarring. Some of her life line on her right hand had burned away, but the nurse guaranteed her that it wouldn't have any impact on her actual life.

"Where should we work today?" I asked Odelia.

Odelia pointed her bandaged hand at the far corner next to the plastic yogurt containers filled with dead dandelions. Together we sat on the floor, leaning against the wall where the wind whipped through the cracks.

I opened the math textbook onto Odelia's lap and said, "The wind sounds like a howling dog," when in reality it sounded more like a long scream.

"It sounds like that song my grandfather liked so much," Odelia said, referring to Ray. "That one by Chopin," which Odelia pronounced "chopping."

Although I could not make out any discernible melody coming from the wind, I knew that Odelia's grief could conjure wishful thinking. Hallucinations. Even the serene mind was capable of finding meaning in randomness. Just like the pareidolia I often saw in the chance faces of tree trunks, Odelia was hearing her own special patterns in the world, in meaningless noise. Piano strings in the wind.

"My mother—" by whom Odelia meant her grandmother, Sophie Florence, "prayed all night for rain." Odelia lifted her bandaged hands so that I could turn the page of the textbook. "She told God I need to get cleansed."

"What you need," I smiled, "is to multiply these numbers."

"Numbers are boring."

I said, "Tomorrow we'll start geometry."

"Ay-ha, Teacher. More math?"

"But not just numbers," I said. "Shapes too."

Odelia grumbled, "Why can't we read a story?"

I didn't answer. All I wanted for Odelia right now was calm and peace and stability. Stories were words, and words were the fault lines between the conscious mind and what slipped beneath. Who could know what emotions would be loosened by even the simplest of tales? Story was conflict and friction and uncertainty.

It was the counsellor from Port Hardy who told me to bring normal things to Odelia's days. Katerina the counsellor was a serious yet optimistic woman who had visited the village regularly for the past ten years to work with the people. Since the fire, Katerina had come on the mail plane three times to meet Odelia inside a small office at the Tawakin Health and Wellness Centre where they talked and played games and did art therapy. Katerina would put a straw in Odelia's mouth and ask her to blow pictures into a plate of sand.

"It is good for Odelia to watch the little grains move under the blows of her own breath. It soothes her in here and in here," Katerina had pointed to her chest and her head as she spoke to Sophie Florence and me with her heavy Dutch accent. The three of us had sat together in the church a week earlier and spooned salmon onto fresh bread and drank tea. "Also the sand art is temporary, so Odelia can erase the whole thing and start over. That is good, yah? Freedom to express? I think this is true. But," she shrugged one shoulder, "I don't get the chance to decipher the drawings, you know? Children, they very much encrypt their selves in art."

"Has she told you yet?" Sophie Florence asked.

"How the fire started? Not a hint." Katerina sipped her tea. "Has she been eating well?"

"Hardly. Some days not at all," said Sophie Florence, her mouth full of fish and bread. She looked outside through the crack between the church doors where Odelia sat on the front step with a colander of snowball hydrangeas. "Do you think she'll ever tell you?"

"Eventually she'll find a way to tell her story," Katerina said.

"Maybe some things aren't meant for me to know," Sophie Florence said.

"Maybe Odelia doesn't know," I said.

"Maybe Odelia doesn't know that she knows," Katerina said.

We ate the rest of our sandwiches in silence. We slurped our tea and clinked our cups on their saucers while the wind whined through the seams in the walls. Through the crack in the door, I could see Odelia swaying back and forth as if dancing to music in her own head. All I could think about was how many cracks there were. Too many. And that strange smell of something foul in the air. No way would Child Protection Services put Grace in Sophie Florence's care now. Where could Grace go? Where could Sophie Florence and Odelia go?

Finishing her sandwich, Katerina sucked the mayonnaise off her fingertips and looked around the church. "Everywhere there are little flowers," she said. "Pretty."

"No, they're not," said Sophie Florence. "They're all dead."

I nodded at the pulpit. "Some are still alive."

"Barely," said Sophie Florence.

"Those hydrangeas in the bowl outside," said Katerina. "They're beautiful."

Sophie Florence snorted. "That temporary nurse replacing Bernie for a couple of weeks, she gave those to Odelia. Carolyn."

"Caroline," I corrected.

"Caroline," said Sophie Florence. "Rhymes with swine. Did I think I'd be able to keep Odelia's hands clean? Not only because of the burns but supposedly there's an outbreak of scabies, too. That's what that woman asked me. Can you believe that?" She looked at me. "Has Odelia ever come to school dirty? No, never. Of course I can take care of my own granddaughter. I can keep her hands clean. What kind of question is that?"

Katerina moved her teacup in a small circle and watched the specks of tea leaves swirl in the bottom of her cup. "I think there are only two kinds of questions. There are questions intended to understand, and there are questions intended to destroy."

Sophie Florence sighed. "There should be plenty of questions going on here. The RCMP came, but not much was investigated. Someone living on a reserve is ten times more likely to die in a house fire. The federal government doesn't even collect proper data. They see our houses as kindling."

Later, as Katerina headed back along the road to catch her float plane, I ran to catch up to her. In the aftermath of the fire, Hannah's sentence was still weighing heavily on my mind. Indeed, the fire and the murmurs of accusations blaming Hannah for starting it, which I refused to believe, convinced me that now was not the time to bring the sentence to anyone who could, accidentally or otherwise, leak that information down the hill.

Pulling the paper from my bag, I showed Katerina and explained how it came about. "I don't quite know what to do," I said. Then I clarified, "Well, I do, technically, and I am aware that I might have already put myself into a world of professional trouble by sitting on it up until now, but it's just such an unusual case. Isn't it?"

Katerina nodded. "It's not completely unheard of, but you're right, it's statistically very low. I've seen Hannah once before in my practice, but only once because her mother won't allow it. I can share one thing with you, though I can never say it with 100 percent certainty, and that's that I am quite confident she is not suffering any such abuse at home that would perhaps cause a copycat outburst like this."

Just then, the plane at the end of the dock started its propellers and the pilot waved at Katerina to board. Turning to me, she handed me a business card and said, "Call me if you need to." She started up the dock, then stopped and took a few hurried steps toward me. "I have hope for Hannah, and I should know. Hope is bred in my bones," she said with a smile. "I used to be a nurse before becoming a counsellor. Whether it be a dire prognosis, or a crippling injury, or a chronic illness, nurses aim to instill hope. Teachers—" She turned and nodded at the pilot who was tapping his watch. "Teachers, they aim to instill faith."

"Hope, too," I said.

"Perhaps. But what is hope without faith?" Katerina asked.

"Faith in what?"

"Faith in themselves, of course," Katerina said, turning to walk away. "Not an easy thing when your students suffer from trauma. Trauma in their personal lives. Trauma in their genetic makeup. And make no mistake, it's there. Whether they know it's there or not. Whatever the mind forgets or refuses to remember, you can always find the imprint of it, like a fossil, somewhere in the body."

*　　　*　　　*

"I'll finish two questions if you pick buttercups first," Odelia whispered to me a week later. Odelia looked at the mattress in the corner where

Sophie Florence sewed sequins, as she did every day, onto the black fabric draped over her legs. "I want to put them around the bed so she can see how they light up like candles at night."

I tapped the textbook. "First the questions, then the flowers."

Initially, Odelia had asked me to gather the flowers out of the goodness of my heart, but soon she bargained. She offered two geometry problems in exchange for the last of the daisies on the school field. She finished one page of sums for the golden buttons we put in Dixie cups along the kitchen counter. She subtracted numbers for rattlesnake root from the stream at the Mossy Spot. Eventually we traded arithmetic for floral arrangements each day: tansies among the mouse turds, hawks-beak on top of the Bibles, wild roses on the cedar pulpit. This growing collection for me was torture and I only imagined it to be worse for Odelia. I thought how only a couple of weeks ago Odelia was drawing flowers instead of just sticking them in containers only to watch them wilt and die. But there they were, right there in the corner and on the pulpit and the windowsills, and I knew what I felt was guilt. Guilt for not helping with the house fire spread like a stain inside me, and I did not want it; it was of no use to Odelia.

Today I finally asked Odelia, "What do you want so many weeds for?"

"If you want to collect something," Sophie Florence said before Odelia could answer me, "let's get over to Toomista and find us those teeth."

"Teeth?" I asked, startled.

"For our dance shawls," Sophie Florence explained.

I nodded, pretending to understand what she meant.

"I can't go on a boat," said Odelia. "Nurse Caroline said—"

"Never mind what that nurse said, she don't know anything about it," Sophie Florence mumbled, holding a needle between her lips as she unspooled an arm's length of thread. She then took the needle from her mouth, moistened the end of the thread and poked it through the eye of the needle. "You're supposed to do normal things, that's what Katerina said. Besides, you could use some fresh air. I'll wrap your hands up good and tight so they keep safe."

"Can Teacher come, too?" Odelia asked. "But only if there's no math."

"Why not?" Sophie Florence shrugged. "We'll go tomorrow."

After Odelia finished her homework, Sophie Florence stood in the middle of the church and asked Odelia to sit in the chair there. I took the textbook from Odelia's lap and helped her to her feet. Sophie Florence swiped her hands across her apron, and flour as fine as ash puffed into the air. She pulled a pair of scissors from the breast pocket as Odelia stepped across the creaky floor, moving slowly through one of the four banners of sunshine that stretched from the windows. Dust motes floated in the light.

"Can I keep the purple parts?" Odelia asked before she sat down.

The ends of Odelia's black hair, which were twisted into two long braids that reached the small of her back, looked as though they had been dipped in purple, the ends not yet grown out of an old dye job.

"Sorry, little bebba," said Sophie Florence, "the purple parts have to go."

"Please," said Odelia. "I like it. I look like a fox."

"A fox?" Sophie Florence smiled at me.

"Uh-huh," said Odelia. "Nurse Caroline said so."

Sophie Florence frowned. "That nurse said you look like a fox?"

"It's a flower," Odelia said. She sat facing me.

"A foxglove?" I asked.

Odelia wrinkled her nose, no.

"Phlox?" asked Sophie Florence.

"Phlox," Odelia nodded. "I like those flowers. They spin at your feet."

"Uh-huh," said Sophie Florence, lifting Odelia's braids and letting them fall down the back of the chair. "Sit up straight, bebba."

"You going to do it real short?" Odelia asked.

"Yes, bebba."

I moved to the pulpit where I stood fidgeting with the Bible there. I couldn't bear looking straight at Odelia while Sophie cut off her locks. Her phlox. Sophie Florence worked the scissors through one of

Odelia's thick braids, the blades brushing against the nape of her neck. I scratched my fingernail against the corner of the Bible, fanning the pages like a deck of cards, as I listened to Odelia's faint whimpers and sniffs, the scissor blades scraping and snapping together.

The braid fell, and the pink bobbles on the elastic, still wrapped around the braid, clattered on the floor. I was stunned at how short Sophie Florence had cut Odelia's hair, that she just lopped off the entire braid like that. After both braids were cut and the loose hairs swept off the back of Odelia's shirt, Sophie Florence sat in the chair and held the scissors up to me.

"Cut mine," she told me.

"What? But why?"

"This is what we do," she said. "After a loss."

I felt a rush of anxiety. Please don't make me, I thought. Nonetheless I walked behind Sophie Florence, taking the scissors as I passed, and looked down at the long hair flowing in gentle waves. Black, streaked with silver. Smelling of soap and salmon and bread.

I draped a thin veil of hair over my palm and snipped along the bottom. It sprinkled to the floor beside the braids that lay twisted like dead branches.

"Don't be shy," Sophie Florence said. "Grab it and chop it off. All of it."

Hesitantly I grabbed a fistful of hair. Some of it got stuck between the blades. I wriggled and tugged the scissors until they came free, several long strands still wrapped around the blades. At the ends of these strands were white follicles, pulled out from under Sophie Florence's scalp like bulbs fresh from the earth.

"I'm so sorry," I said.

Sophie Florence rubbed the sore spot and touched the ends I had cut.

"Shorter," she said.

I cut until Sophie Florence's hair was no longer than her thumb.

"Shorter," she said.

Resting the blades against her head, I cut more.

"Shorter," Sophie Florence said.

"But I can see your scalp," I said.

"Good. The greater the loss, the shorter you cut."

*   *   *

Early that evening we took Sophie Florence's skiff to Sennick River. Again, Odelia begged for me to come along, and it warmed my heart that she had and that Sophie Florence agreed. Their hair filled a plastic bag. The river was only ten minutes up the coast from the village. When we arrived there, the estuary was a swirling mess of colliding currents as the outflowing river wrestled the incoming tide. Sophie Florence cranked the throttle to motor through it. Upstream, where the current was gentler, we stopped and dropped the small anchor. Overhead the curved hemlocks leaned away from the banks, leaving only a narrow strip of sky visible.

Sophie Florence untied the plastic grocery bag and turned it upside down over the side of the skiff. The hair—Odelia's pink-bobbled braids and Sophie Florence's loose tresses—spilled onto the water. As I watched it turn slowly in the current, I thought of Sophie Florence's buoyancy, and Odelia's too, and how they kept afloat under the weight of life in a remote village where houses were built like shanties and fire services meant a hose in a wood box at the corner of the dirt road and where the losses numbered like the hairs on a woman's head. A thousand strands of lost childhoods, lost histories, lost traditions, lost Nuu-chah-nulth words, lost lives.

Daylight started to sink near the horizon, the trees turning black, masking the red sun like thick smoke hiding fire. Sophie Florence pulled up the anchor, started the motor and headed downstream. Near the mouth of the river, the serpentine strands of black hair were picking up speed, uncurling and lengthening, flowing to the ocean.

19

The next day was Saturday, and when I arrived at the church mid-morning, Sophie Florence handed me two squares of folded black fabric and said, "Can you help spread these out for me? It'll give us an idea how many teeth we need."

Together Sophie Florence and I spread out the two shawls while Odelia watched. On each shawl there was a large eagle, its unfurled wings glinting with red and silver sequins. Sophie Florence crouched down and examined an eagle's head, which was undecorated except for an outline of white sequins, estimating how many teeth were needed to fill both heads.

"Definitely going to take more than one trip over the next year," she said, walking back to the small kitchen area where she handed me a jar filled with tiny translucent balls. "*Kwaqmis*, for when we get hungry."

We took Sophie Florence's little skiff, flashing with silver salmon scales and coughing out blue and grey smoke. I sat on the middle bench facing the front and Odelia sat near the bow facing me. Sophie Florence steered slowly through the cove, past the houses along the shoreline, past the smoking huts and the skulls of rotting *muwach* flesh that hung over shed doors, past the edge of the village where I could see the top of the old church poking out over the blackberry brambles on the low ridge.

"Feels chilly today," I said.

"Lucky I got little flames in my pocket," Odelia said. Both her hands were wrapped in bandages and sealed inside grocery bags to keep out the sand and salt. With her plastic paws she patted the bulging pockets of her denim shorts. Yellow dandelion heads, flattened and wilted, stuck out the top. "They keep my legs real warm."

I smiled at her wild imagination.

"But you can't have none," Odelia said. "They're just for me."

As Sophie Florence moved the skiff through the narrow mouth of the cove, I asked Odelia, "What's the difference if the temperature was ten yesterday and seven today?"

"It's colder today," Odelia said.

"How many colder?"

"I don't know, Teacher. Four? Three? Three. Also, I said no math today. Remember?"

As we left the cove and started across the open Pacific, Odelia's short tufts of black hair spread out and flattened in the wind like pressed flowers. When I squinted at the watery horizon, white as whalebone in the sun, and at the wrinkled ocean that surrounded us, I half expected to see Odelia's pink-bobbled braids float past. But there were only beds of kelp and otters and three small islands in the near distance.

"What is that?" Odelia asked. She shook one of the Safeway bags on her hands, then peered closely to see through the thin, white plastic. "Brussels sprouts? Yuck!"

"Careful, Odelia," Sophie Florence said. "If that bandage comes undone we might have to go back to the clinic, and we don't got enough gas for that."

"But there's gross pieces of old food in this bag—rotten Brussels sprouts or something. See?" She stuck out her arm. "Plus," she said, "you tied the knots on these bags too tight around my wrists. It pinches. And," she lifted the other hand to her nose and took a big sniff, "in case you didn't know, this bag stinks like pickles. Also, did you forget? Nurse Caroline says I'm not supposed to get my hands—"

"But I say different," Sophie Florence said.

The shadow of Waas Island, the first in the triangle of islands, slipped over the skiff. As we entered the narrow channel between the towering sea stack and the stone cliff on the corner of the island, the water became glassy and shallow. Sophie Florence cranked the throttle down, slowing the skiff so suddenly that the jar of fish eggs rolled off my legs and landed inside a coil of rope. Odelia almost slipped off her seat. Some of the dandelions spilled out of her pockets and tumbled into the murky finger of water in the middle of the hull.

"Check that side, Odelia. Tell me if we get too close to the rocks," Sophie Florence said.

I also searched the surface for shadows. Spectres of eelgrass swayed silently under the boat.

Sophie Florence called out. "Odelia? Did you hear me?"

Odelia looked at the dandelions. "I was saving those special."

"We'll get more," I shrugged.

"But I wanted those ones."

"Then we'll dry them out on the rocks when we get to Toomista," I said.

"No," Odelia said. "They've gone out. They're no good no more."

✳   ✳   ✳

The teeth, according to Sophie Florence, always washed onto the northeast shore of Toomista Island, but we dragged the skiff onto the south beach where the tide didn't churn and froth but drifted gently onto the rippled sand.

"I want those ones," said Odelia. She was surveying the field above the ridge of the beach. A river of flowering thistles snaked between the abandoned houses.

"Then let's go get some," I said. "Seize the day. *Carpe diem*."

"I don't like carp," Odelia said matter-of-factly. "Only salmon."

I laughed, then looked once more at the flowering thistles on the field above us. I said, "They'll look nice in the church."

"They're stars," Odelia said. "We'll put them in the windows at night."

Odelia and I walked across carpets of dried kelp and around logs of driftwood to the field while Sophie Florence remained on the beach to collect beach glass while she waited for us. The windows of the houses were dark and empty as usual. Eye sockets of weathered skulls. The ashes in the fire pit where we had burned elder Candice's creations had been flattened by rain. Odelia sat on the bottom step of a house beside the jar of fish eggs and poked her toe into the split seam of an old abandoned doll while I ripped flowers off thistles and tossed them into a fish bucket.

"Sometimes stars explode, right Teacher?" Odelia said.

"Some do, yes. When they die," I said.

Once we had collected enough flowering thistles, we walked with Sophie Florence around the corner of the shoreline to the low-lying steps of black basalt. At the top, Odelia pointed with her plastic paw to the strip of beach below. Two walls of rock formed a small canyon in which the rising tidal water sucked and swelled. A giant choir of wind whistled below.

"The teeth are down there," Sophie Florence said. Out of her pocket she pulled out a shell and held it up for me to see, pinching it lengthwise at its ends between her index finger and thumb. "Dentalium. Tooth shell. Indian money, we also call it, on account of it being used for trading. Usually they're a bit smaller than this beauty, about the length of a fork tine and not much wider, pointed and curved slightly. Some a bleached white like this one, but lots of other ones are stained green. No matter. You should know, it can be pretty frustrating searching for them. It's real easy to mistake an urchin spine or tiny triton for the teeth."

We descended the stone steps to a dry patch of shore above the tideline. The ground was a deep and dessicated mixture of small minerals and skeletons: smooth chips of seashells and mauve urchin spines, pockmarked pieces of coral and broken bits of bone, smooth shards of glass in blues and greens, the paper-thin crusts of crabs, shreds of sponge, ribbons of dried seaweed.

I set the bucket of flowers on the ground and kneeled down. The loose mixture gave way to the shape of my knees. Sophie Florence picked a spot about fifty feet farther up the shoreline. I plunged my hands down deep and gathered armloads of the beach, pouring it into a pile. The tumbling pieces clicked like children's play money or midsummer dragonflies. Sweeping away the pile one thin layer at a time, I scanned the shapes for teeth. I scooped handfuls of the broken mosaic into my cupped palms, sifting it between my fingers.

"Are you paying attention, Odelia?" I asked.

Odelia didn't answer. She squatted next to the bucket of thistles.

"Odelia, you're supposed to be helping us look."

But she ignored me and continued to gaze into the bucket.

After another fifteen minutes of searching, I asked her, "You hungry?"

"Yes," said Odelia. She rocked backward off her haunches so that she sat in the sand. The wind rustled the plastic bags on her hands, which rested limply over her thighs.

"Sophie Florence!" I called out, waving the jar of fish eggs. "Hungry?"

Looking up from her stooped position, Sophie Florence shook her head and went back to sifting the beach.

Sitting next to Odelia, I unscrewed the lid on the jar of fish eggs. There was no spoon, so I blew sand off a broken piece of a clam shell and used it to scoop up some of the tiny translucent balls. I lifted it up to Odelia, who closed her small lips over the shell and pulled the eggs into her mouth. As Odelia chewed the salty roe, she looked at the rock walls below. They were capped with a rippling carpet of dried grasses and swaying blots of red petals open wide to the sun. I lifted another spoonful of eggs to Odelia's mouth. This time Odelia took it without looking, her eyes focused on the tops of the rock walls.

"Those ones glow red," she said after swallowing.

I turned and watched the flowers shift in the wind, soft blurs of crimson. "Maybe when your hands are better you can draw a picture of those flowers," I said. "Instead of math."

"Instead of math?"

"Instead of math."

"I could write a story about them and make pictures. Could I do that?"

"Yes," I agreed. "You can write a story about them."

"I'm going to start thinking up my story today." Odelia smiled and took another mouthful of roe. Her lips smacked with chewing as she pointed to the ground. "Look, there. Right there."

"Where?" I put down the jar.

"Right there. No, there!"

Finally I saw it. A large dentalium, nearly as long as my thumb, a hollow shell curved slightly and tapered to a point. The tooth shells would represent the feathers on the eagle's head, and when it came time for the memorial potlatch in a year, Sophie Florence and Odelia would wear these shawls to dance and celebrate life. Maybe this was the gift of mercy that kept Sophie Florence and Odelia afloat under the weight of tragedy: this ability to transform one thing into something else. Sorrow into stories, tooth shells into celebration, haircuts into catharsis, rain into purification, flowers into stars that light the night.

Odelia said, "We'll need lots more to fill the head. And don't ask me to guess how many more, Teacher. The answer is lots more."

Something in Odelia's words made me think of the large beads of rain that knocked against the woman's hollow skull and spilled into her gaping mouth and along the ridge of her broken teeth. As I thought of this, I found myself fabricating a connection between Odelia's hands and Hannah's hands, and once that connection had been made, I could not let go of the question forming in my mind. How many children had found her?

Watching Odelia's face closely, I said, "Maybe we'll find a silver tooth for the eagle's head."

Odelia did not hestitate to answer. "We won't find it here."

"Maybe a wood tooth, then."

"Won't find that here either," she said in a surprisingly casual tone.

"Where would we find them?" I asked.

Now Odelia said nothing.

"Do you have them, Odelia?"

"Have what?"

"The teeth," I said. "The wood one and the silver one."

Odelia set her plastic paws on her hips. "Did you know that dandelions are called that because their skinny petals look like the teeth of a lion?"

I smiled. "I didn't know that. So, do you?"

"Do I what?"

"Have the teeth. The wood one and the silver one."

Odelia sighed impatiently. "You can't have both of them. It's impossible. They don't work properly if you have both. You have to choose only one."

"Why can't you take both?"

Odelia sighed again. "You have to choose. You can become whatever you want or you can get whatever you want. You can't have both."

"I see," I said. "Which one did you choose?"

"I don't got even one of the teeth," Odelia said.

"Who does?"

Odelia shrugged one shoulder. "Don't know."

"If I had the teeth, I know which one I'd choose," I said.

Odelia lifted her face as though curious.

"Not the silver one. I wouldn't choose to get whatever I wanted. Sure, it might sound like fun," I said, thinking about how much Grace wanted to get her mother back. "Having things, especially if they're things that aren't right for you, can end up feeling like a prison. So I would choose the wood tooth. That way, I could become whatever I wanted."

Odelia said, "That's what I was going to choose, too."

"But the teeth weren't there, were they?"

Odelia lowered her face.

"You can still have hope, Odelia," I said. "You can still choose to become whatever you want. Even without the tooth."

Odelia shrugged, looking unconvinced.

"Did you go with Hannah?" I asked.

"She went by herself," Odelia said softly.

"Did you also go by yourself?"

Odelia's mouth, wrenching into a look of shame, gave her away. Had she seen my drawings there? I pressed, "Did you also go?"

Odelia didn't answer, her eyes cast down at the sand.

I tried a different line of questioning. "Do you think Hannah has one of the teeth?"

"Somebody has them," Odelia said with a trace of bitterness.

I lightened my tone of voice. "Which tooth do you think Hannah would choose?"

"She said she liked the story about the Devil best."

"Because he was so powerful? Or because he was so clever?"

"She felt bad for him. Because he was kicked out of Heaven. Nobody wanted him." Odelia paused. Her mouth trembled. "Do you think I started the fire because I looked for those teeth? Do you think I started the fire with my flowers because I didn't show *isaak* for the dead?"

I screwed my face up in confusion. "What?"

Odelia held out her plastic paws and examined them, front and back. Then she said, "I don't want to talk about this no more."

I nodded, then turned back to my search in the sand. My thoughts moved like the tide, back and forth, wondering who else had found the woman, who else knew which of the children had gone, who else knew for certain that I had gone. I wondered if it was *numak* that put that rock in front of my house, and *numak* that caused the fire, and *numak* that took Grace away from her home, and *numak* that damaged both Odelia's and Hannah's hands.

Bits of something white fluttered past my head and interrupted my thoughts. I looked up to see Odelia standing on top of the basalt steps with the bucket by her feet. She scooped out some of the flowering thistles with her plastic paws and tossed them high into the air.

"Look, the stars are falling!" Odelia shouted. She launched another bunch into the air and watched them spiral to the ground. "That's what I'm going to make my picture story about, when my hands are better.

Instead of math."

"About falling stars?" I asked.

"About a girl who lives in a special castle," said Odelia. "Because she's a princess but she's sad because she can't go outside because there's something wrong with her."

"What's wrong with her?"

Crouching to gather the flowers off the ground, Odelia paused and squinted her eyes. "I haven't thought up that part yet."

The wind started to blow harder, whipping around the trees that crowded the middle of the island. It pushed some of the flowers down the steps and sent a spray of sand across the shore.

"Some people bring the princess presents so she can have the outside inside," said Odelia. "Let's see. She gets flowers, lots of flowers, and she plants them in the carpet and when they grow they spin in colours at her feet. Sometimes it even rains flowers! And trees, too. Those big crying trees—"

"Weeping willows?" I asked.

"Yup, weeping willows with branches like this—" Odelia made sweeping motions with her arm like she was outlining the spokes of an umbrella. "They bring her stars and then she has the whole sky inside her castle and the silver stars go whizzing over her couches and over her chairs and then they die. But the presents are a secret. They're just for her. The end."

Sophie Florence had since moved farther down the shoreline away from us. She sat in the sand and studied the bits of beach cupped inside her palm.

"Do the presents come from her great-uncles?" I asked. Then I corrected myself. "From her grandpas?"

Odelia nodded.

"Her *naqcuu* grandpas?" I asked.

Odelia nodded again.

I drew in a long breath. I had the urge to sprint along the shoreline through the deep, dessicated sand and shells and grab Sophie Florence to hear Odelia's story. But I didn't want to disrupt the moment for fear that Odelia might not tell her story again. Presents from Sophie Florence's brothers. I thought how Katerina was right. Children, they encrypted their inner selves in their art. I imagined the pictures Odelia would draw for her story, now knowing that sometimes flowers were just flowers, and sometimes flowers were stars in the night. And sometimes flowers were ground spinners and flying spinners, spitting fountains and jumping jacks, palm trees and spider's legs and horsetails encased in cardboard, dry waterfalls of red and Bengal fires of blue burning potassium nitrate and copper; sometimes they were Catherine wheels and delicate, lacey Saxons, and repeaters that ignite tiny mortars, and magnesium rods that flicker and sparkle, and Roman candles with small, bursting balls of light. They were artificial satellites, celestial bonfires, drunken displays of fireworks inside a clapboard castle, pyrotechnic supernovas exploding into tinderboxes of carpet and curtains and couches while Beethoven and Vivaldi and Strauss played.

Odelia smiled proudly. "Pretty good story, right Teacher?"

"Yes, it is quite the story," I said.

I took a moment to gaze at the mounds of sand where all those teeth were buried among the other husks of life deposited on these shores each day and I remembered the resolve I had felt in that icy cold shower, when my purpose in life had come to me clear and sudden. I had been sure about myself in that thin slice of time like never before, and as I stepped toward Odelia, I tried hard to feel as sure again. Hesitantly, I lifted my arms, then put them down, then raised them again and wrapped them around Odelia. I felt her small arms wrap around my waist, the plastic bags on her hands rustling against the back of my jacket, and as I hugged the girl with my whole heart, relief washed over me. The fire was not started by Hannah. Not by angry spirits either. I thought about the careless fire and I felt how alive Odelia felt in my arms. I didn't stop. I didn't let go. I kept holding on to this girl, and I imagined the energy of my care, which was not at all a dark energy like Ernie claimed but a radiant one, sure as can be, warming Odelia like sunlight, blooming her like a flower.

It was many hours later when I returned home, first sitting with Sophie Florence in the church to share Odelia's story with her, but not before first fetching Gina, Lizzie and Margaret so that Sophie Florence could have all the support she might need. Once I had finally returned home, I found myself restless and needing to stay busy, so I decided to move the chickens from my classroom to their new coop. I carried out this task on my own, walking back and forth across the road fifteen times with a chicken in my arms. Moving the chickens to the coop was not straightforward. The birds grew nervous in their new setting, and the next morning I got up early so that they could hear the comfort of my familiar voice when they awoke. I wanted to be there to reassure them that everything was okay, knowing that they would feel disoriented when they woke up in a strange place. With a soothing voice, I talked to the chickens, telling them how well they were doing in their new coop, promising them that they were safe in their sturdy little house. Like every good teacher, I did a head count and took attendance of all the Henriettas. As I opened the door leading to the caged run, the chickens peeked out, apprehensive to walk down the narrow ramp. Eventually, with my encouragement, they all emerged into the world.

20

Meet the Teacher Night started at six o'clock the next night, but most parents didn't show up until well past seven-thirty. The students came, too—some of them looking eager to show their parents around the classroom, others less so. I was stunned that the event was still happening in light of the recent tragedy, but Mr. Chapman said that it would be good for the parents, and I got the distinct sense that while tragedies devastated the community, they were embedded in the soil of Tawakin life, and as such, life mostly carried on as usual. Of course, typical of any parent-teacher night, only those parents who didn't need to come showed up. Which meant, primarily, that neither Chase nor Patty was there. Other parents used their absence as an opportunity to complain that Hannah frightened the other children. They spoke of how Hannah had tormented the other children recently by circling her boat around them in the cove and how if something wasn't done about Hannah soon, one of the other children was going to get seriously injured. They even discussed holding a community meeting to vote on whether Hannah should leave the village. But not all the comments I overheard were about Hannah.

"Look at this. Michael's not doing too well in science."

"Better the truth than those fake grades most kids get here."

"That's right. An A in Tawakin is a C out in town."

"My oldest daughter tried going to college. She got laughed at by the professor, that's what she told me when she came back home. I wish the school done a better job of getting her ready."

"This school is the worst."

"For real."

"I heard she yells at the students."

"She better not."

My spirit cracked into shards. I wanted to defend myself, but I couldn't risk getting in a public dispute with parents, and anyway the commotion of so many different conversations and comments made it impossible to address them all. I wanted to say, do you all know how close I've come to quitting? Is that what you want? Another teacher to leave your children? The complaints were hurtful enough to hear. But that I yell? I never yelled. I tried to hold on to Joan's pep talk from earlier that day. Don't take their comments personally, she had advised. No matter how good the school became, Joan added, the parents would never stop blaming the teachers. Where else could they find a scapegoat for the struggles of the community and the troubles in the homes? To make things worse, Joan explained, there had been a long history at the school of blatantly racist teachers and principals. And all their students were related to somebody who went to residential school.

All of a sudden one of the dads called out to me from across the room:

"Teacher, you been getting the knocking on your door?"

"Yeah, Teacher," another man asked, "you had any weird stuff happen?"

"No," I replied, perhaps too quickly, too brusquely. "Nothing at all."

"How did those rocks get at your place, then?" a woman asked.

All the parents stopped what they were doing and stared at me.

I tried not to look flustered. "I don't know," I said.

"What'd you do, Teacher? You do something bad?"

"No." Again, the word came out of my mouth too forcefully.

A man smiled at another man. "I think Teacher did something bad."

A woman near me murmured what sounded like, "She never even came down the hill to help with the fire."

I wasn't certain what she had said until someone else asked, "Yeah, Teacher. How come you never came? You too busy to come help us out?"

I wiped my sweating palms on the sides of my pants. I shifted my gaze around the room, trying to keep my composure as I decided how to respond. Finally I said, "I'm sorry. I really am. Truth was, I was dead asleep," and immediately I cringed and wished I had chosen a better word than *dead*.

A man with a friendly face wiggled his eyebrows. "You hiding a man up there, Teacher? Is that what's getting you so tired?"

The room erupted with laughter.

My face burned hot with embarrassment. While I was horrified that something so sexual about me had been said in front of students, I was thankful for the comic relief more than anything.

"Better start getting more sleep, Teacher," the man with the friendly face said. "Because *something* must be making you real tired."

I wanted to scream. I wanted to say, "Yes, I am tired. Of course I am tired. All day long I plan and I prepare and I think about little else except your children. And then I teach. I teach and I worry. I worry about your children. I worry I am not enough."

Instead, I just looked at the man and smiled.

✳   ✳   ✳

After the last of the parents had finally left Meet the Teacher Night and I had finished putting my classroom back to normal, I went into the office to check my pigeonhole before leaving. The lights in the office were off, but the glow of light coming out of Mr. Chapman's open door illuminated the main office. When he saw me, he waved me over enthusiastically and asked how the evening went as I entered his office.

"Pretty good," I said, not wishing to bring up the small inquisition about the stones in front of my house or my failure to assist with the fire. I stood just inside the doorway and rested my arm on the top of the filing cabinet. I motioned at the book splayed open face down on his desk. "What's that you're reading?"

"Plato," he said.

"Pegged you more of a Spinoza guy," I joked.

Mr. Chapman pointed his index finger upward. "Consider this," he said. "Can one apple be less of an apple than another apple?"

"I don't think so," I said. "An apple is an apple."

"What if the apple changes somehow," he asked.

"It's still an apple," I said.

"How about a child? Can one child be less of a child than another child?"

"Of course not," I said.

Mr. Chapman squinted one eye. "Are you certain? One child cannot have more essence of child-ness than another?"

"No, one child can't," I said. "I am certain."

"A child is a child is a child. Is that what you're saying?"

"Yes, that is what I'm saying."

"Interesting. And yet—" he cut himself off as he pointed at the top of the filing cabinet.

Next to my elbow was a glass frame standing upright. Inside the glass frame was a tiny hand-drawn map. "What's this?" I asked, picking it up to study it closer.

"That is a map I drew of Bodder," he explained. "You'll note the school and my house labelled at one end of the town, Louise's Store, the Super A and Suicide Hill at the other end."

It was a very rudimentary map, hardly better than a child could make. Unsure what he was hoping I'd make of it, I continued to examine it with feigned interest.

"See that X on the road near the school?" he asked.

"Yes."

"That was where I saw the boy that morning."

I shook my head. "The boy?"

"It was nearly nine in the morning. But the sky was still black. Not a hint of sun. I couldn't see much of anything through the jaundiced halo of the streetlight and the heavy snowflakes that flecked my vision with white every time I blinked. At first I thought the boy was a dog, the way he scrambled over the snowbank on all fours. But it was a boy I saw, I'm certain of it now, and truth be known I was certain of it then, too, only I'd refused to believe at the time that any child would dare go outside, not the day after Louise's body had returned to town."

"Louise, the store owner?" I confirmed as I slipped into the chair on the other side of his desk, setting the framed map on my lap. "The one who died by suicide?"

Mr. Chapman nodded. "None of my students attended school that week. I was still required to show up for work, of course, and so I sat in my classroom alone every day as the morning bell rang and was followed by silence, no clamour of chairs and swearing and Mr. Chapman this and Mr. Chapman that, not since all the children in Bodder were quarantined to their homes in order to protect their soft, loose souls. It was a boy I saw that morning, and in all probability I couldn't have seen that the boy's feet were bare, not from where I stood half a block down the street, but I was convinced that was exactly what I saw, not only his feet but his toes. How they were blackening with frostbite."

"Oh my gosh. Who was it?" I asked.

"Tomas Whitehead." He enunciated the boy's name carefully. "Tomas, it turned out, had become so hopeless that he ran away and hid all day and all night in a tree well in the snow on Suicide Hill. It was minus thirty-seven that night. When they finally found him, he had a bad case of hypothermia. He almost died. They managed to nurse him back to health at the clinic, but his feet. The frostbite had killed his flesh. Why didn't he have boots on? He had a thick wool hat and many layers of sweaters, two pairs of mitts, long johns, a snowmobile suit over top of it all. All that and no socks, no shoes or boots? It made no sense. Anyways, he was shipped out to the hospital up in Whitehorse so they could monitor the frostbite. In the first few weeks it's difficult to tell the difference between good tissue and dead tissue after a frostbite injury, so I was hopeful. They waited eight weeks before deciding that amputation was the only option. The gangrene was going to spread. You know what he told his foster mother? And all the nurses? You know what he told everyone who visited him?"

I shook my head slowly. My voice was still breathy. "No. What?"

"He told them that he ran away because the homework that night was too much. It was too much. I had put so much pressure on a child that he thought his only choice was to run away in the dead of winter. On a night when evil spirits were gathered in town around Louise's body. I took a child with hope and I made him hopeless."

The quiet that followed fell heavily. The ticking of the clock on the wall in the front office filled the empty space, making it painfully obvious that I didn't know what to say in response to his story. It had taken a turn that I was not expecting.

Finally Mr. Chapman broke the silence. "Anyway, I was broken after that. Was certain I would never want to be inside a school again. But instead I went the other way. I burnt myself out trying to help, fix, save, build hope in every kid in my class. I tried every way I could think up. I experimented. I spent my evenings poring over research to find new methods. I became so obsessed I lost all hold on myself." He exhaled a long breath, letting his lips flap together. He straightened a calculator on his desk. "But really, what does it matter what I saw or didn't see? The point was that I thought it was real yet I did nothing. I didn't call for the boy. I didn't follow him. I just stood there, frozen. There are few things in this world more agonizing than regret, especially when that regret has to do with a child and how you failed. It's a barbed quill that can't ever be pulled back out of the flesh."

21

The next night I awoke to a thunderous clatter. At first I thought it had come from the VHF radio. As my senses grew sharper, I realized it came from the baby monitor perched on my dresser. There was no mistaking the frantic flapping of wings, the terrorized sounds of squawking. Something was wrong with the chickens. The squawking rose to a high-pitched crescendo as things or bodies crashed into the walls and floor of the coop. I stared wide-eyed into the dark, the only light coming from the tiny red dot on the baby monitor. I remained there, listening, unsure what to do. Then the squawks quieted. Some of the frantic sounds faded into the distance while some cut off suddenly, like a switch had been flicked. There was no way I was going out into the dark not knowing what had caused such a wild frenzy.

In the morning, I went to the kitchen window to see the coop door hanging from its hinges. Smears of brown and red marked the outside walls and the ground in front of the door. A snowy bed of feathers spread across the long grass.

I couldn't be sure that whatever had done this wasn't still inside that coop. I got dressed and knocked on Joan's door. No more than ten minutes later, Joan and I stood in front of the chicken coop.

"That's definitely blood," Joan said, looking at the outer walls of the chicken coop. Then she pointed to the grass near the road. "There are streaks of blood up there, too."

"Do you think they're all dead?" I asked.

"Only one way to find out."

Slowly we inched toward the coop door. I listened for any sign of movement. When we reached the doorway, we both peered into the dim space. With the exception of feathers, hundreds of which stuck to viscous smears of blood on the walls and floors and in the nesting boxes, the coop was empty. A chicken foot was on the floor. On the chicken wire next to my head was something that looked like a small eyeball.

"What am I going to tell the children?" I asked.

"Shhh!" Joan put her finger to her lips. Her eyes darted around as she listened. Leaning back, Joan looked around the corner of the coop into the woods. "Hear that?"

I cupped a hand around my ear. Tiny bursts of high-pitched cries came from the woods. "What is that?"

"Survivors."

I followed Joan along the rock face. We found a spot easy to climb and ascended up the rocks to the woods. I volunteered to check along the perimeter of the woods, leaving Joan to bravely search inside the forest. We both walked as softly as we could but the ground was covered in things that crackled and snapped. With every noise our footsteps made, me on the outside of the forest and Joan nearby on the inside, I heard frightened squawks.

"There!" Joan called.

I could see her just through the trees. She motioned for me to circle one way while she went the other. We hid behind two trees. Joan signalled a count of three with her fingers. Leaping out of our hiding spots at the same moment, we pounced upon the chicken, which flapped and cried out as we held onto it tightly.

"What do we do with it?" I asked. "The coop is useless now."

Joan squinted in thought. "I've got an idea. But you're not going to like it."

Inside my trailer, we put the chicken into my empty bathtub and closed the door. Then we headed back out to the woods in search of more survivors. After two hours of searching and cornering chickens in the woods, we had managed to rescue four out of the fifteen chickens. The rest, we assumed, had perished.

"So," I said as we stood outside the closed bathroom door and listened to the traumatized chickens try to settle in the bathtub, "think I could shower at your place tomorrow morning?"

"We'll see," Joan teased.

Later that afternoon, Joan made an arrangement with Nurse Bernadette, who was about to head back from visiting her sister in Duncan, that the chickens could be relocated to her nurse's outpost on Hospital Island. They would be safe there: no bear or any other predatory wildlife had ever swum across to Bernie's place. I had to endure only three days, four at most, with the chickens in my bathtub.

* * *

Getting some sleep did not help me figure out how I would break the news to my students, nor did it make me feel rejuvenated to take on another day.

"Something stole eleven of our chickens."

In the end, that was how I put it to the class.

"Are they dead?"

"I think so," I said.

"Are they all dead?"

"Four lived," I said.

"Where are they?"

"In my bathtub," I said.

"Which ones?"

"Which ones?" I asked.

"Which Henriettas?"

"Oh, I—" I considered lying to the children. Henrietta #5, Henrietta #11, Henrietta #7 and Henrietta #3. Those were the survivors, may the other Henriettas rest in peace. Instead I shook my head and said, "We shouldn't speak their names until the chickens cross to the other side," which I didn't mean as a joke though I couldn't help but smile.

"Somebody should tell Odelia," Hannah suggested.

I nodded. "I will, yes. Smart idea."

"It's not a smart idea," Hannah said. "She drew all them pictures for the chickens. She must have liked them lots. Even a dummy would know somebody should tell her. It's an obvious idea."

"We should have a memorial," Kenny suggested.

"We should," Hannah agreed.

"Shouldn't we wait a year?" I asked. "Isn't that what we're supposed to do?"

"We should do it now," Kenny said. "You won't be here next year."

"You don't know that," I said. "I could be."

Hannah scoffed. "You won't be here. We should do it today."

I felt a little hurt by this, which provoked me to pose a question I immediately regretted asking, for who knew what unkind responses I might receive. "Do you want me to be here next year?"

"Yes," Kenny said.

Several students nodded. Hannah did not nod, but she also did not make any of her usual snide comments. Hannah said nothing, which said everything.

"Let's have a memorial," I said.

The children decided that the brooder should be the site of the service. They pushed aside some of the desks and pulled the kiddie pool, still layered with wood chips, to the centre of the classroom. Gathering around it in a circle, they looked to me to say something.

Cradled in my clasped hands like a Bible was the Gordon Korman novel I'd been reading to the class, *The Chicken Doesn't Skate*. Not sure what to say or sermonize, I adopted Mr. Chapman's Biblical cadence. "Is a chicken a chicken?" I started, having no idea where I was going with it. "One chicken does not have more essence of chicken-ness than another."

The children hung their heads. Two of the younger ones sniffled. Hannah stood back, slightly outside the circle, while Kenny looked close to tears.

"You came into our lives and you made a great big fussy noise," I continued, searching around the room for ideas, words, phrases, but nothing more came to me. "But we loved you still. *Chuu*."

Everybody stayed quiet. I looked around at their lowered faces and realized that there were days in a classroom where the feelings were truly one and the same, days when what one person celebrated or suffered was felt by everyone.

✳   ✳   ✳

When Dawn Jimmy showed up to teach Language and Culture in the last block before lunch, I stepped into the hallway and peeked through the open door of Joan's classroom. Joan was seated in a tiny chair in the corner. All the children sat cross-legged on the carpet in front of her. She held open a picture book, *Harold and the Purple Crayon*. As she read the story, the children gasped with glee. They interrupted Joan with questions and comments about the story, eagerly urging her to turn the page. I wished to hear more of that wonder and delight in the voices of my own students. Was it a matter of age? Were younger children naturally more open to the wonders of the world? Or was it because primary classes revolved so much around story?

At lunch I got an idea, a little something to take the children's minds off the chickens. I went into the school kitchen and searched for ingredients, then spent my lunch making batches of special paint.

"What are we doing?" the class asked as I placed a large sheet of newsprint paper on each desk.

"Class," I said, "I didn't want to tell you about this until I was certain I could get hold of it. Last month I ordered one of the rarest kinds of paints available in the whole world. It came from Paris. Everything is fancy in Paris, even their paints. Many famous painters have come from Paris. Anyhow, it was very expensive. It is used for a special style of fingerpainting. You might think that only little kids fingerpaint, but it is all the rage in Paris right now."

The class looked at me with a bored uncertainty.

I charged on. "One thing you'll notice when I give you a small bowl of this paint is that it only comes in one colour. Brown. The result on the page is beautiful, a kind of sepia monochromatic effect."

"A what?" Hannah sneered.

"You'll see," I said. "Of course, I want you to be very careful with the paint because it was incredibly expensive, as I said, plus it took a lot for me to locate a store willing to ship any of this rare paint to me. But there is an even more important reason I need you to be careful. And please, please listen closely to this."

The students were now riveted to my words.

"This paint is very toxic. If you get any of it near your mouth, you will be poisoned," I spoke slowly. "I shouldn't even be letting you use it. But I trust you, and I know you'll be able to use this without any trouble. So, please do not put your fingers anywhere near your face, please. If your parents knew I was letting you use paint that was this poisonous, they would be furious with me."

All the students nodded with excitement at the prospect of using something that should be forbidden in the school.

"We'll be careful," Kenny said.

I passed out plastic bowls of the brown paint. Students got to work quickly and eagerly, their eyes lit up by the sight of the special paint. Fingers dipped into the bowls and swirled with creative abandon. Except Hannah, who chose to keep her hands covered as usual. She watched with keen curiosity, though, as the other children lost themselves in a state of artistic flow.

"You know," I said. "I forgot to eat lunch. I'm so very hungry."

I grabbed Hannah's bowl of paint, dipped two fingers into it and as the class turned to watch, stuck both coated fingers into my mouth.

"Teacher!" several kids exclaimed.

"What are you doing, Teacher?" Kenny cried out.

Hannah bent forward and sniffed the bowl. She stuck her tongue over the rim and into the paint, then laughed. She said, "It's chocolate pudding!"

There was an uproar of gasps and laughter and joyous groans.

When I turned around to see the rest of the class, Kenny's mouth was rimmed thickly with pudding. He pointed at Hannah, who had stuck her entire face into the bowl. When she lifted her face up again, there was chocolate on her forehead, her nose, her chin. The others smelled their bowls and their paintings, dragging fingers across the paper and into their mouths or dipping their tongues into their bowls. Hannah threw back her head in laughter.

"Paints from Paris, my ass," Hannah smiled. "Teacher, you're real funny."

*   *   *

The point of finishing *Foucault's Pendulum*, I told myself as I settled at the kitchen table that evening to read, was not to discover the contents of the book, but to persevere. An act of commitment for no other reason than the commitment itself.

Opening the book, I started to read then closed the cover and reflected on the title. *Foucault's Pendulum*. A giant pendulum swinging back and forth. To the onlooker, it seemed to move along its simple, repetitive arc—along the same plane of space, back and forth. What was unseen was the rotation of the Earth underneath it all. Tape a pencil to the pendulum and the truth would be drawn before your eyes: the swinging arc would eventually depict a full circle. The size of the circle itself would differ depending on where in the world the pendulum stood. To you, nothing had changed. It was only an arc. But hidden within the back-and-forth motion of the pendulum was a circle—you couldn't see it when you too were rotating with the Earth. No matter how you thought you were moving through time and space, you might very well be moving in another direction: one you are completely unaware of.

22

On Saturday morning Patty asked over the VHF if anybody had seen Hannah. "Daughter has gone off somewhere. Don't think she's been home all night. Her bed's the same as before."

I sat at the kitchen table and listened closely. Nobody answered Patty.

"She stay at somebody's house last night?" Patty asked.

I sat upright with concern. Hannah didn't show up at school on Friday and it was a strange question for Patty to ask. Certainly Patty knew that nobody allowed her daughter inside their homes. It was the type of wishful thinking that comes from feeling the first stabs of panic.

"I ain't seen her nowhere," somebody replied.

Patty then raised her voice into the radio as though she were calling out the window to everybody in the village. "Anybody see my daughter, you tell her to get her ass home. Daughter! You hear me? You get home right now!"

I squeezed my hands into fists. There was something disquieting in Patty's voice that alarmed me. A tremor of fear vibrating under the surface of her breath. I could hear it through the static of the radio and even through Patty's booming demands.

As I retrieved Hannah's notebook from the top of the fridge, I felt apprehension pour through me.

I opened the notebook.

I like to rape.

My heart beat so hard I could feel it against my ribs. I stared at the sentence that had troubled me to the point of telling nobody about it except Katerina. I had carried on as if my silence erased its existence. A tree that fell in the forest did not make a sound if no one was around to hear it. And a child who wanted to rape did not act out if no one knew of their impulse. What had I done? I knew, I *knew*, that my inaction was wrong, yet I kept carrying on with it anyway. What had Hannah done? What had I done by doing nothing?

Rape. Such a small word in my mouth, just one syllable that I could remember first hearing on the news as a child. I had asked my mother what it meant. It was something men did, that was how my mother explained it in that flustered voice she used whenever she didn't want to talk about something. It was something men did. To women. But my mother wasn't telling the whole truth: it wasn't only to women. But to children too. To girls. And to newspaper boys.

I returned to the kitchen and looked at the sentence again.

It was not something only men did.

I paced around the trailer, thinking of Hannah's sentence and longing for ambiguity. I rearranged the rows of seashells on the sill. I drank cups of coffee. I stood beside the open refrigerator and ate forkfuls of salmon straight from the jar. I wanted the meaning of that sentence to become indeterminate, to grow fuzzy around its edges, to open itself up to wider interpretation. I hovered over Hannah's notebook, staring at it intensely as though by sheer will the meaning would change. I backed away and viewed it from various angles as if it were one of those optical illusions where the images were reversible. Two silhouettes that formed a vase. An old lady that transformed into someone young and beautiful. A duck that was actually a rabbit. Nothing more than perceptual switches. I wanted Hannah's sentence to be like that: subject to perception.

And it was in the moment that I propped it up against the back of the counter and viewed it from the other side of the kitchen when I saw something I hadn't seen before. I exhaled, a long, shuddering release of pressure within me. Each letter was a piece of the puzzle, and as I disassembled those pieces, I finally saw Hannah's intention.

I knew where Hannah had gone. Taking only a small backpack of things, I drove the school boat out of the cove and across the open ocean, past the island with the cave of old bones, past the island where Grace's grandmother was buried, past the island with the abandoned, wind-cracked houses where Odelia and I had collected stars. When I reached the cove of the tiny island that hid Hannah's favourite spot, I dragged the school boat ashore and threw down the anchor. Hannah's kicker was there, pulled onto the beach between the tall grasses and piles of driftwood. Otherwise, the island was desolate. Nobody to see or hear us.

Behind the sun-bleached whale rib, which leaned against a cedar tree, there was a small trail in the forest that was nearly hidden by tangled branches and old man's beard. I wriggled through to find Hannah beside the fallen totem poles in the grassy clearing. She mustn't have heard my footsteps because she didn't turn to look. She ran her bloodied hands over the faces of the figures on the poles, which were barely visible, rotting and moss-masked, as if she was searching their ovoid eyes for secrets from other times.

Without a word, I sat on a fallen cedar about thirty feet away from Hannah. Out of my small backpack I retrieved a book and my pair of special reading glasses. In a voice soft yet loud enough for Hannah to hear, I read the opening line of the story.

"Once there was a tree…"

I turned the page and read the next line, only I changed the character from a boy to a girl for both our sakes. Here and there I added my own spin on the story, but mostly I stayed true to the original.

"…and she loved a little girl."

I continued. Page after page. Hannah didn't move except to continue running her uncovered hands along the faces on those totem poles. Was she even listening? Had she heard me at all? I pressed on. I read about how the girl would come every day and collect the tree's leaves and how she would turn the leaves into crowns and pretend to be the queen of the woods. On some days the girl climbed the tree's trunk and swung from the branches and ate its apples. The girl was all alone in this story. She played hide-and-go-seek with the tree. Did she not have any friends? I had read the book at least a dozen times. I had never considered before how lonely the child in the book must have been. Did the child not belong anywhere except with this tree?

And when the child was too tired from fitting into this world, I read with some improvisation, she would sleep in the tree's shade. The child loved the tree very much. And the tree was happy, too. But then time passed, as it was bound to do, children growing up to not be children anymore, as they were bound to do, and the tree found itself all alone. So when the girl who was not really a girl anymore came back, the tree asked her to climb and swing and eat her apples. The girl said no, she was too big for climbing and swinging. She wanted money now. So the tree gave her its apples to sell, and it made the tree happy to be so giving to the girl.

The grown girl stayed away for another long spell, which made the tree sad. When the girl finally returned, the tree "shook with joy," I read. Again the tree asked the girl to climb and swing, and again the girl said she had no time for such things. She wanted a family to love, who would love her, a place where she could belong. She had to build a house for her dream family. So the tree gave her its branches for building, and it made the tree happy to be so giving to the girl.

When the girl returned a third time after many more years away, the tree was filled with so much joy it couldn't speak a word. Finally the tree asked the girl to come and play. But the girl, who was an old woman now, was too sad to play. All she wanted was a boat that would take her far away from everything. So the tree gave her its trunk for carving out a canoe, and it made the tree happy to be so giving to the girl.

"But not really," I read.

When the girl was very, very old, she came back once more. The tree apologized sadly to the girl because it had nothing left to give her. It had given the girl everything it could. All that was left of it was an old stump. The girl told the tree that that was all she needed now. A quiet place to sit and rest. So the tree invited the girl to rest on her stump, and the girl did. And it made the tree happy.

I closed the book and stared at its bright green cover. A small sound pulled me out of the story world. In my transfixed state, I hadn't noticed that Hannah had moved from her spot next to the totem poles. She sat cross-legged in the grass in front of me. The grey lines and knots of scabs on Hannah's uncovered hands looked like the bark of a tree. Hannah had the look of somebody entranced, of somebody who had been transported to another place and time. Her eyes were red with crying.

Quickly Hannah wiped away the tears. "I seen a show once where these prisoners made shivs out of soap. You think soap could cut a person's skin?" She dragged her finger slowly across her wrist.

"I don't know," I said, feeling strange that Hannah didn't act surprised to see me. "Never thought about it. Have you thought about it?"

"My grandma says people like me get sent away to turn into trees."

As I peered at the scabs on Hannah's hands, I remembered having lunch in the church with Katerina and Sophie Florence, and how Sophie Florence had said that the nurse expressed extra concern over Odelia's hands due to a possible outbreak of scabies in the community. All the rubbing, the slamming of her hands against the walls and her desk—it made sense to me now. Hannah had been suffering from the unbearable itchiness of mites.

"You have scabies, Hannah. Lots of people get it."

"But my grandma told me the stories," Hannah said. She held up her bare hands to me and tears returned to her eyes. "My skin is turning into bark."

"Your skin is not turning into bark. You won't turn into a tree, I promise. We'll go to the nurse. She'll tell you it's scabies. She'll help you. You'll see, Hannah."

"What if you're wrong?" Hannah asked.

"Let's find out if I'm wrong. Don't do anything until we find out, okay?"

"Everybody blames me for the fire. Everybody will blame me for this, too."

"I don't blame you. I know it wasn't you who caused the fire. Sophie Florence knows it wasn't you," I said.

Hannah looked all around. "This is my favourite place in the world. If I'm going to become a tree. I want to be stuck here forever."

"Is this where you slept last night?"

She pointed. "Over there between the totem poles."

"You're not turning into a tree, Hannah. I promise," I repeated. I nodded at Hannah's hands. "Nobody can blame you for this. This could happen to anybody. It's not even your fault if you gave it to somebody else."

Hannah looked at her hands with worry. "It's contagious?"

"Very," I said. "You didn't know. You're not to blame."

But I knew Hannah was right. People would point at her parasitic hands as though she alone was to blame for a common contagion like scabies. How often, after all, had they accused her of taking things that weren't in fact missing? How many times had they attributed every bump, bruise and scrape on their own children's knees to Hannah? They clicked the locks on their doors whenever she wandered the village alone. They yelled at her from their windows, their words sliding back and forth between English and Nuu-chah-nulth, words slippery and sharp, air squeezing out either side of raw glottal stops.

Hannah climbed to her feet and returned to her spot on the grass where she stretched out on her stomach. I put the book and my reading glasses on the fallen tree and lowered myself onto my stomach next to her.

"What kind of animal you gonna be after you die?" Hannah asked.

I thought for a moment. "I don't know, a tiger maybe?"

"Bullshit. There ain't no tigers here. You don't get to pick. I'm gonna turn into a killer whale. Everybody in my family becomes a killer whale when they die." Hannah checked my face. "Do you believe me?"

"I believe you, Hannah."

"You don't believe me," Hannah said.

"I do believe you."

Hannah said, "One day, when my dad's dead and I'm dead, him and me are gonna swim the ocean together, that's what he said."

"That sounds nice." Then I thought for a minute and added, "When I die, I want to be put inside the moon."

Hannah nodded.

As we fell into a long spell of silence, I thought about Hannah's sentence and wondered how I could find out the truth from her. I could not simply ask Hannah because if my theory was correct, the question would make the girl defensive and volatile. It would embarrass her, and she would take it as another sign that she was no good. In my head, I started to frame the question in various ways, playing with the possible outcomes in my mind.

Hannah pointed to the figures carved into the totem poles. "One time I seen one of these creatures turn real. Do you believe me about that, too?"

"I believe you, Hannah."

"You don't believe me," Hannah said.

"I do believe you."

"If you believe me, then come over here," Hannah said, and she walked to a patch of tall grass farther away from the totem poles. She lowered herself back onto her belly and parted the grass with her sore hands. "I'll show you."

Away from the totem poles, we hid on our bellies in the tall grass. Hannah's long arms near mine, the terrain of her hands colonized by those unyielding, unforgiving mites. My pale hands were open like clamshells, while Hannah's fists were closed tightly. Lying there, I realized that we were both truly waiting for something magical, for something supernatural to happen to the cedar figures. A transformation of some sort, just like the stories Nan Lily told the children on Hot Breakfast Day, of Raven and Son of Deer and Mother Turned Into a Bluejay.

"I don't want my skin to turn to bark," Hannah whispered.

"It won't, Hannah, I promise," I whispered back.

Hannah didn't respond. She watched the totem poles.

I asked, "Do you believe me?"

Hannah scratched at her irritated hands for several moments. She lifted her eyebrows. "I believe you."

Next to me, Hannah looked as long as a cedar tree. The type of tree cedar pullers stripped to make hats and baskets. For years, long strips of Hannah had been pulled, pulled away and woven into something new. But into what? Into a basket that carried nothing except the memory of cousins who tied her to a chair where they threw insults and rocks at her as a small child. And not even the same cousins, Sophie Florence had pointed out, who had kept Hannah in the water under the dock. The drawings of death in her desk drawer and her question of shivs as she made wrist-slicing motions crowded my thoughts. I looked at Hannah and suddenly envisioned her in some year to come, tying her own rope and climbing her own chair and transforming her cracked and forsaken hands into black fins that would glide her into the milk-washed horizon of the cold Pacific, and the vision weakened me to the bone. Seeds and spores and aphids floated in the air above, twisting the sunlight into a golden kaleidoscope. The edges of everything around me grew fuzzy. The silence between us stretched out into long moments of watching the serene space before us. At last, I asked what I'd come to find out.

"Hannah, do you know how to spell 'fat'?"

"R-O-Y-S-T-O-N." Hannah laughed.

"Seriously. I'll buy you a chocolate bar from the store if you try."

"Two chocolate bars," Hannah said. "And a pop."

I sighed. "Alright, Hannah, two chocolate bars."

"And a pop."

"And a pop."

Hannah bit her lip as she thought. "F-A-T-E."

My face dropped toward the grass. I let my head hang limply from my neck as relief coursed through my shoulders and my neck. My mouth pushed out a gasp of air that explosively turned to laughter. I covered my mouth to contain my catharsis and as I looked up, I suddenly recognized that Hannah's hiding spot was the most beautiful place I'd ever seen, a place of possibilities, a place of optical illusions where totem poles became living creatures and every image was reversible, a place where vicious words revealed themselves to be the innocent errors of children who have never known silent ease.

"You were close, Hannah," I said. "On Monday I'll teach you again about silent *e*'s."

Hannah shrugged.

I said, "You'll learn to read, Hannah. You will."

Hannah gave me a sidelong look of scorn. Then her eyebrows crumpled, as though something had occurred to her. "How did I get scabies?"

"I told you, it's very contagious. Could have been from anyone."

"What if I didn't get it from another person?"

"What do you mean?" I asked.

"What if I got it because I did something that gave me bad luck?"

"You mean Fossil Island?" I asked.

Hannah shot me a quick glance. "I got scabies for nothing."

"Why did you go, then?"

"Because he said I could become whatever I wanted."

"Who said?"

Hannah picked at the grass. She scratched at her hand.

"Who said?" I repeated.

"He said sometimes you needed to make big moves to get what you want," Hannah said. "Sort of like playing the King's Gambit. But in real life."

"King's Gambit? What's that?" I asked.

"The most dangerous move in chess," Hannah said.

I felt a rush of anger flood my cheeks. I sat up. Then I stood up. I paced through the grass. I was unable to concentrate on anything. Not on the golden kaleidoscope. Not on the totem poles. Even if every carved character came to life right in front of me at that moment, I might not have noticed. I was thinking about Mr. Chapman, and I struggled to reconcile the man who spoke so sincerely about Tomas Whitehead, the man who wrote poetry and read Plato, with the man who told the children these stories with a silver tongue. Why? Why would he do such a thing? If it was just a whimsical story that would be one thing, but he told stories that set children against the teachings of the elders—and since he had done so by making the girls promise to keep it a secret, he must have known it was improper. Disrespectful.

I didn't know what to do with myself. Marching toward the edge of the woods, I said, "Come on, Hannah. I want you to hear something."

Hannah followed and watched me as I listened to the trunk of a cedar. After a few minutes, Hannah also pressed her ear to the trunk.

"What are we trying to hear?" Hannah asked.

"Its heartbeat," I said.

Hannah wrenched back. "Like a person's heartbeat?"

"It's not really a heartbeat. It's just the water pulsing inside the tree. But I like to imagine that it's a heartbeat."

"But then it's just a lie," Hannah said. "Why would you believe in a lie?"

"Because sometimes I want the world to be different than it is."

"Sometimes I want to leave the world," Hannah said.

"Oh?" I tried to hide the worry in my voice.

"Sometimes I want to be up there." Hannah looked skyward.

"In Heaven?"

Hannah shook her head. "Outer space."

"Like an astronaut?"

"I saw that on a show. It had this woman on it. She was the first black woman to become an astronaut. Mae Jemison." Hannah recalled this with the steel-trap precision of somebody who has long practised distracting people from the fact that she couldn't read or write. "She said that out there in the universe she felt at ease. She could just be herself. It was right for her to be there. She belonged there as much as any speck of stardust. That's what she said."

Hannah sat down on the log next to the book. I sat down next to her, so close our shoulders pressed lightly together. It occurred to me that Hannah had scabies, but I was willing to take the chance. We sat like that for a very long time. Neither of us said a word. Neither of us moved except for Hannah's scratching of her hands. I thought about the nightmare Hannah had been living with all on her own, believing that she was turning into a tree like those who were sent away, unwanted, and I soaked in how alive the child felt next to me. I kept my shoulder where it was, never losing contact with her.

23

Ernie Frank stood on the shore of the village next to the dock with a huge eagle wing in his hand. With his other hand, he motioned for me to come to him. I had returned from Hannah's special place after getting her to radio her mother and promise to return home by evening at the latest. Behind Ernie was his sister, sitting on a large log of driftwood. She did not say a word as I approached.

Ernie motioned his head at his sister. "Diane says she can still see the black aura around you. And I can feel it, too. The dark energy. We're going to cleanse you."

"Now?" I asked.

"Now."

"Here?" I asked.

"Here."

I swallowed hard. All the houses set on the ridge above the shore would be able to see us from their windows. A few people worked on their boats while others walked along the dock. They would probably stop to watch the spectacle. In the yard on the ridge above them a group of small children played. Not far down the shoreline, three teenagers, one of whom was Kevin Sam, hung out on a jumble of driftwood. I didn't care to have any of them watching me. What was even involved? Did I have to stand or lie down on the ground? Feeling ambushed into something I didn't know anything about, I gave Ernie a look of doubt. "Right here?"

"Right here." Ernie tugged on my backpack, which was slung over one shoulder, and slid it off my arm. He set it on the ground and lifted my arms so that I stood with my hands pointed out from my sides like bird wings. "Close your eyes and keep them closed the whole time. Relax."

I took one last look around the shore and the village. Some people stood at their living room windows and peered out at us.

Reluctantly, I closed my eyes.

With great force, Ernie brushed the eagle wing across the inside of my right arm. He moved it rapidly, frenetically. The feathers were stiff and the shafts, while hollow, stung my skin slightly. As he brushed, I couldn't help but wonder about the darkness inside me. What was it? Where had it come from? What would it feel like when it rose out of me? I envisioned the darkness seeping out of my skin, rendering itself visible for everybody to scrutinize. Like apparitions floating out of my pores and telling everybody my secret story. A theatre of shadow puppets whose script would reveal what a bad person I truly was underneath it all.

Now Ernie brushed down my right side. Hard.

I shook with vulnerability. A vague sense of shame washed over me, and I was surprised to find myself holding back an intense need to cry, as if the eagle wing was loosening something inside me. For a second I forgot where I was, but then I could feel my feet firmly planted in the rocky sand again. It happened like that several times over the next minute: seconds of drifting into a trance, a hypnotic state, only to sense my surroundings once more. Finally I drifted into a trance and remained there. Images came to me unbidden. Images without language. Images in their purest sense, arising straight from my subconscious, manifesting as metaphors, appearing to me only in my dreams and in the visceral sensations of my body. In this state I understood fully, as if I'd always known deep down, that there in my subconscious was every single thing I'd ever experienced in my life. Every single thing from the inconsequential to the monumental. Every story I'd ever known, every story I'd ever lived, every story I'd ever heard, every story I'd ever read.

I could not make sense of what I saw, but I could feel the truth of it all. The images were not something I watched but something I received through no specific sense. I absorbed each one as if through osmosis. The first things I envisioned were things I seemed to carry inside me which did not belong to me yet had taken root. Imprinted upon me like a stamp on a page, scallop fossils on the shores, a black stain of a beetle on a board. Ghostly resonances, the sticky residue of things upon life, things gone but never erased, and when they wafted before my mind's eye, I could hardly bear it. Visions of people that were familiar yet faint as thin mist.

I lost all physical sensation of Ernie's brushing the moment I saw the image of an elderly lady collapsing on her kitchen table into a pile of silver and blue beads. As the woman's heart stopped beating and her jaw fell open and her skin sagged toward the linoleum, her molten spirit poured out, transparent yet visible to the ten-year-old who stood in the kitchen doorway and watched her grandmother's soul spread across the table and absorb the colours of the beads like cobalt ions added to the glass. An amorphous pool of energy in search of a new shape—some sort of mould in which to vitrify. For the next several years the grandmother's viscous spirit would ask the girl to help her find her new shape. She would whisper into the girl's ear. She would enter her dreams. She would try out possible shapes right in front of the girl—spheres in the seas and prisms in the sky—as if the edges of her soul were transformed by an invisible glassblower. At times the girl would refuse to help, first out of fear and later selfishness, but in the end it was this shared search that would save the girl from being beaten at a house party on her nineteenth birthday.

I then saw four men die in a house fire while a ten-year-old girl escaped by crawling under the smoke, her hands blistered with the circles of doorknobs. All of the men were the girl's great-uncles. One of the men was especially close to the girl and loved her with all his heart, his every intention for her good and true even when it was fool-ish. As this man's skin seared, his silica-dry soul spilled out like sand and melted in the fire and in the heat of his anguish, then cooled rapidly and shattered into a million shards. Restlessly, endlessly, these fragments tumbled over one another. A river of glass in search of a new sound—some kind of sonata with which to soothe the girl all her days. For several years the uncle's echoing soul would ask the girl to help him find a new sound. He would jangle softly in the girl's ear. He would add soundtracks to her dreams. He would try out melodies as the girl walked to school—in the wind and between the stones under her steps—as if each piece of his glass spirit were cast by an invisible bell maker. At times the girl would tune out this music, first out of denial and later anger, but in the end it would be this shared search that seven years later helped her to save another girl from hanging herself in the forest near the bleached whale rib.

From around the farthest corner of my mind, a boy appeared. He pulled a wagon filled with folded newspapers down the sidewalk, the wheels thumping on the seams between the squares of concrete. A noise filled my head. It was the sound of a car engine and as it approached, I was floating into the air high above the street. From the shelter of the sidewalk, the boy was sucked up by the mightiest of winds and pulled into the car, his skinny body torn into several pieces under the strange and unnatural force. As the boy's heart ripped apart and his soft jaw pulled open and his threadbare skin unravelled in the wind, his soul—soft and loose and glinting like quartz—slipped out and, like desert sand struck by lightning, solidified in the suddenness of bright light. A figurine of glass. For many years he visited the girl who painted giraffes in his memory and who kept her gesture drawings of him—the boy as motion—hidden under her mattress. He interrupted her thoughts. He woke her in the night. He tricked her sleeping mind with the illusion of being flesh and blood, the light refracting through his delicate, glossy soul and splitting into colours saturated and vibrant, as if new life had been breathed into his transparent form by an invisible mouth. More than anything the girl wished he would go away. Sometimes he would disappear for a few days, sometimes more than a week, only to return again. Sometimes the girl denied his existence, out of both disbelief and guilt, though occasionally she acknowledged him, and it was in these moments that she questioned why the world no longer made sense.

Ernie was brushing my legs now. For a brief, lucid moment I had the sense that everything I was seeing was a double narrative: the actual moment and the future moments that shed greater light and understanding on the past. How much of what I was seeing was accurate, I could not tell. Yet everything had truth in it. I knew that.

The boy had come to George Ellerson's to deliver the newspaper. The flung newspaper landed with a thwack on the concrete next to the car and slid, spinning, just inside the door of the garden shed at the back end of the carport. George flinched at the sound the moment he landed his boot down on Marvin Gardens. The boy appeared in the doorway. None of them knew his name. He lived on the adjacent street, and back then children were territorial about playing on their own streets. Look what you made me do, George said to the boy. I didn't, the boy said quietly. Then he asked George why he didn't let the beetle live. It's just a stupid beetle. No, it was a living thing. The boy with the stoop of doubt in his spine appeared devastated. What do you care so much for? It's only a stupid beetle. I'm going to Africa one day. That's what I'm saving all my paper route money for. I'm going to see a whistling thorn tree and the ants that make music by chewing holes in the branches. And the quiver tree, the fever tree, the baobab tree, the ones that look upside-down, the sausage tree with fruit so big it can knock a person out cold. And giraffes. My favourite animal. I'm going to see lots of giraffes. I'm going to travel across the grasslands. In a safari hat. It's my dream. George scoffed. Who cares about that?

Foliage and botanical species floated across my mind. Sprawled across my bed with library books about giraffes by Anne Innis Dagg. Diaries from great treks across the savannah. Field guides on African trees. My mother and I stretching canvas over wood frames. The viscous swirls of acrylics on a palette held to my arm with my thumb. Bleak images of suburbia. Empty parking lots with weeds in the cracks of asphalt, blue and rusted garbage dumpsters, long coupe and sedan cars from the late 1970s, early 1980s. A brown Oldsmobile with a broken tail light. License plate EEG 842. Out of the dumpsters grew African trees and across the asphalt wild grasslands sprang to life. Giraffes drove the brown Oldsmobiles that parked and waited in the empty lots, their necks curving out of the open windows. Everything lush and beautiful, tangled in vibrant clusters and coloured emerald, bronze and gold.

My mother's voice. You might be only a child, but even children need visions for themselves. Become something, Molleigh, that lets you keep the dreams and destinies of children safe. Do this, and redeem yourself.

I wanted the cleansing to stop. My head grew warm. I had the urge to sit. I wished to open my eyes and see only the contours of the world. Everywhere there were shadows. Shadows crisscrossing my path. Shadows played strange tricks on the mind. Every artist knew how easy it was to be misled by shadows. Shadows were followed solely by the eyes, and the eyes were the most gullible victims of cruel illusions. But touch the contours of a figure and it would always feel the same, whether it was cast under light or fallen under shadows.

But I couldn't move. I couldn't make myself come back out into the world of my five senses. I saw my bed next to the window, from where I watched other children play while I refused to leave my house. Go out and play, my mother implored me. No. At night, the Beast kept me from sleeping. I clutched my pillow and tried to keep myself from screaming. When I finally fell asleep, the Beast entered my head. He dragged the boy out of the brown Oldsmobile with the broken tail light. Into the dark woods that reminded us of the darkest places of our minds. A boot smashing down without a care for his sprayed and sticky state. A thrill. A spectacle for amusement. Amorphous, shifting images of blood and crying and begging and indifferent laughter, the imagined sounds rising to an unbearable crescendo in my head. I tried to lift my hands to my ears, but I couldn't make them move. A slight moan of anguish come out of my mouth as Ernie brushed up my left side. Then children playing hide-and-go-seek and capturing grasshoppers inside plastic ice cream pails, the lids punctured for air. For breathing. For staying alive.

The woods where my favourite tree stood. If that tree fell in the woods and nobody was around to hear it, it would make no sound. If I didn't admit to seeing what I saw while up in that tree, if I didn't let it come out of my mouth, it never happened. My elbows on the window ledge. Bluebottles lay belly up, dessicated, in the window rail. I looked onto the sidewalk. There was the boy pulling his wagon. He stooped to take hold of a newspaper, rolled it tight, and arched his back to hurl it end over end onto our front step. The boy was motion. Movement. One unit of energy. He was going to Africa. It was his dream. It lived inside him like a pancreas or a liver.

But nothing lived inside the boy. His lifeless body was found covered in leaves in a dark woods far from my street. Telling nobody, not even when the television reported him missing, not even when the television reported the discovery of his body, it gave me nightmares every night and made me feel like nothing I did in life would ever matter. It was all senseless, meaningless. Nothing I did would ever make a difference when I had failed to make a difference to someone who needed it most. I chose not to tell a soul. But I was only a child. I chose to turn it into art rather than life. I chose not to help. I shut myself away, disconnected myself from others, disconnected myself from my own heart. But I was only a child.

My paintings, the ones my mother turned toward the wall. The blue dumpsters behind Safeway. A brown Oldsmobile. The details of a license plate number done in a thin bristled brush.

My mother reading to me every night, but once we'd finished *The Story Girl*, she read nothing to me at bedtime but the Bible. It was a children's version, as large in area as my mother's lap, so large that when she spread the pages open it looked as though she were reading a cartography guide. Inside, the coloured drawings scared me so much that I insisted on facing the wall away from my mother. Bloodied sacrifices of small creatures. Wrenched mouths of parents and children drowning in a great deluge, people clawing their way out of the water and onto stones drenched by rain. Shadrach, Meshach, Abednego and clever Daniel. All thrown into the fiery inferno of Nebuchadnezzar's furnace, the heat so great that the guards themselves were burned to death by the flames. The picture in my children's Bible nothing but shades of orange, the boys' shadows of agony on the stone wall.

It was me who knew something and would tell no one, and it was my mother who knew I knew something, and because it was me not my mother who kept myself confined to the house that summer, my mother dwelled on the passages about atonement. Peter, telling me that by his wounds you have been healed. Hebrews and the promise of eternal redemption. Leviticus. For the life of a creature is in the blood, and I have given it to you to make atonement for yourselves on the altar; it is the blood that makes atonement for one's life.

Up in the tree. A bird's eye view of my quiet street and surrounding neighbourhoods. I saw roof shingles and treetops and rectangles of mowed grass and the circle of asphalt where I played road hockey with the other kids. I saw the field of hydroelectric poles and the empty parking lot behind Safeway where I was not allowed to cut through on the way to school. No one to see them. No one to hear them. Blue dumpsters. A brown Oldsmobile. I looked through the pair of pocket binoculars I'd ordered from the back of a *Richie Rich* comic book. The boy pulled his wagon across the asphalt. The Beast sat in the front of the Oldsmobile. A broken tail light. EEG 842. Beautiful British Columbia. The Beast offers the boy something. Come in, you can get whatever you want. Money? For what? Africa? Why, yes. Get in the car. Your wagon? Get it later. Get in the car. The boy nods and opens the passenger door. No, I think. No, don't. You aren't supposed to go that way. Not behind the Safeway. Then there was only the wagon. And the blue dumpsters. Cracked asphalt.

All these buried memories, I could feel them coming out of the shadows of my existence, unknown crevices and corners of my flesh and bones where all this had been stored, little scars marking the rings of my heartwood over the years. Please stop, Ernie. I wanted to return immediately to the world. From out of the depths of myself. Anywhere but this place where everything was amorphous and ambiguous. Why did he get into that car? Why did he choose to risk himself like that?

After nothing but blackness and foggy memories for years and years, the suddenness of everything appeared to me like a secret hidden at the edge of my mind. The order of the images hadn't always been right, and some of the things I remembered people saying were never said, or at least not in so many words, and true, some of what I saw might have been planted there years later by my guilty conscience, but none of that mattered. It was truth, and truth was something that existed beyond fact. As Ernie stopped brushing, I felt a lightening in my flesh and bones, and my arms, as if they had a mind and a wish of their own, lifted a little toward the sky. Those dark currents that moved invisibly underneath everything, rolling the round pebble of my life downstream, were still there, but so too were sun-rippled streams of blue and green. Behind me the tide washed ashore, and I could hear the word *chumiss—chumissssss*—as the ocean brushed against the stones and sand.

*   *   *

My legs were weak as I walked away from Ernie and his sister. My entire body shook. I felt hollowed. It was as if I had experienced a spiritual enema. Cleansing yet violating. Every pore on my skin saturated with forgotten memories. It wasn't the Beast of BC who undid my mother to the point that she no longer wished to talk about the destinies of children. It was me. I had undone my mother. Like Odelia, my art had been my way of telling my story, my way of speaking what I could not say with my tongue.

At home I dug out a tiny key from a canvas pencil case inside one of the moving boxes. Then I pulled the wood box from underneath my bed. I had been scared all these years to open the box, to discover secrets I had always sensed were there. But those secrets had been brushed out of me with an eagle wing. There was nothing more to fear. I turned the key and lifted the lid. Immediately I was stunned by the colours. Emerald, bronze, gold. Blues and browns. Layered over an underpainting of dirty grey and dusty black and the decay of rust. Inside the box were my paintings of dumpsters and cracked asphalt, giraffes driving brown Oldsmobiles. Also inside the box were my binoculars, the pair I'd ordered out of the back of a *Richie Rich* comic, and my magnifying glass, the one I used to burn grasshoppers with the sun's concentrated rays. Between the layers of paintings was my thin sketchbook. Inside were the gesture studies of the boy. The boy as movement. The boy as motion. A single unit of energy captured on the page in seconds. I took a pair of scissors and punctured the canvas, then cut out one of the giraffes that stood inside a blue dumpster. I taped it to the kitchen window behind my glass balls and willow charcoal sticks, on an edge of the world where dark rainforest met ocean, the precise place where two unknowable things came together.

24

The next day Kevin Sam was coming to take the chickens over to Nurse Bernadette's place. Chicken poop now covered my bathtub tiles like a Jackson Pollock painting, and the stench of ammonia and hydrogen sulphide, reminiscent of urine and rotten eggs, filled my house. As a thank you to Kevin, I planned to surprise him by opening the gym that night for as long as he wanted. As I lay in bed that morning, I realized how crucial the community was to my success. Kevin boating the chickens away. Bernadette helping with a new coop. Ernie Frank and his sister cleansing me. Sophie Florence and the other women lifting me up and making me believe I could make a difference to the children of Tawakin. Even Chase Charlie coaxing a promise out of me.

The night before I had slept better than I had slept in years. Everything that had ever haunted me had stopped trying to get my attention and was finally resting too. When I awoke, I felt the impact of the cleansing, physical and emotional, easing. I knew that the shock of remembering what I had witnessed and my failure to speak out would eventually lessen, in the most minuscule of increments. And I accepted that it would lessen, no matter how tightly I held onto grace and mercy.

Later that afternoon, I knocked on Mr. Chapman's house door. I needed to confirm for myself if my suspicion was right—if he was the one who had told the children the strange stories of the woman in the box with the baby. I reserved some doubt. Anyone could have used a chess term like the King's Gambit, true, but the reference made me realize that Mr. Chapman's chess club provided him with weekly opportunities to feed the children tales without any other person knowing it.

"Molleigh," he said cheerfully. "Come in."

In his living room there was only the table and chairs, plus a coffee table and a futon couch that sunk into a deep V. I left my coat and boots at the door and took a seat at the table.

"Coffee? Tea?" he asked.

"No thanks," I said.

He took a seat across from me. "What can I do for you?"

I opened my mouth to start, then I hesitated. This seemed easier when I mentally rehearsed it at home. With both hands, I fiddled with two corners of a cloth placemat on the table.

Mr. Chapman gave me a puzzled look. "Is something wrong?"

"I'm just going to come out with it," I said. From my spot at the table I could see out his big window. Mr. Chapman's trailer was the farthest up the hill from the others, which gave him a view of all our homes, the school and a good stretch of the logging road. I kept looking out the window as I spoke. "You're the one who told the kids the story of the woman in the box with the baby, aren't you?"

He laughed. "What? I have no idea what you're talking about."

"The silver tooth? The wood tooth?" I watched his face this time.

He rubbed his chin. Then he shook his head slowly. "No, don't know about them. As principal is this something I should be concerned about?"

"You really don't know anything about it?" I asked.

"No. But I'd be grateful if you could explain it all to me."

Accepting that my suspicion had turned out to be wrong, I felt relieved. Not only because my suspicion about Mr. Chapman was wrong, but because I could share the story, unburdening myself. Without further hesitation, I told Mr. Chapman every detail I knew about the promise of the silver tooth and where it had come from, as well as the promise of the wood tooth and where it had come from.

"And some of our students went there because of these stories?" he asked. "When they weren't supposed to?"

"Yes," I said, without divulging which students.

"So they believed these stories?"

"Yes."

He rubbed his chain again. "Interesting."

"Well, I suppose I better leave you to your Sunday," I said, standing up from the table. The chair slid back with loud squelch.

"You ever seen rats put inside jars of water, Molleigh?"

I grimaced at him. "What? No. Of course not."

"Back in the fifties at Johns Hopkins School of Medicine, they put rats into glass jars and then filled the jars with water. One rat in each jar. They couldn't climb out since the walls of the jars were too tall and too slippery. To make it even more challenging, they blasted water from overhead. That way, they couldn't just float there without trying much. It was literally sink or swim. Then they timed how long the rats swam before they drowned. They had no chance to rest, no food, no real hope of getting out of the jar. Some of the rats kept swimming right to the very end. Other rats seemed to give up much sooner. Could rats have beliefs? Could rats have hope?" He asked these questions as if they might intrigue me, and inspected my expression closely before continuing. "To test this, they didn't put the rats into the jars right away. First, they held each rat and then let it squirm to freedom. They did this many times before putting the rats into the jars. They turned on the overhead water jets for a few minutes and then took the rats out and put them back into their cages. They went through this whole process many times. At last, the rats were put into the jars for the true test. Sink or swim. Guess what happened."

I didn't want to guess. I shrugged. "Don't know."

"Not one of the rats in the second experiment gave up swimming. No matter how exhausted they became. There was no chance for escape. Do you know why these rats never gave up, Molleigh? Because unlike the first group of rats, these rats were held and released, put in the jars then released. They were shown the promise of freedom. Do you know that on average they swam for sixty hours before finally drowning out of sheer fatigue. Sixty hours! Those rats believed they could survive their terrible conditions. More than that, they believed they could free themselves from their prisons. They made the choice to swim because they believed they had the choice."

"I see," I said out of politeness. It was an interesting anecdote, albeit one filled with cruelty, but I couldn't see his point of telling it to me.

"But how do you get people to believe they can escape their jars of water?" Mr. Chapman asked.

Again I shrugged.

"Stories," he said. "That's why I find this woman in the box with the baby situation so interesting. Stories are the only thing that make you believe. It's true. People become the stories they hear over and over. Even with religious beliefs it's true, isn't it? Nothing but stories in the Bible. Do you know why stories have that power? Because they suspend your disbelief, and by suspending it, the story can slip into your subconscious where it's played like a movie over and over again, even if you don't realize it."

I thought about how entranced the children became with the tale of the teeth, and how Hannah became lost in the story of the people exiled to the woods, believing that her skin was hardening like bark, her arms straightening into branches, her legs thickening into a trunk. It had slipped into her subconscious, playing over and over again like a movie, making her fear that this was the inescapable fate for all the unwanted. I myself grew up believing I could become whatever I wanted because my mother had convinced me it could be this way. It was stories that made me believe this. All those stories. The ones we'd made up together. The ones we'd read together. Stories of hope and belief and possibility.

Mr. Chapman said, "Take a homeless person. What do most people think or shout? 'Get a job! Just do it!' Think you can sloganize a person into believing they have a choice? Think you can just feed them a couple of anecdotes—there was this guy once who did this thing and so you can do it, too? Anecdotes are not quite stories. They are full of small words and small ideas. None of that will make a person believe they have a choice. I mean, haven't you ever wondered as a teacher why some kids and not others seem to believe they have a choice in life?"

"Just about every day," I said.

"Story is *the* single most powerful thing in this world. Nothing is more powerful than a story. A story can transform hopelessness into hope."

I leaned forward over the table in astonishment. "It *was* you."

"Hardly," he said with a dismissive flap of his hand. "But it would make for a great experiment."

I was still eyeing him with suspicion. "Our students aren't rats."

"Of course not," he said emphatically. "But think what an experiment like that could teach us about belief and choice. About how to instill hope in the hopeless. Besides, it's not as if the students were put into jars of water. They were just told a story."

Something out the window caught my attention. I turned to see a number of people walking up the road. At first I thought it was only about a half-dozen or so people, including Sophie Florence, Lizzie, Margaret and Gina. But more people followed. I spotted Odelia and Hannah trailing behind Sophie Florence. I watched as more and more people appeared. They didn't stop coming around that curve. I looked at Mr. Chapman, whose view out the window was blocked by the wall. Within a few minutes, however, the sound of people shouting could be heard clearly from our spot inside. Mr. Chapman gave me a confused look and leaned past the wall to the sight of the entire village gathered outside his door. Over one hundred people standing together in a narrow stream that flowed out of his small front yard and onto the road.

Sophie Florence stepped forward out of the crowd. There she was, the soul of Tawakin. The heart of the school. The feeder of all the children. Grandmother, auntie, friend to all. I beamed at the sight of her, her hair buzzed to her skull, her bottom lip protruding in thought. She climbed the steps and knocked on the door.

Mr. Chapman's face went pale. He did not get up from his seat.

Sophie Florence knocked again. This time an impatient rapping.

Mr. Chapman rose from his seat and his chest heaved with a deep breath.

By the time he opened the door, Sophie Florence had descended the short staircase to stand once more with the village. From my seat I could observe both the crowd out the window and Mr. Chapman directly in front of me. He held onto the doorknob, his body swaying almost imperceptibly. He surveyed the crowd, saying nothing.

"One time there was this principal who told the kids that they were bad because they were dirty Indians," Sophie Florence said to Mr. Chapman. "He called them all kinds of hurtful names every day, and every day they came home in tears. We told the principal to leave our community and never come back, and he told us that the school was a public one and that we didn't have any say in whether he stayed at the school and lived up the hill. One morning lots of us"—Sophie Florence gestured at the crowd of people—"stood at the bottom of the hill and blocked the way to school. The children arrived with their backpacks on, and they asked us why we wouldn't let them go past to school. We told them, we will always fight to keep our children safe."

"Why are you here to tell me this?" he asked.

"I bet you think you done nothing wrong," Sophie Florence continued, "but us telling our stories is us telling about our land. Our home. Us telling our stories is us remembering who we are and how we are supposed to be. Our stories are *haa-huu-pah*, our teachings, and when you tell stories that shadow over our stories, you are crushing who we are, our ways of knowing and being."

The crowd erupted into a roar of cheers and whistles.

Taking a few steps toward the trailer, Gina pointed her finger angrily at Mr. Chapman. "You might not be like those principals before who said them real awful things to our children, so you probably think we're overreacting or something, but we ain't. We are sick and tired of people like you pushing your ideas and your stories. We got our own histories. Our own ways."

Mr. Chapman raised his hand, signalling for them to settle so that he could say something. When the crowd was slow to quiet down, Sophie Florence raised her hand to them and they stopped.

"I think there's been some kind of mistake here," he said. "I haven't pushed any histories or stories. I have the utmost respect for your ways."

Several people in the crowd threw back their heads in disbelief. Margaret and Lizzie took a few steps forward, each of them guiding Odelia and Hannah by the shoulders. Lizzie said, "These two girls have told us the truth. About the stories you told them at chess club. About the woman in the box with the baby. About the silver tooth and the wood tooth, and about how you told it to them many, many times. They told you that no one is allowed on that island and you kept telling the story anyway."

A murmur of voices rippled through the crowd.

"The only thing I'm guilty of," Mr. Chapman said, "is trying to give the kids some hope. Don't you want them to have hope?"

"You need to leave!" Somebody yelled.

Mr. Chapman's sighed. "I can't just up and leave," he said, almost sounding irritated. "I can't leave the school without a principal."

"We will survive without you," Sophie Florence said. "We always do. Teachers and principals come and go all the time. We know how to handle people like you, Mr. Chapman."

Several people hooted and hollered their support of these words.

"But—" Mr. Chapman was flustered. "This is ridiculous. I don't deserve to be kicked out."

Wheels crunched up the road. It was Chase Charlie's pickup truck. He pulled over next to the crowd and hopped out. He undid the rope that held the passenger door closed and set the entire door on the hood. Then he took a wheelchair from the pickup bed and unfolded it. In his arms he lifted Nan Lily from the passenger seat and set her carefully into the wheelchair. Everybody watched as he pushed her across the yard to the bottom of the front steps.

Mr. Chapman swallowed hard, his pointy Adam's apple sliding down and back up his translucent neck.

Softly, Nan Lily spoke. "You took a story that was ours, and you told it however you wanted for your own benefit. You told the children that it was a very old secret, the story you told them. You were right. It is a very old secret, one that not even these people here know. It is a story held close to our chests, we elders, and now that my sister is on her journey, I am the only one who knows the story. Sometimes I tell bits of it now and then but not much. You told our children a false version of our stories. And you gave our children a false version of their future. You are every lie ever told to us. You are every thief who has stolen from us." Nan Lily paused to wet her lips with great effort. "Stories are the heart of this world. But there is a dark side to telling stories, a side our people have known since missionaries came to tell us stories. Stories like yours. Stories of false choices and false futures."

Sophie Florence pointed at Chase and gave Mr. Chapman a choice. "Either you pack your things tonight," she said, "and be on Chase's boat first thing in the morning, or we will block all the children from coming to school. We'll do it tomorrow and the next day and the day after that. You can explain to the superintendent why no one came to school all week. Or you can go away and forget all about us. Because we will certainly forget all about you."

The next morning, he was gone.

25

On the day Grace Henry returned to Tawakin, I stood between Sophie Florence and Gina. Gina, who had gone through the necessary bureaucracy to become Grace's temporary guardian without a word to anybody. A stealthy angel in disguise. This had both delighted and astonished me, given Gina's standoffish attitude with adults and children alike, and it only proved to me that you can never really know what a person looks like on the inside. Together, we waited on the dock with dozens of other people. In the far distance was a large cedar canoe with tall, curved ornamentation at the bow and stern. It entered the mouth of the cove by the strength of two women who paddled steady and in perfect tandem. A small hooded figure sat in the middle. In this type of situation, children always returned to the community by canoe, Sophie Florence had explained. Never had the cove looked so large to me. Between us and Grace, a thousand choppy waves to slow the reunion.

In a whisper, Sophie Florence told me: "When a child returns, we wrap them in a blanket made just for them to show them that they are safe back at home and that we have hope that they will become a good story."

A story of hope and possibility, I thought to myself. This was what I had already decided, that I would search for stories of hope and possibility to fill their school days. Stories that would make them believe that they had choices in life, that would help them dream up their own destinies. I asked Sophie Florence and Ernie Frank and Nan Lily about this, if it was okay that I shared all kinds of stories with the kids. Yes, they said: stories from the elders, stories from the community, stories from books, stories from around the world. All of it was good, so long as their stories remained their stories, told by them.

The journey by canoe must have taken the women an hour, if not more. The stretches of open ocean they had faced along their route made the sight of their canoe stirring and sacred to me. With my eyes transfixed on the small figure, the image of whom made my heart swell so much it hurt, I reflected on something Gina had said on the walk down to the dock. I had asked how I could support Grace at school following this difficult time.

"You teach who you are," Gina had said with a shrug.

I gave Sophie Florence a puzzled look.

Sophie Florence smiled. "Who you are is how you teach, that's all there is to it. Your schooling, your degrees—that stuff is good. You can have theories. Methods. The very best ways of doing things. But in the end, when you're standing in front of your class, it's just you. You're it. You and everything about you. You teach who you are."

There was a time when I would have, upon hearing such a statement, fished for their opinion of me. Did they mean that I taught who I was, and that I was somebody who mattered? Was I somebody they thought was good for their children? But I was different then.

When the canoe neared the dock, I didn't know what to do with myself. I noticed how all the others fidgeted, their feet shuffling on the dock, so excited were they for the girl's return. Several people clasped their hands over their mouths to smother gasps, tremulous giggles, crying. I felt divided, as though I shared what was going on here but also not. This incredible moment of Grace's return, of which I was a part and apart. Quietly, I receded into the crowd as Grace was given a hand out of the canoe and onto the dock. Every single person took a turn hugging Grace, who was beaming with what looked like joy and relief, each hug enveloping the girl with immense love.

After a long time, Grace finally made her way through the crowd until only I remained. Grace smiled and reached into her jeans pocket, pulling out a folded piece of paper. Standing close to me, Grace opened the small paper and displayed it on her open palms. It was my drawing of her with the small circles of white light like stars dotting the universe of her dark eyes. Those tiny constellations that made Grace's charcoal gaze appear hopeful, as if everything bright and good and new in the world was ahead of her.

"I kept this under my pillow the whole time," Grace said.

I wrapped my arms around Grace and hugged her tight. What incredible joy to hold the girl in my arms after nights of worrying about her, projecting her loneliness, her fear, her sorrow. With Grace's small arms clinging tightly around me, I felt as if I had the entire world in my arms.

✻   ✻   ✻

As I ate my dinner that evening, I heard the murmur of voices outside. After looking out the windows and the door and seeing nobody, I tried to pinpoint where the voices were coming from. I wound up in the bathroom, which was finally empty of the chickens since Kevin Sam had boated them over to Nurse Bernadette's place on Hospital Island. Unfortunately, no matter how much I'd scrubbed the tub, it still stank of chickens.

While I could tell that the voices were those of children, I could not at first recognize who was out there. It sounded like two or three children.

"Help! Help!" It was Hannah's voice, but she didn't sound distressed.

Standing on my toes, I tried to peek through the window. Whoever was there must have been pressed against the side of the trailer because I couldn't see any part of them.

Outside, I stepped softly to the back end of my house and peered one eye around the corner. Sitting in the grass with their backs against the trailer were Hannah, Grace and Odelia. Grace was in the middle with a book open on her lap.

"Keep going, it's still your turn." Grace nudged Hannah with her elbow and pointed at the page.

Hannah looked at the spot above Grace's finger. "The skkkk—"

"Sky," Grace said.

"The sky," Hannah repeated, "is failing."

"Falling," Odelia said kindly.

"Falling," Hannah repeated.

Grace tilted the book the other way for Odelia to see better.

"And along the road," Odelia read, "they met—"

"Louder," Grace said, "or they won't hear you."

Odelia raised her voice. "They met Turkey Lurkey. And Turkey Lurkey said, Gobble gobble gobble! Hello Chicken Little, Hello Henny Penny, Hello Goosey Loosey. What in the the world is wrong with you?'"

"Oh, Turkey Lurkey. Haven't you heard?" It was Grace's turn to read. "The sky is falling! The sky is falling! Gobble gobble gobble! Oh that's terrible! Can I go too? And they all went down the road saying—"

The three girls read in unison: "Help, help the sky is falling! Help, help the sky is falling!"

"What are you doing?" I called out.

The girls spun their heads in my direction.

"Reading to the chickens," Odelia said. "We figured they might be bored in your bathroom. Plus, you said chickens love stories."

"That's true," I said. I hadn't yet told the class that the chickens had been moved to the nursing outpost, and I wasn't about to mention it now. Not when Hannah was there, being included, reading and willing to let Grace help her. "What are you reading to them?"

"*Chicken Little.*" Grace held up the book to show the cover. "We thought they would like another book with chickens in it."

I agreed. "There's far too many books about people. Chickens should get to see themselves in stories."

✻   ✻   ✻

I went back into the house to finish my dinner, now turning cold, but I really didn't care. From the table, I could hear the murmur of their voices as they took turns reading to my empty bathroom. I thought of Mr. Chapman and the story he had told the three girls and I wondered why he had done it. Was it purely a source of amusement for him? Or was it an experiment in belief and hope as he indicated? An experiment born from his time in Bodder and his obsession with turning the hopelessness to hope? Was he here just to do this research? Or was it a distorted effort to redeem himself for not following Tomas Whitehead into the forest? At school that week, Grace showed up early with an envelope in her hand.

"I got a letter from my mom when I was away," she said, sitting cross-legged on the Read-Aloud Rug. "Want to read it?"

"I sure do," I said, putting on my special reading glasses.

I stood next to the window. I started to read the letter.

Deer Grace—

"You're not supposed to read over there," Grace interrupted. "You're supposed to read over here. On the Read-Aloud Rug."

"It's fine where I am," I assured her.

"But I'm already sitting on the rug. How come you can't meet me over here?"

I smiled. "You're right. I can meet you where you are."

I sat down next to Grace. As always, I paused to puzzle out misspellings and occasionally stumble over missing punctuation, but nonetheless I read with an air of great importance.

> *Deer Grace, I wont be cumming bak to Tawakin. I like your new name. It means to get love and mercy even if you dont deserv it. I know it mite be hard to believe rite now, but you will half a special life. You will. I can feel it.*

I folded the letter and carefully slid it back into the envelope with the stained ring of grape juice. "Do you want to answer your mom during writing today?"

"No," Grace said.

"No?"

Grace wrinkled her nose. "I got a different story idea I thought up."

26

In the corner of the gym, the men and boys stood in a circle holding large rawhide drums, some decorated with pictures of eagles and killer whales. Chase Charlie sang something in Nuuchah-nulth all by himself, his voice, robust and mesmerizing, filling the entire space. The other men and boys then repeated the line together as one harmonized sound, their voices lifting and falling and lifting like waves. Their drums started right after that, a slow, throbbing pulse of thunderous booms that reverberated against the walls. It sounded as if the gym itself had transformed into a massive heart that beat blood into life. The power of it made my skin prickle. I watched from my spot against the wall. Rows of chairs filled half the packed gym. Many people had walked up from the village and now sat in those chairs. Some were seated on the benches along the side and back walls, while others like me who couldn't find a seat stood around the perimeter. Despite the energy that vibrated around me, I stifled a yawn. I was exhausted, having stayed at the school cooking with the women until three in the morning. You got to do it like that. That was what Sophie Florence had reminded me. You got to host a meal for the community. The ancestors get upset by stuff like that, disrespecting the dead, and if you don't apologize for it out loud in public so that everyone hears it, including the ancestors, it can cause a lot of trouble for the whole village.

From the back door of the gym, Hannah entered the gym dancing. Girls and women followed Hannah one at a time in a long line, also dancing their way in. They wore black shawls, some with red tassels along the fringe, each one with a unique image—eagles, thunderbirds, wolves—decorated in sequins and tooth shells and bits of felt. In their hands they each held a long cedar stick. They used these sticks to paddle through an invisible ocean as they danced forward until they had formed a large circle in the empty half of the gym. Hannah, no longer wearing that oversized shirt, held her stick with her bare hands, no longer contagious, though the patchy residue of medicinal ointment was still visible.

"They've chosen Hannah to be lead dancer," Nan Lily said to somebody seated next to her. I couldn't tell if Nan Lily was making a declaration or questioning the decision. Then she added, "She is the best dancer I've seen since her father Chase, and he was the best dancer we'd seen in a long time."

I watched Hannah dance. She moved with a tidal grace, her motions strong and confident. I got the sense that the others were striving to feel Hannah's timing in their own arms and in their own feet. She moved softly, effortlessly, as though she floated across the floor, and her face lifted to the sky, her chin protruding into an angle of pride and certainty. There was both a peacefulness and a power to her movements, the sense that she was at harmony with the world, simultaneously in command of her actions yet willingly surrendered to unseen currents. Whatever Hannah was feeling, she belonged there on the dance floor, anybody could see that.

All those studies at my university about how to treat trauma, I reflected back on them for a moment, about how movement exercises could help a person feel grounded and attuned to their feelings. The answer, I realized, was already built into their culture.

As I continued to watch, the flour dust from the floor wafted up in small puffs as Hannah led the dancers—including among others Sophie Florence, Gina, Lizzie, Margaret, Odelia and Grace—around their circle. The synchronicity between the drumming and Hannah's feet was perfect. Whenever the boys and men stopped singing—these boys who otherwise kept their faces hidden under hoodies every day at school—and only the sound of their drumbeats could be heard, the girls and women also stopped moving forward, but continued to paddle with their sticks, each one of them sneaking a sidelong glance at Hannah, for once not out of fear but fellowship. I glanced back at the drumming circle in the corner where Chase drummed with the others. It was the first time I had seen him without his green ball cap covering his eyes. Never once did he stop watching his daughter.

When the song ended, I went to Hannah and said in a matter-of-fact tone, "You're pretty good at dancing."

She said, "My father's voice moves my feet."

*   *   *

With the women's assistance, I had made the lunch that would be served to the community at the potlatch. When it was time to announce that lunch was ready, I walked to the middle of the empty dance floor. I could feel everybody watching. My heart fluttered like a small bird in my chest.

I said, "I am standing before all of you because I need to apologize for something I have done. I went to the woman in the box with the baby. I saw the woman and her baby and I am the one who upset the ancestors. I am truly sorry. I offer you the lunch today to apologize for my wrongs."

I felt something brush against my arm. I turned to see Grace and Odelia standing next to me in their dance shawls. Something brushed my other arm. I turned to see Hannah.

With her head bowed to the floor, Grace spoke almost inaudibly. "It was me, too. I went to the woman in the box with the baby. It wasn't Teacher's fault. It was mine. She was just trying to make sure I was okay. I am sorry."

I put my hand on Grace's shoulder and smiled. Odelia and Hannah then expressed their apologies. Out of the corner of my eye, I noticed people standing behind us. I turned to see Sophie Florence, Gina, Lizzie and Margaret standing shoulder to shoulder behind us on the dance floor, their hands clasped in front of them, a quiet stance of support. Nan Lily then clapped her bony hands together, and I tensed. Nan Lily was the person whose reaction I feared most.

The elder smiled and said, "This calls for the fire dance before we eat!"

Everybody laughed, and the men started to drum a fast beat. The dancers ran in between the rows of chairs, pulling spectators onto the dance floor. Hannah went straight to me and took me by the hand. I shook my head. I couldn't dance. I didn't know how.

"You have to come, Teacher," Hannah said. "If you're asked to come on the dance floor, you have to come. If you don't, you have to pay money or do something silly by yourself in front of everybody. That's the rule."

Reluctantly, I went onto the dance floor with Hannah. We danced in a large circle and while I didn't understand the nature of the movements at first, I soon realized that the entire dance was a story about enjoying a fire on the beach after being chilled and how the flames kept scorching our bottoms. Everybody moved as one into a tight circle around an invisible fire, then turning to fan the flames off their backsides. Dancers bumped and crashed into one another, laughing, moving their bodies playfully, clumsily. I noticed that Hannah watched me out of the corner of her eye, and each time I was uncertain about where to go or what movements to make, Hannah swooped in quickly to demonstrate for me, making sure that I was not lost out there on the floor.

As we all ate lunch, I remembered my drawings impaled on those trees in the forest, artifacts of my past self. It was remarkable how many people in this world wished things were different but didn't want to change. I didn't want to be one of those people. I wanted to be larger than that.

At the table next to me, Joan said in a low voice, "Look around us. All this suffering and in the middle of it all, their brilliance. I mean, take a look at your students. Grace's writing and Odelia's art and Hannah's dancing. Just think of it. One day, Grace might publish stories—"

"Not just stories," I said. "Stories that will turn the nation inside-out with her voice."

"And Odelia. She might make art one day that captures the imaginations of millions," Joan said.

I nodded. "Art that will show people how to see the world in a brand new way."

Who knew what my students might do. What they might become. Who was I to guess? All I knew was that I would stay so that I could love them and teach them and make sure they crossed the graduation stage one day with dignity, purpose and options. As I sat inside a school that felt forgotten by the rest of the world, I hoped that some of my students might burn the government down to make way for the others. Burn it down to the ground for only ever pretending to believe that a child is a child.

I reflected on the promises I had made this week to Grace and Odelia and Hannah. That I would stay. I had to stay. I wanted to stay. Part of me still worried how long this could last. How long could I stay in a place where I had little opportunity for a wide social life, or perhaps even a partner? In a place where the morning bell brought broken hearts every day? How long could I live in a place where I was never not the teacher? Where the boundary between my personal and professional life had disappeared altogether? Maybe that boundary couldn't exist. Maybe it shouldn't exist. Maybe in a place like Tawakin, I reminded myself, the only way to make a difference was to immerse myself, my whole self, so deeply, so fully into their lives that there'd be no boundary. No divide between Molleigh and Ms. Royston. How could there be any other way?

*   *   *

When I returned to my trailer early that evening, I heard a loud rustling of leaves at the edge of the forest overhead as I turned the key in the lock. I scanned the top of the neighbouring rock face. The woods were thick, and it was hard to imagine any creature bigger than a marten squeezing out of the entangled branches, shrubs and brambles. I caught a glimpse of fur. I looked closer, waiting. Then I looked over at those two rocks, still there. Perhaps I would never know how they got there. Nor would I know who was responsible for all the mischief down in the village—the knocking, the moving of furniture—but I was more open to the possibilities of things unseen in this world. I looked back again at the woods for signs of movement. The air seemed charged with an awakening, as if something stirred, faintly, then simply turned to illusion, leaving me alone again. I mouthed to myself: *aalth-maa-koa*. The forest next to my trailer was quiet and still, barely a breeze of movement in the branches. Somehow it looked not as dark to me now. It felt as though the darkest places of my mind were less dark now, the woods no longer reminding me of those frightening things I carried.

And then there it was, almost the same colour as the giant stone on the tree stump behind me. A wolf. It stood perfectly still on the edge of the rock face and stared down at me. I didn't move a muscle. I stared back, mesmerized by its eyes. To see a wolf, Sophie Florence had said at the funeral, is one of the greatest gifts. The invisible force in my mutual gaze with the wolf was electrifying, and for a moment my understanding of life and the world expanded. Everything became clear. I would throw my whole heart into it. Until they graduated. I would stay here, and I would say to them, I am still here, and I will walk with you into the middle of dark forests. If only to be present with you. Because it was about connection.

It was always about connection.

Acknowledgements

I raise my hands in gratitude to every teacher, educational assistant, counsellor and youth care worker in this country. Especially those who are anything like these amazing educators:

Amanda Bartle, Colin and Kristi Teramura, Hazel Quash, Jackie McDonald-Read, Dani Beattie, Greg Elliott, Michelle Wood, Jana Fox, Kari Duffy, Julia Jacobs, Angela Gadd, Darrel McLeod, Helen Jones, Monique Comeau, Simone Randall, Janis Deming, Natalie Jack, Janice John-Smith, Daisy Hanson, Lynn Norbjerg, Cari Bell, Tara Forbes, Heather Wilke, Travis Gronsdahl, Stephanie Brown, Shannon Atkins, Tim Coy, Clayton Panga, Larry Lamont, Rayna Hyde-Lay, Wendy Milne, Francis Perkal, Chad Ganske, Catherine McGregor, Allyson Fleming, Ross Davidson, Ross Wheeler, Stu Banford, and my amazing agent Carolyn Forde's favourite teachers, Dave Hamilton and Brenda Burke.

Klecko to the trailblazing educators Linda Kaser and Judy Halbert for their relentless work to ensure that every learner crosses the stage with "dignity, purpose, and options." Thank you, Linda and Judy, for inspiring me to be the best educator I can be and for allowing me to use your phrase. And thank you to every teacher who participates in the Networks of Inquiry and Indigenous Education.

Klecko to my son-in-law, Leroy Jack, who was a teaching assistant in my classroom, and my daughter, Emma Vallee, who often taught in my classroom, and who both now are the first teachers of my beloved grandchildren.

Meduh to my student, Josh Dragos—Chi'yone Cho—whose kind presence in my classroom is still, to this day, one of the greatest highlights of my teaching career, and whose death at the end of my last year teaching in Dease Lake is still, to this day, the greatest sorrow of my teaching career.

To the victims of he-who-I-refused-to-name: rest in peace.

Lastly, as always, to my mother, Lynn Manuel, whose joy of teaching and writing led me to where I am now. I miss you.

Nick Caumanns photo

Jennifer Manuel has achieved acclaim for her fiction, including the Ethel Wilson Fiction Prize for her debut novel, *The Heaviness of Things That Float* (2016). A long-time activist in Indigenous issues, Manuel has taught elementary and high school in the lands of the Tahltan, Nuu-chah-nulth, and Cowichan peoples. She lives on Vancouver Island, BC.